A Seamless Murder

A MAGICAL DRESSMAKING MYSTERY

Melissa Bourbon

AN OBSIDIAN MYSTERY

OBSIDIAN
Published by the Penguin Group
Penguin Group (USA) LLC, 375 Hudson Street,
New York, New York 10014

USA | Canada | UK | Ireland | Australia | New Zealand | India | South Africa | China
penguin.com
A Penguin Random House Company

First published by Obsidian, an imprint of New American Library,
a division of Penguin Group (USA) LLC

First Printing, January 2015

ISBN 978-0-451- 41721-3

Printed in the United States of America
10 9 8 7 6 5 4 3 2 1

For sewing enthusiasts everywhere,
and for those who love a little magic in life

Acknowledgments

As always, a big thank-you to Kerry Donovan, Isabel Farhi, Maggie Powers, the amazing art department at NAL for the cover of *A Seamless Murder*, surely the best one yet, and to Holly Root for continually championing my work. Also, a loving thank-you to Carlos, A.J., Sam, Jared, Sophie, and Caleb for their ongoing support. I couldn't do all that I do without you. I love you all!

Cassidy Family Tree

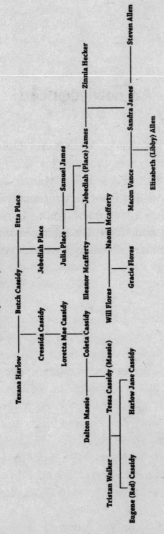

Chapter 1

Aprons aren't couture garments. They aren't even knock-off couture. But it was looking as though they were going to be my next project. Seven individual and unique aprons for the members of Bliss's Red Hat Society chapter, to be exact.

I had to laugh. Last week I'd been creating a suit for a Fort Worth woman who wanted a highly tailored linen ensemble—not an easy task. But as my great-grandmother, Loretta Mae Cassidy, always said, success is something you have to work for. Harder than you may want to, most times. That linen suit pushed me to the edge of my ability, but I ended up on the other side a better dressmaker and tailor. In the end, the outfit could have competed with any high-end handmade Italian design—and come out on top. And I'd made it, not in Florence, Rome, Milan, or New York, but in little ol' Bliss, Texas.

Now, standing on the sidewalk in front of Bliss's

United Methodist church, I agreed to create aprons for the local group—women who celebrated life at every age and who spent their time together in fellowship and friendship, and I was good with that. Working in the fashion industry in New York had taught me to expect surprises. Living back in my hometown of Bliss had taught me to embrace them. After my great-grandmother's death, I'd moved home to live in her old yellow farmhouse right off the town square. I'd opened up Buttons & Bows, a custom dressmaking shop, and had since made two bridal gowns and countless bridesmaids' dresses and homecoming frocks, as well as designs for town events such as period dresses for the Margaret Moffette Lea Pageant and Ball and a Christmas fashion show.

But at the moment I needed to focus on the bevy of red-hatted, purple-dressed women who had surrounded me. They had presented me with a task—to do something completely different from anything I'd done before.

I was ready for the challenge—or lack thereof, considering that an apron pattern didn't require any advanced sewing skills. I homed in on Delta Lea Mobley, my neighbor—and apparently the leader of Bliss's Red Hat ladies, all of whom currently stood in a half circle around me, looking expectant. Delta was a robust, rosy-cheeked woman with lots of soft curves, but her personality didn't quite match. Although she looked like a middle-aged Mrs. Claus, there was no twinkle in her eye, no laughter in her voice, and no spring in her step. She had a serious demeanor and was known to get to the point in conversations—two characteristics that had helped her to gain a reputation as a no-nonsense businesswoman.

Her sisters, Coco and Sherri, on the other hand, had the same huggable shapes, but each had a joyful and friendly personality their sister lacked. Unfortunately, though, neither of them happened to be anywhere near the church or the big white-tag sale tent set up in the church parking lot. So I was stuck with Delta.

"Harlow, I know you're a big-shot fashion designer and all, and at first we thought Jeanette Mayweather could make them, but her mother has pneumonia. Do you think you can handle making these aprons?"

So I was the second choice. Not surprising, given the animosity between my family and Delta's. Nana's goats had destroyed the Mobleys' foliage more than once, and it chapped Delta's hide that she had to share a property line with a goat farm. The granddam of Nana's Sundance Kids herd had led the other goats straight into the Mobley yard on more than one occasion, and I'd had a few run-ins with my neighbor since I'd moved back to Bliss, mostly because of Nana's goats. Delta; her husband, Anson; her daughter, Megan, and her husband, Todd Bettincourt; and her mother, Jessie Pearl Trapper, all lived next door to me. I knew I was responsible for the goats' trespassing simply by association. At least in Delta's mind.

"I thought—" She broke off, then waved her hands at the other Red Hat ladies. "*We* thought you could probably make aprons, too. I'm not sure how creative you can get with them. We want something more than burlap sacks, you know."

"I'm not a big shot, Delta," I said, knowing her abrasive attitude didn't spill over to the other women in her Red Hat group.

Cynthia Homer, her ginger hair shimmering in the soft light of the morning, sucked in a bolstering breath. "We're *hoping* you'll be able to fit it into your schedule," she said, shooting daggers at Delta. "We'd be honored if you'd do our small project, in fact. Just tickled pink."

I ignored Delta's mean streak and mustered up a healthy dollop of sweetness, dropping it into my voice. "I'd love to make y'all some aprons," I said, knowing the moment I spoke that it was absolutely true.

The tense expressions on the women's faces relaxed. Cynthia clasped her hands together. "Harlow Jane, that's wonderful. They're for our first ever progressive dinner. Of course, you'll have to come to that, too. Bring that nice fellow of yours."

I would gladly bring my boyfriend, Will Flores, anywhere, but I had no idea what a progressive dinner was.

"It's a dinner party on the go," Delta said. She must have recognized the confusion in my expression. "The dinner is broken into courses. We start with appetizers at one house, then move on to soup or salad at the next, and so on. By the time the evening is over, we've been to five or six houses and had a full meal."

"It's a dinner party on the move," Randi Martin said. "Shakes things up a little bit."

Cynthia extended her index finger and counted the women surrounding me, her mouth moving but no words coming out. "With everyone, that'll be seven aprons. We need 'em finished a week from next Friday for the dinner. Can you do that?"

I barely stopped myself from sputtering. "Two weeks?"

They were just aprons, but still, I had other obligations. Although I could push off the good-luck outfit I was putting together for my grandmother for her upcoming Sundance Kids open house—that wasn't for another month, and I hadn't quite decided what to make for Nana that would suit her.

"That should be a piece of cake for you, Harlow," Delta said, shouldering Cynthia out of the way. "Especially for something as pedestrian as aprons. Why, I've seen you whip out homecoming dresses and those bridal gowns in a matter of days. Aprons have to be the easiest thing on the face of the earth for someone with your sewing finesse."

I couldn't decide whether she was trying to be nice now and I'd just been imagining the healthy dose of sarcasm I'd heard in her voice a minute ago or if she really was just wickedly nasty. Maybe it was a genuine compliment and she *was* trying to butter me up, but I wasn't sure.

What I couldn't tell her was that my hesitation wasn't due to how easy or difficult the aprons themselves would be to make. She was right. I could pull off a period dress in a day if I had to. My hesitation stemmed from my magical charm. I had inherited a family charm that enhanced my dressmaking skills, but I had to get a sense of someone's personality before I could select the right design for them or even pick out the best textiles to use. Two weeks did not allow for much time to get a reading on seven women—not to mention that I had made a commitment to volunteer at the church tag sale.

"Of course, if you *can't* do it . . ." she said, trailing off.

And just like that, I recognized that she was challenging me for some reason. She wanted me to fail.

"Oh, I can do it," I said, realizing a second too late that I'd fallen smack into her trap, hook, line, and sinker.

She shook her head and directed her gaze toward the porch roof, as if she didn't believe I could make seven complete aprons in time. "I don't know. . . ."

"Well, I do." This time I was fully aware that I was being played.

But Delta Lea Mobley would not get the better of me.

Or maybe she already had.

"If you're sure," she said, still not sounding convinced, but I noticed the corner of her mouth quirk up and her eyes crinkle just slightly, and a new thought crossed my mind. Maybe she really wanted me to make the aprons, and she just didn't know how to get past the Mobley-Cassidy family feud.

"Enough, Delta, good Lord," Cynthia said, batting Delta's arm. Her jaw was set, her mauve-colored lips thinning with her aggravation. "They're aprons for a dinner party, for pity's sake, not *Project Runway* extravaganzas."

"And Harlow said she can do it," Georgia Emmons said. Georgia looked like a former beauty queen with her long eyelashes, thick auburn hair, and hourglass shape. She was like an ageless Mary Tyler Moore.

They were talking about me as if I weren't right there front and center. I wanted to wave my hands and shout,

I'm here! I can hear you! But instead I kept my mouth shut. I knew the Red Hatters were showing me their support, but I felt I had gotten a glimpse behind the curtain, seen a softer side of Delta. Or at least as soft as she was able to show me. She was always tough as nails, but she had a heart.

They were all so different, but the Red Hats united them, and I could tell they were a tight group of friends. Figuring each of them out and making their aprons would be a fun task, and I was already anticipating the challenges and end results.

"Right," Bennie Cranford added. "We're not walking the runway, it's just dinner. Well, not really *just* dinner, with the down-home theme, but you know. This isn't Dallas high society."

Randi Martin hung back, clearly uncomfortable at the direction of the conversation. She wrung her hands in front of her without saying anything. Her short, spiked silvery hair made her long, narrow face look longer and more narrow, her tan skin accentuating the map of wrinkles. She'd enjoyed too much sun during her salad days, and now her skin was paying the price. "Harlow said she'd do it, so you can stop arguing," she finally said, her voice small. If someone yelled, *Boo!*, I was afraid she'd clutch her heart and keel over. Still, most of the ladies acknowledged her with a nod. She had made a good point.

"You know me," Delta said brusquely. "No holds barred. Life's too short to not say what you mean. Harlow," she said, turning to me, "I'm pleased you'll make the aprons. Do us proud."

"Delta thinks she should say every thought she has

just the second she has it. Not always a good thing," Cynthia said.

"No, it's not," Delta admitted. Under her breath, she muttered, "I've learned that the hard way," but then she smiled.

"Water under the bridge," Randi said, squeezing Delta's upper arm.

Cynthia nodded. "Like Delta always said, this town leaks like a sieve. It's a lesson learned. You have something to hide, you best do your business in Granbury or Glen Rose, or some such. There aren't any secrets in Bliss." Cynthia stepped closer to Delta, leaning in and lowering her voice a touch, although we could all still make out what she was saying. "You know that now."

I didn't have a clue what they were talking about, but that's what came with years and years of friendship. It was almost like a secret language between tribe members, and no outsider could decipher the true meaning of what was being said.

After another minute of whispering, they turned back to me. "All set, then? Seven aprons by next Friday?"

"I'll start planning them right away," I said. "I'll be in touch."

"Harlow," Delta said, recovered from whatever pall had slipped over her a moment ago, "I'll see you later at my house. We can talk about my apron then." I was happy to oblige, but I didn't have time to say so before she turned on her sensible flats and marched off in the direction of the cemetery.

Chapter 2

Throughout my childhood, my great-grandmother was an ever-present part of my life. She was even the person who had taught me to sew, but, more important than that, she had taught me that I could achieve whatever I set my mind to. She hadn't wanted me to leave Bliss, but when I'd set off for college to study fashion design, she walked me to Mama's car, planted a kiss on my tear-stained cheek, and said, "Darlin', don't let nobody trespass on your dreams."

In our family, our magical charms varied from person to person, and hers had been to bring whatever she wanted into reality. It was a lot of power for one person, but Loretta Mae had always used it wisely.

When she'd finally given in to her charm, wishing I'd come home, she had known that Bliss was where I was meant to be. She'd known before I did. She just helped me get here a little faster than I might've done on my own.

Her homespun advice always came back to me at odd times. When I walked into Buttons & Bows yesterday to find I'd left the pillows askew, my workroom a mess of fabric, and the breakfast dishes in the sink, her voice sounded in my ear. *When your refrigerator is full and your bed is fresh, you feel cared for when you walk in the door.*

I'd spun around, thinking maybe it hadn't been a memory of Meemaw I'd heard in my head but her effervescent voice in my ear. After all, she had stuck around as a ghost in the house she'd left to me, even if I couldn't see her half the time and our communication was mostly limited to clanking pipes, cryptic words written in the steam on my bathroom mirror, and low moans.

But Meemaw hadn't been whispering in my ear. She had been MIA, in fact, for two days. If I were a betting woman, I'd lay money that she was holed up in the attic looking through the buttons, lace, trims, and fabric collected up there. She didn't need to come down for food, she couldn't leave the house, and she didn't sleep, so she was perfectly content escaping into the sewing world she'd left behind.

Now, as I stood on the sidewalk in front of the square white Craftsman-style house next door to mine, another of her wise sayings came back to me. *Brighten someone's day with your smile and your words.*

I frowned. Talking to Delta Lea Mobley wasn't going to brighten *my* day, so I wasn't sure how my forced smile and falsely cheery words would brighten hers. But I had an apron to make. The first of seven, so there was no time for hesitation on my part. A Jeep drove past, pulling around the corner and into the side driveway. Like so many corner houses in the Historic District, there was no driveway in front of the house. It hid on the side, letting the house itself be front and center. I knew the Jeep belonged to Mr. Mobley, even though I had never actually met Delta's husband. Was he a stronger personality than she was, or was he a carpet she walked all over?

I couldn't put it off any longer. I marched up the brick walkway, past the mailbox, past the Aggies flag and the flowering shrubs, mounted the steps to the front porch, and knocked on the edge of the screen door. Delta could be sweet as pie when she wanted to be, but she'd held tight to her grudge against the Cassidys for so long, I feared that trying to let it go might do her in. She might look like a rose. She might smell like a rose. But underneath it all I'd seen a mess of thorns, and I didn't know if her stem could ever be stripped clean.

There was no answer, so I knocked again, louder this time.

Still nothing. I opened the screen door and pressed my ear to the door listening for any signs of activity inside the house. It was utterly quiet. "Delta Lea Mobley," I said to the empty porch, "if you stood me up, so help me I'll—"

I raised my fisted hand to knock again, rapping my knuckles against the solid wood door. As they came down a third time, the door wrenched open. "You'll what?"

I stumbled backward, my knee buckling and my ankle twisting, but I caught myself and straightened up, wondering just what kind of game Delta was playing. Had she been standing on the other side of the door listening to me grow frustrated? I wouldn't put it past her.

"I won't be making your apron," I finished. I almost jammed my hands on my hips, but Meemaw's voice echoed in my head. *Smile, Harlow. Brighten her day.* Pasting a smile on my face, I said, "But here you are, so let's get started."

There wasn't much measuring to do. I just needed the waist, the length of her body from waist to knee, and another from waist to neck. What I ended up using would depend upon the vision I got for her. Half apron or full? Ruffled or tailored? Floral or striped? I didn't imagine her spending much time in the kitchen, and when I looked at her now, my charm failed me. I got no image in my mind's eye of what kind of apron would suit her. She was a mystery.

"You're letting all the bought air out. Are you coming in?"

Her words were blunt, but the edges of her voice had a buttery softness. She was trying hard to be sweet. It just didn't come naturally where the Cassidys were concerned.

"Harlow?"

I blinked, focusing on her standing there holding the door open wide. I'd been woolgathering, as Hoss Mc-Claine, Bliss's sheriff and my mother's husband, would say. "Yes, coming."

Inside I noticed two things right away. First, it was so dimly lit that I had to blink and strain for a moment before my eyes adjusted to the light. Anyone who stayed holed up in here a good part of every day would be in need of a healthy dose of vitamin D to replace lost sunlight. And second, the place was jam-packed with antiques. A veritable eBay store, right next door to my house. Who knew?

Delta weaved around the sideboards, ancient chairs, ottomans, and the rest of the scattered furniture, leading me deeper into the maze. "So you collect antiques?" I asked, making small talk.

She stopped short and looked at me over her shoulder. "My daughter, Megan, does. She sells items online and at local flea markets with a friend. Her husband got her into it, but she loves it."

As she turned back around and walked on, I took it all in. Ornate hat trees, small chests, figurines, lamps, period chairs. It went on and on and on. Megan needed to clear out her merchandise right quick or they'd be overrun.

Delta rounded the corner, disappearing behind a table stacked with upside-down chairs, but I stopped to look at a curio cabinet filled with collectible figurines. One in particular caught my eye. It was a delicate ceramic woman. I wanted to say she was a dressmaker, but I couldn't be sure.

"My mother collects those. Lladrós," Delta said, coming back to me.

"They're beautiful," I said. The only things I collected were buttons, trims, fabrics, and the occasional old pattern, but these figurines were exquisite. Perhaps someday when I had more free time, I could start a new collection for myself. . . .

"They're meant to stay in the family." She considered

me, and then looked at the Dressmaker, as if she'd made up her mind about something. "You'll have to look more closely at them one day. Like everything in here, they have a story to tell. Now, are you coming?" she added, a slight abrasiveness returning. I suspected it was taking a great deal of resolve for her to be so nice to me, and it was wearing thin.

"Mother," Delta said as Jessie Pearl came into view. "Harlow Cassidy is here to take our measurements."

This time I stopped short. *Our* measurements? I'd signed on to make seven aprons for the Red Hat Society ladies. Now, just hours later, Delta was adding her mother to the mix. I had a sinking suspicion in my gut that if I wasn't careful, I'd end up making double the number I'd initially agreed to.

"Um, excuse me, Delta?" I said, moving forward again, turning at the table and chairs. "I can't—"

The words caught in my throat when I saw Jessie Pearl reclined in a blue corduroy easy chair that looked like it had seen better days. *She* looked like she'd seen better days, too. Her snow-white hair was usually curled and soft, but today it was frizzy and wiry. Her skin seemed to hang loose on the bones of her face, the wrinkles pulling it down. But it was her leg, wrapped in a heavy blue plaster cast, that took me off guard. I didn't see Jessie Pearl very often, but the sight of her laid up with a broken leg made my frustration with her daughter over adding an apron to my task list evaporate.

"Miss Jessie Pearl, what happened to your leg?" I crouched in front of her, resting my hand on the arm of her chair.

The look she gave me made the hair on my arms stand up tall, as if it had happened just minutes ago. "Let me tell you," she began.

Delta came to an abrupt halt in the doorway, turning on her heels. "She doesn't need to hear the whole sordid tale, Mother. She's here to talk aprons."

"That's right, Delta Lea mentioned you were going to whip some up for her Red Hat group. Although I still can't figure out why, exactly. It's just the women and their husbands."

"And the pastor, and Jeremy Lisle," Delta said.

"Ah, well, Randi doesn't have a husband. Maybe one of them will be suited to her. 'Course maybe her being single is a good thing. Not all women are meant for domestic life."

"Mother, that's enough," Delta said, a faint scolding tone in her voice.

Jessie Pearl lowered her chin to her chest and closed her eyes for a beat. "Randi's very nice," she amended, "and single is fine. No judgment here."

She turned back to me, refocusing. "Anyway, mighty nice of you to make a bunch of aprons, Harlow Jane, even if it's a bit ridiculous."

The cat had my tongue for a few seconds before I mustered up a response. "It's my pleasure, ma'am. It oughta be fun figuring out the perfect fabrics and patterns for all y'all."

I cringed at the double *y'all* I'd thrown into the conversation. I'd all but lost my Southern accent when I'd gone away to college, but since being back in Bliss for the past year, I'd managed to pick most of it back up. It slipped in when I wasn't looking, and it seemed here to stay.

I maneuvered myself onto the seat of a nearby chair to settle in for the story of Jessie Pearl's broken leg. "Fridays are my chore day, you know. Every Friday I take mop to bucket and clean the floors. I do the bathrooms, dust the shelves, and once every six months, I flip the mattresses. Used to be that I had some help, but since we've all bunked up together, that stopped." She gazed up at Delta. "Whatever happened to that girl who used to come in and help once in a while?"

"You know you scared her away, Mother," Delta said, meeting my eyes and shaking her head. The message was clear. Jessie Pearl's memory was slipping.

I came back to the statement that had caught my attention. "You flip the mattresses?" Meemaw had come from the generation of mattress flipping, too, in the days before Tempur-Pedic and pillow-tops. The concept wasn't unfamiliar, but I had to admit that I'd never flipped a mattress in my entire life.

"Of course. Used to take the area rugs outside and would beat them to smithereens, too. I'll tell you this: Young people today don't know the meaning of clean. Why, Megan and Todd bring in these old antiques and wipe them down, but I tell them over and over it's not enough. You have to get the corners and use lemon oil—"

"Mother," Delta interrupted.

I sensed that this wasn't the first time they'd had this discussion, and I also suspected they'd never quite see eye to eye on cleanliness. Jessie Pearl came from a different generation and did things differently. Meemaw had been the same way, and her sense of order and cleanliness, even amidst the creative chaos of a sewing room, had spilled over to me. But that wasn't true for a lot of people, and it looked like Delta's daughter, Megan, may have missed those lessons.

"So," I said, getting back to the broken leg, "you were flipping a mattress?" I fluttered my hand so she'd continue even as I imagined the frail, elderly Jessie Pearl heaving a heavy mattress up and over. I couldn't quite picture it.

"Mattresses have gotten a good sight heavier over the years, let me tell you."

"I'm sure."

"I managed to flip Megan and Todd's, although it's a full-sized. I turned my own. It's an old twin, nearly as old as me. Easy as pie."

I knew she was exaggerating, but had she really been sleeping on the same mattress for as long as all that? I shot a glance at Delta, but she was focused on something in the kitchen.

"It was Delta and Anson's big lump of a mattress that nearly did me in, do you know?" She curved the fingers of one hand and lifted it above her head as if she were trying to block an imaginary mattress from falling on her head.

"I've told you to leave it be," Delta said, her head snapping back to look at us. "It doesn't need flipping."

Jessie Pearl balked. "You said no such thing. You said Anson wanted the thing flipped."

Delta pivoted toward her mother. "Anson may have

wanted it flipped, but you certainly don't need to be the one doing it. Mother, you're eighty-three years old. Your mattress-flipping, rug-beating days are behind you."

A faint red blush stained Jessie Pearl's cheeks, and her lips tightened, the lines on her face deepening into harsh crevices. "They'll be behind me when I'm dead."

I stared at Jessie Pearl wondering how I could have possibly misjudged her and the muscles she apparently had under the saggy skin of her arms. "So you lifted their mattress by yourself?"

She uncurled her fingers and fluttered them at me. "Pshaw. It wasn't anythin'. You just have to work your way under one corner with your arm, then your shoulder. Once you're under it, you climb on the box spring, lifting as you go, and then—" She clapped her hands as she said, *"Bam!"* I jumped. "It falls. Then you do it all again, only this time around, you have to pull it back up onto the box spring. It gets tricky, but I have a method."

"That method stopped working when the mattress fell on you and you were trapped, you mean." Delta still kept one eye on whatever was occupying her in the kitchen, but she seemed to have her full attention on our conversation. I got the impression she didn't want to leave me and her mother alone where we could have an unmonitored talk.

"I've been flipping the mattresses for years and years. Longer than you've been in the world," she said. "Haven't I asked for help? Good thing for me Megan and Todd showed up when they did or I might still be under that bed and you'd all be talkin' about me at Christian Brother's Mortuary instead of talkin' with me right here, right now."

"We're glad we showed up, too!" a man's voice called from the kitchen.

So Todd was in the kitchen.

Jessie Pearl grinned, exposing the outline of her dentures. Her smile was contagious. "This time the dang thing felt like it was alive. I thought I was going to be smothered. Todd was trying to help, and I couldn't even hear him. Megan screaming at him to hurry gave him the gumption he needed to heft it off of me."

"It is a good thing they got here when they did," I said.

"And now they're makin' supper for us tonight. Sweet, right? *They're* the ones who need aprons. They'd actually use them."

I ignored that hint, not wanting to take the apron count up to ten, and instead I focused on Delta's hyper-attentiveness to the kitchen. Had Todd and Megan been in the kitchen the whole time, or had they come in from a back door?

More than wondering when Todd and Megan had started cooking, I was curious about Delta's attentiveness to them. Did she not want a mess left after they were done? Was she trying to learn what was on the menu? My own interest was piqued. If there was anything that could help me pinpoint the style and fabric choice for Delta's apron, it was a glimpse into her kitchen.

"Very sweet," I said, wishing someone would come over next door and make me dinner. With all the tasks on my plate, cooking was going to go by the wayside. At least I had the progressive dinner to look forward to.

Jessie Pearl continued on as if there hadn't been a break in the conversation. "You'd be surprised at what I can do, but this time . . . this time it was different."

"You're eighty-three years old, mother," Delta said. "You had no business trying to flip it."

"I was a suffragette, I'll have you know. I've always been a doer, not a watcher. I know what matters, and I'm not afraid to stand up for what I care about."

Miss Jessie Pearl directed a stern glare at her eldest daughter. I'd wondered a few times how in the world she could have given birth to Delta, but for a moment, I saw the likeness between them. Jessie Pearl had gumption, just like Delta did, and they were cut from the same cloth in a way I had never noticed before.

"Like I said, there wasn't anyone to help. If you want somethin' done, do it yourself. That's a rule I've always lived by, and I ain't about to change it now."

"'Course she has so much money, she couldn't spend it all if she tried," Delta said to me, but to Jessie Pearl, she said, "Good for you, Mother. Now, do you want Harlow to make you an apron or not?"

The wrinkles on her forehead deepened as she slipped into thought. "I don't know if true suffragettes wore aprons."

"You were born too late to be a real suffragette, Mother," Delta said, rolling her eyes.

Jessie Pearl drew her lower lip up and over her upper lip, ignoring Delta, so I jumped in. "I bet a good many of them did," I said. "Women don't like to be defined by just

A SEAMLESS MURDER 21

one part of themselves. They shouldn't be. We're layered, right? Complicated. We can wear aprons and still believe in equality."

Another of Meemaw's tidbits of wisdom.

"That's true enough," Miss Jessie Pearl mused. "I suppose so, then. I'll have plenty of people to cook for during the holidays. Coco can help. She's the only one who can cook worth anything—"

Delta scoffed, but she didn't rebut by saying that she herself actually *could* cook.

"Her corn-bread dressing is every bit as good as mine," Miss Jessie Pearl said to Delta, "and didn't she decide to add dried cranberries to it? Perks it up with a special something, do you know? Todd's gonna help this year, too. Learn the family recipes. I'd bet a turnip and a dollar that he won't catch the oven on fire," she added, looking directly at Delta. The sentiment was clear. Apparently at some point, Delta *had* caught the oven on fire. I couldn't even imagine how that could happen, so I left it alone.

Delta pinched her lips together, but she held her tongue.

My stomach grumbled. Loudly. "Sounds delicious," I said. I made a mental note to add dried cranberries when I made my own corn-bread dressing at Thanksgiving.

I looked around for Anson Mobley, just wanting a glimpse of him, but he was nowhere to be seen. He must have come through the kitchen and snuck down the hallway to the bedrooms before I'd come in. I masked my disappointment at the missed opportunity. I'd have to meet him another time.

"Have I shown you my runner collection?" Jessie Pearl continued.

Delta sighed. "Mother, for pity's sake, Harlow doesn't want to see some old, stained runners. She's here to talk aprons."

I waved a hand in the air. Textiles were my passion. "Actually, I'd love to see them. Loretta Mae had embroidered runners. I have a few of them tucked away for safekeeping."

Delta threw her hands up and turned her back on us. "Great," she muttered, but she indulged her mother, disappearing and returning a minute later, her arms laden with a stack of folded white cloth. "These are just a *few* from her collection," she said, as if she couldn't believe how many runners her mother had made over the years.

I touched the first one, letting the pads of my fingers gently rest on the soft cotton. Images of the past didn't fly at me like they did for Gracie Flores, the newest discovered member of the extended and convoluted Cassidy clan and my boyfriend, Will Flores's, daughter. Will, who just happened to be the man of my dreams, had adjusted to both of the women in his life having magical charms. He was a keeper, as Meemaw would say.

Even though I didn't have Gracie's charm of reading the fabric, an overall peaceful feeling enveloped me. I could feel the love Jessie Pearl had woven into the runners she'd embroidered.

"Take a look," Jessie Pearl said. She took the top runner by one of the embroidered ends and spread it out over her lap. "These are May baskets," she said, pointing to the designs on either end of the cloth. "This was one of the first pieces I ever completed on my own. My aunt taught me. Once I got going, I didn't stop."

"Ha. That's the understatement of the century," Delta said.

I could hear low voices coming from the kitchen, followed by the faint rustling of plastic bags and the slamming of cupboard doors. "But I needed olives," a young woman's voice said.

"Go get them for her, Todd," came another woman's voice. "Megs and I need some girl time without you."

So someone else was in the kitchen, too. My guess was that it was Megan's friend and business partner.

A man's voice said something in response, and then the reverberation of another slammed door, followed by giggling. So Megan had won the olive argument, and Todd was going out to the market.

"If I had to count, I bet I've made a couple hundred over the years—"

"At least."

"You appreciate the art of handwork, Harlow, don't you?"

"I sure do, ma'am. And these look like they were made with a lot of love." I picked up another runner. The stitches were smaller and more precise on this one. They were also varied, a mix of lazy daisy stitches, back stitches, traditional straight stitches, outline and blanket stitches, herringbone and broken chain, and even bullion knots. Not a piece made by a beginner.

I folded the runner and started to lay it on top of the stack, but she pushed it back toward me. "Take it."

"Oh, but I can't. These should go to your daughters. Your granddaughter."

Jessie Pearl laughed, waving away the very idea. "What are they going to do with them? There are hundreds of them. Sure, Coco and Sherri might keep some, but Delta and Anson don't want any, do you, Delta?"

Delta shook her head.

"And Megan might keep one, but she'll put the rest in an estate sale or sell 'em at the flea market, like everything else around here."

"But—"

Jessie Pearl pressed her chin to her chest, looking up at me through her thinning eyelashes. "These are yours," she said, and I knew she wouldn't take no for an answer.

I nodded, holding my hands out so she could hand me a few. She took a few minutes to look at the folded stack on her lap, finally withdrawing eight runners and handing them over to me. "You take good care of them, Harlow."

I blinked away the sudden dampness in my eyes and nodded. "I sure will, ma'am."

"Finally," Delta said. "Can we talk aprons now?" She'd been standing sentry in the doorway between the living room and the kitchen. When I stood, she turned abruptly and walked out of sight.

I gave Jessie Pearl a little wave, but she was already back to her runners, muttering to herself as she looked at each one. If she was like me, then each design told a story and each runner represented a moment of time in her life. I wanted to stay and hear what she had to say, to listen to her stories, but Delta was done waiting. As I entered the kitchen, she was already talking. "I want something dramatic," she told me. "Something that will go with my kitchen and will . . ."

She ran her hands down her sides, but trailed off. An image suddenly popped into my head of her in her signature black pants and a patterned blouse, her standard outfit as a realtor. She must have a closet full of pretty blouses, and another full of the exact same pair of pants. In the vision, she also wore a frothy apron made with silk organza, a silk dupioni, and ruffles out of tulle and chiffon. I actually had every single one of the fabrics I was picturing. None had enough yardage to do anything significant with, but an apron? It could work.

Not the most practical of fabrics, either, but I got the feeling from looking around her dramatic black and white kitchen, and from what her mother had said, that she didn't actually do a lot of cooking, so impractical could work.

Megan greeted me, introducing me to her friend. "Harlow, meet Rebecca Masters. Rebecca, this is Harlow Cassidy. She runs the dressmaking shop next door."

On the surface, they were opposites. Megan's shoulder-length blond hair was pulled back into a ponytail, she had on minimal makeup, and she wore jeans and a T-shirt. She looked ready to dig in and work. Rebecca, on the other hand, had applied a heavy layer of foundation, blush, and mascara. She had short curly brown hair that looked artfully messy. It worked on her, giving her the look of a pixie or fairy with her delicate features and petite frame.

"We're going to sort through the back room today," Megan added, looking at her mother.

Delta glanced from Megan to her friend. "You're going to work in that?" she said to Rebecca. She wore a flirty dress with a full skirt. It hit her mid-thigh, and her flats had pointy toes. She could have been dressed to go out on a date rather than to work in the kitchen or sort antiques.

"We have Todd to do the dirty work," Rebecca said, nudging Megan with her elbow. "Right?"

Megan laughed. "Right."

Delta looked skeptical. "Doesn't he have a job to find? Resumes to pass out?"

"Bribery does wonders to motivate a person," Rebecca said, giggling again. Megan joined in and they both collapsed against the counter, their giggles turning to full on laughter.

Delta stared at them. "Bribery," she said. "Is that right?"

Rebecca waved her hand in front of her. "No, Mrs. Mobley. We're just playing around. Nobody's bribing anyone. Todd said he's happy to help if we take another load of donations to the tag sale. He loves antiques. Maybe as much as you do."

Delta didn't look appeased. She gave both girls a stern look, and they each straightened up, stifling their still bubbling laughter. "Y'all just steer clear of my things. There's a lifetime of treasures in this house, and I don't want to find anything missing."

"Yes, ma'am," they said in unison.

Megan and Rebecca went back to their cooking, and Delta pulled open a bottom drawer, showing me the aprons she had. None of them looked worn—or even like they'd ever been washed. "And you're sure you want me to make you a new one?" I said after I'd taken her measurements.

She tucked her current aprons back in a bottom drawer, then turned to look up at me. "I'm sure. And I fully expect it to be the best of the bunch."

So that was that. Delta Lea Mobley wanted a showpiece—an apron that would transform her figure and make her curves look a bit more like Jane Russell in her heyday. She wanted her apron to make a statement, and I knew I could deliver.

Chapter 3

I climbed the steps to my porch, pausing at the front door—the entrance to both my home and my dress-making shop—lost in thought. The details of Delta's apron were coming together, but something else had stopped me short the second I crossed the threshold. I sensed something. Not chaos, exactly, but a disturbance in the air. I shut the door behind me, walking around slowly, looking at the sitting area, the coffee table made from a vintage door, its old-fashioned handle still intact. Nothing was awry there. My lookbook of fashion designs lay undisturbed. The retro magazine rack, filled with fashion magazines, sat untouched. Meemaw hadn't left a trail of messages for me to decipher by following the open pages and circled words, as she has been known to do.

My gaze traveled to the far side of the room. The corkboard displaying current and past designs I'd sketched was just as I'd left it. The rack of prêt-à-porter clothing I kept on hand was overstuffed, but it had been like that for the last few weeks as I'd continually designed, sewed, and completed new projects.

But still, I knew *something* was amiss. "Meemaw?" I called out to my great-grandmother as I headed toward my atelier, which at one point in time had been the dining room. I had more use for a sewing and designing workroom than I did for formal dining. It was filled with my Pfaff sewing machine, as well as Loretta Mae's ancient Singer, the machine I'd learned to sew on and would never part with, as well as a large, tall cutting table in the center of the room, and a makeshift dressing area with an antique privacy screen that displayed some of my creations. Along the left wall was a freestanding shelving unit lined with Mason jars, each glass container filled with buttons, closures, bows, and other sewing notions. Jar after jar after jar was lined up.

Upstairs in the attic, another set of shelves held even more jars. A good many of them held vintage trinkets once owned by Texana or Cressida. Each was a treasure trove to be savored and cherished.

On the shelf in the atelier, one jar was turned on its side, buttons spilled out across the shelf like a can of spilled paint. Meemaw. Who knew what she was up to? Since it was already dumped out, I spread the contents of the jar across the shelf, taking a quick look. Nothing unusual jumped out at me. This particular jar held an array of vintage glass and rhinestone buttons. A few pewter, heart-shaped buttons drew my eye, one in particular. It had a pale pink center, and I knew it would be a perfect addition to Delta's apron. The hair on the back of my neck stood on end. Meemaw couldn't have known what I was up to with the aprons, and yet . . .

"Just coincidence," I muttered as I set it aside and cleaned up the rest, replacing the buttons, setting the jar back in place.

"Meemaw!" I called. "I'm home."

The sheer drapes on either side of the one window in the atelier rustled, catching my attention. I looked—and jumped. Thelma Louise, the granddam of my grandmother's goat herd, stood just outside the window, nose to the glass, her dark eyes watching me, her mouth pulled back to reveal her teeth, as if she were grinning. "Skedaddle!" I said, waving my hand to shoo her away.

But Thelma Louise never did anything I told her to do. She'd gone and nearly destroyed a handmade mum during homecoming season, consistently ate her share of my flowers, and generally kept me on my toes. Not the ideal neighbor, but Thelma Louise was a package deal with Nana. Wherever my grandmother was, so were her goats.

I wagged a scolding finger at the naughty animal, warning her to be good, then headed upstairs to the attic to find the fabrics for Delta's apron. The attic was really a big, unfinished room on the second floor. The entrance to it was in my bedroom. And the door was wide open. *Not* how I'd left it. I poked my head inside, drawing in a sharp breath.

Just inside the door were more shelves and more Mason jars filled with more buttons, trinkets, notions, and bows. Several had been tipped over, the contents scattered over the shelves. Further in, stacks of fabric had been tossed to the ground. The drawers to the ancient dresser were pulled open, and all of its contents scattered about.

Meemaw could clean up when she wanted to, but apparently picking up after herself wasn't high on her list of things to do at the moment.

"Meemaw, what in tarnation?"

Once I spoke, the energy I'd sensed when I'd walked in stilled. The air stopped moving. It was as if Meemaw was holding her breath, waiting for me to leave. I couldn't even fathom what she was up to.

"Meemaw, I'm not going anywhere until you tell me what you're doing," I said. On a really good day, and when she seemed rested and full of energy, she could almost take a corporeal form. Her shape became clear, sometimes her clothing was discernable, and I could almost see a teasing smile on her face.

But it never lasted long, and the effort seemed to wipe her out. She was great at making lights flicker on and off, excelled at clanking pipes, could steam up and write a mean message in a bathroom mirror, but actual physical tasks were more challenging. Once she'd managed to make a tornado inside the house with all sorts of my things, and another time she cleaned up a huge mess, but these incidents were few and far between. When they happened, they exhausted her and I saw neither hide nor hair of her for twenty-four hours.

I didn't expect her to suddenly appear before me, but that's just what she did. Sort of.

The air in front of me rippled, and I grew warm, as if a heated blanket had been thrown around my shoulders.

Slowly, a form took shape, the body distorting the air enough that I could tell it was Meemaw.

"Oh my," I breathed. This had happened only when Mama and Nana had been with me—four generations of Cassidy women in the same room. But now Loretta Mae was trying to appear before me. Just me. "Meemaw, what is it? Are you okay?"

A million thoughts raced through my head, beginning and ending with, *Was she saying good-bye?* Was her time on this plane up for some reason, and was this her way of making her presence known before she was gone for good?

The translucent air moved, and the next second I realized she was shaking her head no. I knew instantly that she was answering the question I hadn't asked, and just as quickly I felt relief flow through me. Having her as a ghost might not be as good as having her here fully, but I'd take it if the only other option was not to have her at all.

"Are you looking for something?" I asked. As I asked the question, I suddenly knew just what she was doing.

Cassidy legend held that Butch Cassidy had sent something special to Texana, his wife and my great-great-great-grandmother, from Argentina, but no one knew whether the stories were true, or whether such a treasure really existed. All the Cassidy women, and even my brother, Red, had looked for the mysterious trinket, but no one had ever found it.

When I'd first moved back into 2112 Mockingbird Lane, I'd searched through a good many of the Mason jars, imagining where the notions had come from or how they'd come into my ancestors' possession.

It looked to me like Meemaw was still on the hunt. And why not? She couldn't leave the house, so looking for the elusive gift from Butch to Texana probably kept her ghostly mind occupied.

She opened her mouth, emitting a haunting sound. "Willll." Her voice echoed, sounding more like a moan than any discernable word.

Trying to talk wasn't something she did very often. My heartbeat skittered. "What? Meemaw, what do you need?"

She tried again, but her form in front of me faltered, flickering like a faulty lightbulb. "Wiiiiilllll."

"You need Will?"

"Yyyyyyyy . . ." The distorted air holding onto her shape smoothed, the image of her disappearing.

"Yes? You need Will?"

But before she could answer, and just as suddenly as she'd appeared to me, she was gone. It was as if the light switch had been turned off. I knew she needed to recharge after the effort of appearing to me.

"I'll get him for you," I said to the empty room. I took my cell phone from my back pocket so I could call him once I got back downstairs. Back in the corner, a drawer slammed and something squeaked. In a strange, distorted way, it sounded like she was saying, *Thank you*.

Hopefully, I thought as an aside, she'd get her strength back and clean up the mess she'd made throughout the attic while I sewed. If not, it was going to be a late night for me. Knowing things in the attic were awry would weigh on me. I rifled through the cupboard of fabric next to the shelves of Mason jars, finding two of the pieces I needed for Delta's apron, then I headed back downstairs so I could get to work. It would take a good chunk of my evening, I knew, but I was bound and determined to finish it in one sitting. I wanted her to *ooh* and *ahh*, but I didn't want to spend umpteen hours on the project. I had the other Red Hatters to get to know, so I could make their aprons for them, not to mention the other commitments on the calendar.

I knew I needed to allot my time efficiently because I was recommitted to a fulfilling personal life with Will. I also wanted to build a Web site for the business, to help with expansion, but I never seemed to find the time to work on it. When I came to the bottom step, the sharp scent of chopped onions and garlic wafted to me from the direction of my kitchen. I knew from experience that Meemaw didn't have the ghostly skills to actually cook, try as she might, which meant either Mama or Nana was here, and they had just started making something delicious to eat.

"How did you know? I'm starving!" I said. I half walked, half hopped as I headed toward the kitchen, pulling off my favorite burnt-red Frye harness boots and dropping them along the way. I stripped out of my asymmetrical Ultrasuede jacket, which I'd made for myself in between other projects, and hung it over the ladder-backed chair in what I now used as the dining room. The smoky scent of the paprika and onions hung in the air, and I knew what was on the menu. Chili. My stomach grumbled in response as I passed through the archway to the kitchen . . .

And stopped short.

It wasn't Meemaw—no surprise—but it also wasn't Mama or Nana standing at the pale yellow cast iron stove.

It was Will.

And he wore an apron.

And not just any apron. He wore a manly canvas apron with I ♥ BEEF emblazoned on it. We were in Texas, after all.

"Speak of the devil," I said, tucking my cell phone away. No need to call him since he was already here. "Meemaw's looking for you."

"Is she now?"

"She'll have to wait, though." I sidled up to him, leaned in, and kissed him as he turned to greet me.

He gave me a cockeyed grin and pulled me close. "Tough day at the office?"

"I wish. Tough day at the neighbor's house."

He returned to the stove, stirring the concoction of ground beef, beer, onions, garlic, tomato sauce, and spices. As the ingredients cooked, we chatted, catching up on the routine parts of our day. When the beef had cooked, he scooped up a spoonful and, with one hand cupped under it, offered it to me for a taste.

Gently, I blew on it, and then took a tentative bite. Will liked his food spicier than I did, but he was learning my taste and accommodating my preferences, adding his own extra spice after the fact so we could both enjoy a meal. "That's so good," I said.

"Imagine it over a bowl of Fritos and then topped with cheese and sour cream."

Frito chili pie. A Texas staple, if there ever was one. I

for one discarded all the brouhaha about Frito pie orig-
inating in Santa Fe. They served something similar on a
bed of lettuce. Lettuce? That was just wrong.

I glanced around the kitchen. No lettuce in sight, although I had noticed right away that Will's chili had
beans, and lots of them. Black, kidney, pinto, and one
other that I didn't recognize. Tomatoes and corn, too. In
general, the accepted Texas chili was bean free, but I'd
take Will's version any day.

He served me up a bowl before serving himself, top-
ping his with a healthy dash (or three) of cayenne pepper, and we sat at the kitchen table to eat. "No Gracie
tonight?" I asked when I finally forced myself to stop for
a breath.

"She's out with Shane."

I dipped my chin and gazed at him through my lowered lashes. "So you thought you'd wine and dine me and
then take me—"

The sentence was left hanging when the bag of Fritos
suddenly flew off the counter, the contents spilling across
the hardwood floor. Will and I looked at each other, at
the chips, then at each other again. "Loretta Mae?" he
asked.

"That'd be my guess."

"Guess she doesn't want me to take you ... anywhere," he said, cracking that sideways smile again.

"Whatever are we to do?" I asked, placing the back of
my hand against my forehead in manufactured Scarlett
O'Hara angst.

"Well, I just happen to have my own house—"

The bag of Fritos skittered across the floor, the mess

of chips scattering farther and wider. A low, haunting sound came from nowhere and everywhere at once and sounded like a ghostly voice saying, "Uh-uh, uh-uh, uh-uh."

Seems my great-grandmother didn't want to wait for Will to find her, so she'd come in search of him.

"Or we can stay here and clean up the kitchen," Will finished, adding in a whisper so only I could hear, "and then we can skedaddle to my place."

Instantly, Meemaw shifted to, "Mmm-hmm," and Will and I burst out laughing. I was thirty-two—he had a year on me—and we couldn't even snuggle up properly at 2112 Mockingbird Lane for fear of upsetting Loretta Mae. Not that I wanted a witness to my snuggling with Will, so going to his place always felt like a good idea. If we ever got married, I wasn't sure what I'd do. I couldn't imagine living anywhere besides this house, where I'd practically grown up and where I ran Buttons & Bows, yet Meemaw's presence put a crimp in my romantic life. Plus Will and Gracie had their own home and wouldn't want to uproot themselves any more than I wanted to.

Love was complicated.

Snuggle time with Will at his place would have to wait. We cleaned the kitchen, then Will went off to the attic in search of Loretta Mae. I left him to it, so I could get started on Delta's apron. I plowed through the armoire in the sitting room, looking for the other specific pieces of organza and silk I had envisioned. Once I found them, I sketched out a rough pattern and went to work cutting the underskirt out of muslin. Next I cut the ties from a denim blue silk organza and the waistband out of a pale-rose-colored silk dupioni. I used another polyester organza, this time in cream, for the bottom ruffle, a subdued pink silk chiffon for the top ruffle, and finally, a pop of blue tulle for the center ruffle.

I marked each center point, hemmed each piece of fabric, and layered and pleated as I put them all together. Once the waistband and ties were added, I went on to the finishing touches to add some charm and whimsy. I attached puffy little rosettes at the waist, as well as putting them in a few strategic points on the front where the top layer of taffeta would be gathered and secured with a round puff of fabric with a hole in the middle. These yo-yos, placed every six inches along the lower edge of the taffeta layer, gave the ruffle a scalloped edge. The heart-shaped pewter button at the hemline was the final accent.

By the time it was finished, the apron was gorgeous. A showstopper, which was just what Delta wanted. If only my charm allowed me to sew something specific into the garments I made, weaving in a little compassion, or stitching in a little joy. From what I'd seen, Delta seemed preoccupied and a touch unhappy. But changing something specific wasn't my charm. Once she wore the apron, her greatest wish would come true. I just hoped Delta wanted something honorable.

Will had long since said good-bye, lightly kissing my lips. "Did you find Meemaw?" I'd asked when he was on his way out a couple hours back.

He'd nodded, that crooked grin showing up again, for all the world looking like he was up to no good. "Can't really talk to her, you know. I think she wanted my help fixing a squeaky drawer in one of the dressers. 'Course I could be wrong about that, since she disappeared again after a while. I did clean up the attic a little bit."

He was a hero. He'd accepted not only my charm (and Gracie's), but also the fact that a ghost lived here. Not many men could come to terms with that. My own father hadn't been able to, walking out the moment he'd discovered my mother had a little magic in her.

By the time I placed the last stitch on Delta's apron, it was nearly three in the morning. I could wait until morning to deliver it, or I could wrap it up and go put it on her doorstep. Finishing a project for someone was exciting. It always felt like Christmas morning when I'd discovered the perfect gift, which filled me with anticipation as I waited for the recipient to open it. I wanted Delta to see the apron first thing, so I decided to sneak over in the middle of the night when she was fast asleep. Patience was not my strong suit.

I wrapped the apron in a sheet of textured ecru tissue paper, tying it with a rustic burlap ribbon. The temperature outside had finally dropped, so I threw on a BLISS CHOIR hoodie Gracie had left behind on her last visit, tucked my feet into my slippers, and headed next door. The house was completely dark—not surprising given the time of night. But the front porch, with its overhang, was especially black, and I hadn't thought to bring a flashlight.

It took me all of twenty seconds to drop the pretty bundle on the doormat and hightail it back home. I lay down, exhausted but satisfied. The apron was gorgeous, and I hoped it would help me turn over a new leaf with

Delta. No more family feud. No more animosity. I wanted to see the side of her that her friends knew and loved.

My little teacup pig, Earl Grey, was asleep in his bed beside mine, and I looked forward to nothing but six blissful hours of sleep ahead of me. The week ahead would be busy, but with Delta off my back, it would be nothing I couldn't handle. I drifted off, dreaming of Meemaw and her antics, beautiful fabric, and aprons, and knowing the week ahead would be a good one.

Chapter 4

First thing the next morning I headed to Buffalo Bill's Ranch House, a down-home restaurant on Bliss's historic downtown square. My friend Madelyn had called me while I walked, canceling our breakfast plans. Left to my own devices, I decided it felt like a waffle kind of day. I ordered mine with a side of strawberries and ate slowly, in case my friend's schedule changed and she showed, then paid and left when it became clear she wasn't joining me.

My stomach full, I headed straight to the church to work my shift at the tag sale. The sale itself didn't start until tomorrow, but we were nowhere near ready. "Thank heavens you're here." Georgia Emmons greeted me as I walked inside the enormous white tent that had been set up for the event. "Cynthia and Delta are both late, and the Red Hatters are supposed to be sorting the clothes. Randi's here, but Bennie can't make it, and Coco and Sherri both are scheduled to be here at eleven."

Georgia drew in a breath and continued on. "I'm working on these jeans."

She pointed to the massive stack of denim on the portable table in front of her. The jeans were folded and piled on top of one another. Two stacks, three feet high each. The grimace on her face made it clear she didn't relish this particular job.

I caught a glimpse of my reflection in a full-length mirror leaning up at the end of the aisle. Jean skirt with a flouncy navy cotton ruffle, my red Fryes, and a white blouse I'd made several years ago, knotted at the waist. Clearly I had nothing against denim.

Georgia had on a floral wrap dress in a deep green pattern, and wide-heeled taupe pumps. She looked like she could have walked straight out of the pages of a 1940s magazine. Denim was not her style.

"I can take over," I said, thinking she'd jump at the chance to be done with the jeans. But she surprised me. "No," she said matter-of-factly. Without Cynthia or Delta here to take charge, she'd stepped into the role. Third in command, I reckoned. "It's a dirty job, and I'm already invested in it."

I glanced around to gauge where I should go to help. There were plenty of people sorting things, as well as other people standing around chatting, and I wondered if they might not need me after all. I could go home and start on the next apron. A vision of one for Georgia Emmons had popped into my head. It was flirty, with a ruffle that started mid-thigh. A large fabric flower accented a band of contrasting fabric, and the same pattern created the neck ties and a band around the front. The main fabric would be a pale green background with happy pink flowers, and the contrasting bands would be pink and white polka dots. Vintage, yet contemporary. It would be perfect for her.

"We need more price tags, but they're in my car. I'm up to my elbows in these." She gestured to the massive pile of denim. "Would you mind?"

"Not a bit. I'll get them," I said, already turning to head back to the parking lot. I didn't want to interrupt Georgia's system, and I didn't mind being an errand girl.

"I parked in the east lot," she said, handing me her key ring. "Behind the cemetery. If you cut through it, it'll be faster."

The cemetery was small, shaded by massive oak and pecan trees, and well kept. Tombstones stood sentry at the older graves, while the more contemporary flat markers intermixed on newer plots. Georgia had suggested walking through the graveyard, but I wasn't sure I wanted to take the shortcut.

"Harlow!"

Georgia hollered my name from the tag sale tent. As I turned toward her, she pointed one finger and rotated it in the air, motioning for me to hurry up.

I held my hand up and nodded, telling her I understood. The cemetery shortcut it was.

A three-foot-high black wrought-iron fence that looked as ancient as the graves surrounded the cemetery. A shiver passed down my spine. I'd seen plenty of death, especially since I'd been back in Bliss, but that didn't make the town's graveyard my favorite place to be. If it had been night, instead of morning, dark instead of light,

I would have thought twice about entering. But it wasn't, so I cowgirled up. A tag sale waited for no one, least of all a ninny who preferred to take the long way round. I opened the gate and slipped through, walking along the pathways between the gravesites.

I felt confident in my planned design for the next apron, but I needed to search out the right fabrics. "The fabric store," I said aloud. "We need a field trip." It would be perfect! Each of the Red Hat ladies could pick out just what they wanted, which would help me hone in on the perfect design. Once I had those two elements in my head for all the Red Hatters, putting together the actual garments would be easy as pie.

I walked faster, hearing Georgia's voice in the back of my mind urging me to hurry up with the tags. The parking lot was only ten yards away, but I had to skirt around a digger that was parked smack in the middle of my path. A newly dug grave meant a funeral was imminent. I gave a wide berth to the John Deere, stepping onto a small mound of fresh dirt. As I moved around the backhoe, I caught the first glimpse of a rectangular hole in the ground. Another shiver passed through me. It was one thing to think about death, but quite another to see an empty grave where someone would soon be buried. Someone who'd very recently been a living, breathing being.

More of the hole came into view and I stopped abruptly, gasping and suddenly short of breath. Because inside the hole was a body, and it wasn't just any body.

Inside the fresh grave lay Delta Lea Mobley.

I scrambled down into the grave, slipping on the dirt

and landing on my knees. Yanking my cell phone from my purse, I dialed 911, then bent over Delta.

"Is she breathing?" the operator asked after I told her what I'd found.

I'd put two fingers against the artery in Delta's neck, feeling for a pulse. Nothing. Her face was smudged with dirt, her eyes wide-open, and her mouth agape. I crouched closer, calling her name, looking for signs of life. There wasn't a single one. No breath coming in or going out of her body. No twitching fingers. No movement whatsoever.

"No," I said into the cell phone. "I'm pretty sure she's dead."

Chapter 5

I called Hoss McClaine straight away, and seemingly moments later the whole of Bliss's law enforcement team descended upon the cemetery. Work at the tag sale ground to a halt as the news of Delta's death traveled over there.

"That's everything?" the sheriff asked me after his team hoisted me out of the grave. I shook off the morose veil that had settled over me and told him what I'd seen. People often made the mistake of thinking he was nothing but a country lawman, assuming his thought process was as slow as his Southern drawl, but they were wrong. One too many cow-tippings, times climbing water towers, and trips joy-riding in the backs of pickup trucks on private property when I'd been a teenager meant I'd had my share of run-ins with Sheriff McClaine. I knew he was one of the sharpest knives in the drawer.

But we'd come to a peaceful understanding since I'd been back in Bliss, letting bygones be bygones. I'd outgrown my childish antics, and he'd ... well, he was still the same, but I'd come to respect him. And recently he'd gone and married my mother, making him not only the sheriff, but my step-daddy.

"Yes, sir." I'd told him about sewing an apron for her and delivering it to her doorstep in the early hours of the morning.

"That apron there?" He pointed to another deputy sheriff who was pulling the half apron out of Delta's discarded purse.

"That's it," I said. It was a small consolation to think that she'd liked the apron enough to take it with her to the tag sale, presumably to show her friends. In her last hours, I'd given her a bit of happiness.

"Interesting," he said.

In that one word, I could tell he had prepared a good sampling of questions to start off his investigation. I certainly had questions of my own. Delta had been late showing up at the tag sale. Had she planned to meet someone in the cemetery, and that meeting had turned ugly? Or had she taken a shortcut and happened upon something she wasn't supposed to see?

So far, the sheriff hadn't indicated there'd been foul play, but a niggling in the back of my mind made me wonder. But, of course, I had no proof that Delta hadn't died of natural causes, so I kept my mouth shut. My mind had gone straight to murder as soon as I'd seen the body, but it occurred to me now that it was more likely that she'd fallen. Hadn't seen the hole, or had misjudged her footing, falling and hitting her head.

Madelyn Brighton snapped pictures of the scene. She

was the town's official photographer, and that meant she was called for in moments like these to document the evidence. She came up next to me, still focused on the scene. "You okay, love?" she said in her British accent as she took another series of shots.

I stood back from the grave taking it all in, one arm folded over my chest, the other angled up, my thumb running along my lower lip. "I'm okay," I said, pushing away my worry. "Just thinking."

"About?"

"Wondering how she ended up in the grave, is all. Seems odd."

"That it does. Pretty hard not to see a hole that size. She must have been out here pretty early."

"My thought exactly."

She leaned toward me, lowering her voice so only I could hear. "Are you thinking . . . murder?"

"Mercy, I hope not," I said. That would be far worse for her family than an accidental death. But I couldn't shake the question, and the possibility. Something didn't feel right about the whole situation.

A burst of noise came from an approaching group. Madelyn and I both looked up as Delta's daughter, Megan, walked up to where we stood. She was escorted by her husband, Todd, Rebecca, Megan's friend, whom I'd met the day before, and another man, whom I presumed was Anson Mobley, Megan's father. He was tall and thin, with an abundance of shaggy brown hair blowing in the breeze, his cheeks ruddy from the shock. I'd only ever seen him flying down Mockingbird Lane in his car. Seeing him now, I thought what an odd couple he and Delta must have made. She was on the short side, not more than five feet four inches, but he had to be more than six feet. She'd had dark hair, and his was almost blond. She was robust and he was rail thin. They seemed opposite in every way.

But opposites did attract, or so the old adage said. The sobbing continued, drawing me out of my thoughts and back to the group descending on the gravesite. Coco and Sherri trudged behind Megan, Rebecca, Todd, and Anson, holding on to each other's hands. Sisterly comfort. And behind them came the other Red Hat ladies, each looking incredulous at the unexpected loss of their friend. Each woman was dabbing a tissue or handkerchief to her eyes. Each one was sobbing.

The other people who'd been working the tag sale came to the edge of the cemetery, most staying outside the fence, but some venturing in. The pastor broke through the crowd, making a beeline for the family. He wrapped his arm around Megan, letting her face fall against his shoulder in grief.

There were other onlookers I didn't recognize. They seemed to have come in droves to see the woman in the grave. I knew death brought out the morbid curiosity in people, but it still gave me an uneasy feeling.

I stayed put just until Hoss McClaine gave me permission to leave. "Try to keep out of trouble, Harlow," he said as I started to walk away. The message was clear. It was bad enough that I'd discovered the body. That had happened a bit too frequently. He didn't want me getting wrapped up in whatever had happened to Delta.

But back at Buttons & Bows a few hours later, I was

surrounded by the Red Hatters. They had shown up at the shop in a big group, gathered around me, and started asking a million questions at once, wanting to get the nitty-gritty straight from the horse's mouth. "The sheriff said she fell and hit her head on a rock in the grave," Georgia said.

My imagination was running wild. Did she fall, or was she pushed? I had no way of knowing, so I shoved the thought away and tried to focus on the women before me.

"How long was she there before you found her?" Randi asked.

"Did you see anything, Harlow?" Cynthia asked, but before I could answer, Sherri, Delta's younger sister, burst into sobs and tried to wipe away her flowing tears. "She found Delta, Cyn," she said, steadying her trembling voice. "She didn't see what happened."

"We need to pray," Bennie said softly. "Your poor mother, Sherri. I can't imagine what Jessie Pearl's going through. Megan, too."

"Mother's in shock," Sherri said. She cupped her hands over her eyes, her chin quivering. "She's lost. Delta was . . . was . . ."

"She was horrible to Mother," a new voice said. We all turned to see Coco Jones, Delta and Sherri's youngest sister, standing in the doorway of Buttons & Bows. She had one hand on the doorframe, the other on her hip. Her blond hair curled above her shoulders, and though her eyes were red-rimmed and bright, her voice was steady and indignant. "You all know it. You heard the way she spoke to Mother. The way she manipulated her. I'm sorry Delta's dead," Coco said, "but there was no love lost between us. I'd be lying to pretend otherwise."

Sherri's jaw dropped, and we all looked on in stunned silence as she stared at her sister. "Coco, Delta is dead! How can you even say that?"

Coco trained her eyes on her sister. "And how can you *not*? You heard plenty of times how Delta spoke to Mother. You *know* what she did to us both."

"Shht." Sherri glared at her sister. "Don't, Coco."

Coco's gaze traveled over each of the Red Hatters in a circle. "You can't sugarcoat things and make Delta out to be something she wasn't now that she's dead. I'm not saying Mother's better off with Delta gone, but things could be a might easier for her."

"You sound so heartless," Sherri said, her voice scarcely more than a whisper.

Coco blinked heavily, lowering her chin, almost looking chagrined.

"Will you say a prayer for your mother, Coco?" Randi asked.

"Well, of course. She's my mother and I love her. I loved Delta, too, for all her faults."

That was all the suggestion the Red Hatters needed. The women formed a circle and clasped hands. I stepped back, joining the circle, taking Randi's hand on my right and holding my left hand out for Coco to take.

She'd let the door close behind her, dropping her cloth purse on the loveseat, and stepped into the open space in the circle. She took Bennie's hand, then took mine, our gazes locking for a moment. I felt as if she were trying to send me a silent message, but I couldn't decipher the meaning behind the look.

Randi cleared her throat, squeezing my hand. At first I thought she was gathering strength from me, but she stood up straight, pushed her shoulders back, and exuded more confidence than I'd ever witnessed from her. She'd seemed so timid the last time I'd seen her, but right now her expression was forceful, and I realized she was bolstering everyone in the room. "Divine Mother of us all, your essence is within us and within all things. We ask for your energy and power on this sad day, that you may fill us with your sacred light, and help Jessie Pearl find peace, wholeness, grace, and wisdom during this time of trial.

"We ask that you help each one of us connect with your divine self, that we may be empowered by you and your love, and that Jessie Pearl may receive all your love and grace."

We all stood silent for a moment, taking in the words Randi had offered. It wasn't your typical Baptist or Methodist, or even Catholic offering, and I got the impression that none of the Red Hatters knew quite what to make of the prayer.

Finally, Coco arched a brow. "What the hell was that?" she demanded.

I thought Randi might shrink back from the criticism, but instead, she stood even taller. "You pray to God, I pray to the Goddess," she said. "Jessie Pearl needs all the support she can get. You're her daughter, you should know that."

"Thank you for that, Randi," Cynthia said, clearing

her throat. "Let's have a more traditional offering, too." She went on before anyone else could say a word, her voice ringing out clear and strong. "Dear Lord, we ask that you watch over Jessie Pearl, Sherri, Coco, Todd, and especially Megan and Anson as they grieve the loss of Delta. We ask this in the name of your son, Jesus Christ. Amen."

"Amen," everyone said at once.

And just like that, the little prayer circle disbanded.

If Randi was offended at the second prayer, she didn't let on. "Should we cancel the progressive dinner?" she asked, not really directing the question to anyone in particular, but more to the room at large.

Coco was the first to respond. "No, it should go on as planned. We need to make things upbeat for Mother."

"She needs to grieve, Coco," Sherri said, once again shaking her head as if she just didn't understand her sister.

"And she'll have plenty of time to grieve, but we need to keep things normal. We can't let her sink into her sorrow or we might never get her back out again."

The ladies all nodded in silent agreement. Jessie Pearl was going to need a lot of support as she came to terms with losing her eldest daughter.

"Harlow Jane!" The Dutch door in the kitchen was flung open and Mama's voice rang through the house. "Harlow Jane, I've got news. You'll never believe it. Hoss said that woman, your neighbor? She was murd—"

Mama came through the archway between the kitchen and dining room and stopped short, a startled expression on her face when she saw all the people still gathered in a circle in the front room. "What the devil?" she blurted.

"Mama, this is the Red Hat group I was telling you about." I swung my arm toward Coco and Sherri. "These are Jessie Pearl Trapper's daughters."

Mama sputtered, regaining her composure. "I'm so sorry for your loss," she said to them. "If I can do anythin' to help your mother, you be sure to let me know."

The women all stared at Mama, looking flummoxed. Only Coco had the wherewithal to speak her mind. "What were you saying about Delta?"

I already knew what she'd been about to say. It wasn't hard to fill in the blank on the word she'd cut short. It had been in the forefront of my mind since this morning's discovery of the body. And it had been a word far too present in my life since I'd been back in Bliss.

Murder.

Before Mama could answer, a cell phone rang. Then another. In mere seconds both Coco and Sherri had answered their phones, and they were both listening intently.

"Hit with it? That can't be right, Sheriff," Sherri said. So she was talking to Hoss.

Coco muttered something under her breath and hung up without saying anything more. I suspected the bearer of bad news for her had been Deputy Sheriff Gavin McClaine, Hoss's son. We'd run in different crowds in high school, but he'd found his confidence since he'd joined his dad's posse. Overconfident. If he weren't halfway decent at his job—and in love with one of my best friends, Orphie Cates—he would have driven me completely batty.

Coco and Sherri looked at each other. Sherri's eyes welled with tears. Coco nudged her glasses up with the backs of her fingers, jamming them back into position. And then Coco said, "Delta didn't fall and hit her head. The deputy said she had blunt force trauma to the back of her head."

The women stood frozen, each of them processing what Coco had said.

"What does that mean?" Cynthia finally asked.

Coco scanned the circle, looking at each of the women who'd been closest to Delta. "It means she didn't fall, and it wasn't an accident. It means," she said, "that Delta was murdered."

Chapter 6

A short while later, the majority of the Red Hatters had left Buttons & Bows. Only Cynthia Homer, Sherri Wynblad, and Coco Jones stayed. We sat in the little seating area, Coco on the red velvet settee, one of Meemaw's original pieces of furniture. Sherri sat back on the loveseat, her fingers intertwined in front of her. Cynthia and Mama sat together on the couch, Mama still looking shell-shocked that she'd almost been the one to break the news about there being another murder in Bliss, and Cynthia, if I wasn't mistaken, looking a little bit thrilled to be part of something so out of the ordinary.

I leaned back against the armoire that housed part of my fabric collection, one cowboy-booted foot crossed over the other, my arms folded protectively in front of me. Delta was dead, and my suspicions had been right. She'd been murdered. I felt the warm presence of Meemaw by my side, buoying me in this moment of crisis. Because once again, it appeared that I was in the thick of a murder.

I'd discovered Delta's body.

She'd had in her possession the apron *I'd* just made for her.

She'd been *my* next-door neighbor.

And I was still making aprons for all of her closest friends . . . since, as far as they'd said, the progressive dinner was still on.

I'd been through this sort of thing before, and I still couldn't make sense of how someone could come to the decision to take another person's life. Murder seemed to happen all around me, and sometimes, like now, I had to wonder if it was my ancestor Butch Cassidy's bad karma that kept coming back to me. And I also wondered if helping to solve murders would somehow help right his wrongs from so long ago.

Or maybe I was just plumb crazy.

Coco shook her head. "How will we ever tell Mother that Delta was murdered?"

No one had a good answer to that. Mama shook her head and filled the silence with her own question. "Why would anyone want her dead?"

Cynthia kept her eyes cast downward. Coco and Sherri remained silent.

Coco opened her mouth to say something but closed it again. Whatever her private thoughts were, she was keeping them to herself.

I wasn't a detective, but I'd had enough experience to warrant butting in. "Having an enemy who would want you dead is big. Murder isn't easy," I said to Coco and

Sherri. "There has to be a motive, right? The sheriff'll ask both of you what you think because y'all knew her the best."

Cynthia cleared her throat and looked up, her gaze passing over each of us. "I don't mean to interrupt," she said, knowing full well that's precisely what she was doing, and seemingly relishing the attention, "and I don't want to toss names out, you know, in case they're innocent, but I saw Delta and Jeremy Lisle, over at the Historic District? They were arguing about something. I wonder . . ."

She didn't want to toss out a name, but she'd done it anyway. I didn't know Jeremy Lisle, but I instantly felt bad for him. People argued, but that didn't mean they would kill someone. I wouldn't want anyone thinking I was capable of murder. I'd been through that once before, and it still left a sour taste in my mouth . . . and had lit a fire under my behind. Nothing like needing to clear your name to help you solve a murder.

"Did you hear what the argument was about?" Coco asked.

The corner of Cynthia's mouth lifted in a little self-satisfied smile. It was scarcely noticeable, but it was there. "Something about her position on the Bliss Historic Council."

Sherri's head snapped up. "What do you mean? She stepped down."

Cynthia looked like the cat who swallowed the canary, self-satisfied grin and all. "Maybe," was all she said.

Sherri glared. "If you know something, just spit it out, Cyn."

"Even if I knew, it's not my story to tell. Talk to Jeremy," she said.

"But do you have an idea?" I asked, already making a mental note to ask Will. He was on the Bliss Historic Council as the city architect.

"Like I said, I hate to stir up trouble and drag anyone's name through the mud, but I will say this," Cynthia said, her hand splayed dramatically across her chest. "Jeremy Lisle is running for mayor, and Delta backed the incumbent. Politics. Makes things sticky." She threw up her hands and looked at me. "You really should talk to Jeremy."

"The *sheriff* should talk to him, not me. I don't have anything to do with this." Because I'd had a hand in a few recent cases, people assumed I was unofficially involved in the goings-on of law enforcement in Bliss. But even if I was curious about what had happened to Delta, all I wanted to do, at the moment, was make aprons.

Coco leaned forward, catching my eye. "Harlow, Delta and I didn't always see eye to eye, that's certainly no secret, but she was my sister. She's left behind a daughter and a mother. And you have the gift of sleuthing. For Jessie Pearl, and for Megan, could you ask around and see what you can find out?"

I blinked at her. And blinked again. Still I couldn't figure out what to say. As the seconds ticked past, I wondered if I could blink away the curiosity coursing through me, blink away Coco's wide, crystal blue eyes imploring me to help her mother and her niece, blink away the intent gazes of Sherri and Cynthia, and blink away Mama shaking her head and silently communicating that under no circumstances was I to get wrapped up in another murder investigation.

As it often did, a question surfaced in my mind. *What would Meemaw do?*

I went over the possible answers:

1) Stay out of it—after all, although Delta had been my neighbor, it was none of my business;

2) Ride the sheriff and deputy sheriff's coattails to satiate my curiosity while still staying out of the fray; or

3) Help a friend in need.

I nodded, and for a second it felt as though Meemaw were right behind me, her hands on my shoulders, slowly pushing me forward. She needn't have bothered. There was no question what she would do if she were in my place. Up until her dying breath, she'd helped everyone around her, and if she could do anything to ease Jessie Pearl's pain at losing her daughter, she'd do it.

And so would I. "Yes. I'll see what I can find out," I said.

Mama leveled a *We're gonna have words about this later* look at me. Sherri wrung her hands and fought back her tears. But Cynthia sat up a trifle straighter, her lips thinning as her grin widened. "Excellent. As luck would have it, the Historic Council meets tonight. Jeremy will be there. I can go with you, introduce you around, and you can talk to him. It'll be the perfect chance to find out what he and Delta were arguing about."

Before I could decide whether I wanted to dive right into investigating Delta's death by talking to Jeremy Lisle or if I needed some time to think things through, perhaps while making an apron, Coco piped up. "Well, you certainly don't think I'm going to sit around by myself while you two are out solving Delta's murder. I'm coming, too." She looked at Cynthia, silently daring her to argue.

Cynthia's smile wobbled, but she managed to maintain it. "Don't let me stop you. It's open to the public. Starts at six thirty on the dot."

Coco cocked her head, forcing her own smile. "Wonderful. I'll be there at six."

Chapter 7

Bliss's Historic Council held its monthly meeting on the third Thursday of the month in the City Hall Annex building on Austin Street. It was located one block off the square. Buttercup, the vintage pale yellow pickup truck Meemaw had left me when she'd died, chugged along, bouncing with ancient charm as I passed through the square and headed to my first ever Historic Council meeting.

"I'll pick you up at five forty-five," Cynthia had said before she left Buttons & Bows earlier, but I'd managed to back away, wave my hands, and insist that I could get myself there.

"I don't mind," she pressed.

I'd pointed to Buttercup sitting under the row of possumwood trees along the side of the driveway between the Mobley house and mine. Behind the trees was a five-foot-deep thicket of shrubs Delta and Anson had planted nearly twenty years ago when Nana and her goats first intruded on their property. "I can get there on my own," I said, "but thanks."

Cynthia's chin dropped to her chest as she peered at the ancient truck. One eyebrow arched. "*That* is yours?"

"Sure is. I used to ride all over town in it with Loretta Mae when I was a girl." I grinned, remembering how we'd sometimes head to the outskirts of town to visit some old rancher Meemaw needed to talk to, and how my brother, Red, and I would sit in the bed of the truck as she drove through the pasture, the longhorns and Black Angus cattle within spitting distance.

Mama had sidled up beside me. "You can take the girl out of the country," she said proudly, "but you can't take the country out of the girl."

Wasn't that the truth? If I'd lost my Southern sensibilities during my time working with a renowned fashion designer in Manhattan, Mama might never have recovered. A girl could not hide her Texas heritage, and even though I'd tried to suppress it while in New York, it never really worked. I'd missed the Lone Star State, and my down-home qualities shone through no matter how I tried to lose my accent to appear more sophisticated.

Finally, I'd given up. Even back then, most of my designs were influenced by my Southern and Western roots. Slowly but surely, my slow Texas drawl had returned. It hadn't taken long for me to settle back into life in Bliss, with all its quirks and subtleties.

As I walked into the City Hall Annex, I stood in the hallway for a moment wondering which room the meeting would be in. "Hello there, Sunshine," said a male voice from behind me. A voice I knew well. Will Flores.

His hands settled on my hips, skimming them as I turned to face him, tuning out the other people milling around us. "Hello to you, Mr. Flores."

"Never thought I'd see you at one of our these meetings."

"I like to keep you on your toes," I said before letting my lips brush his.

He grinned. "You do a good job of that. Never know what you're going to be up to next."

Will had been one of the first people I'd met after I'd set up shop in Bliss. He'd had a key to the house, courtesy of Meemaw, and had done handyman tasks around the place, also courtesy of Meemaw. What Loretta Mae wanted, she got. That was her charm, and she used it well. She'd wanted something to develop between Will and me, and she'd set out to make that happen by bartering deals with him prior to her death. She'd arranged for Will to do work around 2112 Mockingbird Lane in exchange for me instructing Gracie, his daughter, on basic sewing skills. Turns out Gracie didn't need my tutelage, but after I got to know him, I didn't mind having Will hang around.

Meemaw had gotten what she wanted. Will and I were going strong, in love, and looking toward a future together.

"About that," I said, lifting my gaze to meet his. "You know Delta Mobley—"

He dropped his hands back to his sides and took a step backward. "Don't do it, Cassidy."

He probably knew he couldn't really stop me from digging into Delta's death, but I had no doubt he felt honor-bound to try. He preferred that I didn't get involved in the mysteries that seemed to abound in Bliss, but he also accepted that I tended to get involved anyway.

I crinkled my nose in a show of contrition. "It's a little bit too late. Coco, Sherri, and Cynthia were over at the house, then Mama stopped by, and, well, before I knew what was happening, I said I'd poke around and see what I could find out."

He cocked his head and gave it a slow, steady shake. "Cassidy, Cassidy, Cassidy. Will you ever learn?"

I closed the gap between us, slipping my hands around his waist. "Flores, Flores, Flores," I said, but instead of shaking my head, I lifted my chin and stood on my toes until our lips touched. "I am learning. Every time I help right the wrongs in this crazy town, I'm learning."

He wrapped his arms around me and grinned. "I meant, will you ever learn to stay out of the crime business?"

"Probably not," I said, then added, "but at least I'm on the right side of it."

His response was an extra squeeze. "Let's keep it that way." A minute later, he led me into a nearby room and to the front row of portable chairs. He sat down next to me. "Since you're here, we should finally finish getting your house designated as a historic landmark. I have Loretta Mae's file, and everything's in order."

I knew that my great-grandmother had shown up at a council meeting about a month before she passed. The house that I now owned was one of the original dwellings off the square and was one of the oldest homes in town. Legend had it that when Bonnie and Clyde went on their rampage through the county, they hung out in Bliss, robbed the bank on the square, and hid out in my backyard. That, along with our connection to Butch Cassidy, made the house all the more interesting. If any house in town had history built into the walls, it was 2112 Mockingbird Lane.

When I'd first met Will, the house was nearly through the historic designation process, but it had been stalled because of the change of ownership. Actually, unbeknownst to me, I'd owned it since I was born. Loretta Mae had deeded it to me the day of my birth. But years later, she'd submitted the paperwork to the Bliss Historical Society in her own name. A minor thing that anywhere else could have been fixed with a little white-out and a ballpoint pen. But in Bliss, it meant we had to go through the entire process again. Something I simply hadn't had time to do.

Whenever it was complete, the house would go on the registry. Pictures would be taken. And it would become part of a book on Bliss history and unforgettable local characters.

Forget about the fact that a ghost resided inside and that the Cassidys, who'd built it, were charmed. My house had a pretty stellar identity all on its own.

"All you have to do is sign the form, since you're the owner," Will said. "Then give the group some context as to your intentions—"

"My intentions?" He made it sound like I needed to explain myself to a judgment committee.

He tilted his head toward the people milling around

the horseshoe tables positioned in front of the room. "It helps them feel connected to the houses they approve," he said, his voice lower than it had been a second ago.

"But they already approved it the first time around."

He nodded, his brows furrowing. "Right. They just want to hear from you before they approve it in your name. Make sure you plan to stick around and honor the Historic District's guidelines."

This was all a little too intense. The house had become my home—and I had no intention of doing anything crazy like painting it purple or ripping out the yard and pouring cement. Maybe the committee, minus Will, of course, was a little power hungry. I thought about Delta and how headstrong and vocal she'd been. She very well could have rubbed someone on the committee the wrong way if they didn't want people voicing their opinions.

I stared at him. "Tonight? Right now?"

He chuckled and took my hand. "Tonight. When you told me you were coming, I added you to the agenda. They can designate, and then we'll get someone out to take pictures of the house. Of course tonight you'll have to give a statement—"

"Whoa, there, back up, cowboy," I said, taking back my hand. "What do you mean, make a statement? I have to get up and speak in front of the committee?"

"It'll be easy. Loretta Mae did it, you know."

Meemaw had stood right here in this room and addressed Bliss's Historic Council? How could I not have known that?

But of course she did. It made perfect sense. She'd almost completed the process before she died. She'd wanted the house designated, which meant I needed to follow through with getting it done. Even if it meant standing up in front of the Council to tell the story of my house.

Will left me to my own devices as he slipped into his seat at the front of the room. He'd blindsided me. Smart man. I might not have shown up otherwise. I looked around at the tables arranged in a horseshoe shape. Will sat on the far side, facing me. Eight other people sat around in their designated spots, all with a name placard in front of them. In the center was Jeremy Lisle. He rapped a gavel against the table, calling the meeting to order. The minutes of the previous meeting were approved, and the first order of business was dealt with. I used the opportunity to observe Will. I'd seen him in his office, working at the Courthouse on the Square, and at his house building architectural models. But I'd never seen him as part of a group like this. I was impressed by what I saw. He was the kind of man who could fit in almost anywhere. He was rugged and had a cowboy swagger, but put him in a suit and tie, and he'd do just fine.

The first order of business was a couple who had put in a request to paint their historic house. Even the paint color had to be approved by the council. A city representative stood at the podium and took the council through a PowerPoint presentation about the Queen Anne house, the acceptable colors, modifications that had been done previously, and her recommendation.

One of the council members raised her hand to comment. "I did a bit of research," she said when Jeremy Lisle called on her. "The green and burgundy color choices fit the style and era of the home. These colors were appropriate for Queen Anne homes, so I think it'll be a nice addition to the Historic District. I recommend we accept the application for a color change."

Jeremy Lisle called for a vote. The council voted with a show of hands. It was unanimous. "Approved," he said a moment later.

That had been easy, I thought, noting that the couple who'd submitted the application had declined to speak. Maybe I could just wave my hand, smile sweetly, and they'd let me slide without addressing them, too. "Wishful thinking," I muttered just as Coco slid into the seat beside me. In the blink of an eye, a vision of her in an apron appeared in my head. It was a full apron with a straight bodice and a ruffle on the skirt. The fabric itself, however, I couldn't see. Blue. That's all I could identify, but it was a start.

She greeted me, then whispered, "I saw Zinnia James back there. We go way back. I sold her and Jeb their first house here in town. That was when Jeb was first starting out in politics, and I was new to real estate. Sold them all their houses, in fact. Zinnia, she's connected to everyone, and I just bet she knows something about the brouhaha between Delta and Jeremy." She glanced behind her. "But Cynthia plunked down right next to me, and then she leaned over and started talking over me," she whispered, "so I didn't have a chance to talk to Zinnia about it. I'll talk to her after the meeting. She comes to all of these, did you know?"

I knew Zinnia James pretty well. She'd been one of my first clients in town, and she had become a mentor and unofficial benefactor of Buttons & Bows, funneling clients and events my way, both of which had helped to keep my shop afloat for the past year. Between Coco and me, I had no doubt we'd get every last nugget of information Mrs. James might have about Delta, Jeremy, and the Historic Council kerfuffle.

But that would have to wait because at that moment, the next agenda item was called. "The designation of 2112 Mockingbird Lane as a historic landmark," Jeremy Lisle announced. "Are the concerned parties present?"

I met Will's gaze, and he gave a slight nod. My cue. I half stood, half waved, and then sat back down. A twenty-something black woman rose and walked to the podium. I recognized her, and the outfit she wore, right away. Janice Sweetwater. She'd come to Buttons & Bows to ask me a few questions about the history of the house, I just hadn't known that information would be compiled and shared in this environment. We'd sat on the porch and I'd told her all about how my great-great-great-grandmother Texana, having adopted the Cassidy name—the only name she'd ever known her true love by—and using Butch's money, had built the house for herself and Cressida, her daughter with Butch, and how it had stayed in the family for all these years.

Now she stood in front of the room, acknowledged me with a little smile, then pointed a small remote device toward the projector. My house appeared on the screen behind Jeremy Lisle. Yellow clapboard siding, redbrick accents, the wraparound porch with the rocking chairs. It was the home where Loretta Mae had taught me to sew.

Where stacks of quilts told the story of the Cassidy women, beginning with Cressida.

When Janice was finished, the committee began asking questions. "In what year was the house built?" one member asked.

"Nineteen oh six," Janice replied. "Built by Louis Sacher, contracted by Texana Cassidy. It's unclear if Butch Cassidy himself ever saw the house, although it's purported that his money funded it. The house has remained in the Cassidy family ever since."

For a moment, I could almost envision my ancestor, Butch, hammer in hand, piecing together the boards of the house just as the love of his life, Texana, and then Cressida, had used fabric to piece together the ancestral quilts I treasured. She'd used bits of old fabric and clothing to tell the stories of her life. These were the threads that bound us all together and were the foundation of our family.

"The application is complete," Will said, after a few more questions had been asked and answered. "The house is a perfect example of the historical architecture in Bliss. It's right next door to the Mobley house, which we designated six months ago."

I shot a glance at Will, and he met it with a small smile. He was laying the groundwork for me.

"We should designate it," he finished.

"Ms. Cassidy," Jeremy Lisle said, looking at me. "The podium is yours."

Nerves had taken hold of me, and my legs felt rubbery. I usually had no trouble addressing a crowd. I'd MC'd fashion shows, taught classes, and had even spoken at a local community college class in fashion design. But this crowd felt different somehow. Even if it was a shoo-in that the historic designation would be approved, I was still worried. I needed to do Meemaw proud.

I stood, running my hands down the jean skirt I wore, to straighten it. Most of my designs had a slight country flair to them, and my current attire was no exception. I'd changed it up by giving the skirt panels and building curve into the hips. Then I'd added a two-inch ruffle along the hemline in a dark blue cotton. It dressed the denim up, but didn't feel overdone.

I had on a cream blouse and had finished the outfit with cream-colored boot socks, the lace and delicate buttons peeking out from under a pair of dark brown boots. Looking at the other women in the room, I knew I could have dressed down in jeans and a T-shirt and still fit in fine. But since I owned and operated a custom dressmaking shop, I was a walking advertisement for my business. If I didn't wear my creations, and wear them well, how could the townsfolk I hoped to woo with my style have any confidence in me?

At the podium, I faced the nine people assembled at the front of the room. I felt Will's gaze on me and drew strength from his support in the same way I drew strength from knowing that Meemaw was still with me. Each of the council members had their attention glued firmly on me. I cleared my throat and launched into my impromptu speech.

"If there is any house in Bliss that should be on the historic registry, it is 2112 Mockingbird Lane. As Janice said, the house has been in the Cassidy family for six generations now, and will be for many more to come. The Cassidys have our roots in Bliss, and we're not going any-where. From the moment the house was built, it was magical." I thought of Meemaw and added, "It still is."

The air in the room grew still. It was common knowl-edge that my family was charmed, but it was a don't ask, don't tell kind of thing. Most everyone in town was aware of the magic that surrounded us. Mama's special orchids, which she grew in the greenhouse on her prop-erty, were in high demand. She was called on to fix dying lawns and raggedy plants, and people seemed to ignore the fact that she never brought tools or soil enhance-ments to do a job. Nana's charm wasn't as widely helpful, but to anyone with a goat, she was a goddess. The cheeses she produced were celebrated for their wonderful vari-ety. And me? Buttons & Bows had acquired a reputation as the place to get custom designs that would change your life.

"The house," I continued quickly, "is everything to my family. Loretta Mae wanted it designated as a historic landmark to share the history of it with the community. I'm here to make that happen."

As the words left my mouth, I could feel my body relax, the nervousness easing out of me.

One by one, the people on the committee nodded. "Not everyone has your passion, Ms. Cassidy," the woman sitting next to Will said.

"I love the house," I said, "and I believe it should be preserved as part of Bliss's Historic District."

With that, I sat back down next to Coco and blew out the breath I'd been holding. She patted my knee. "You

did good, Harlow. You're a natural. Loretta Mae would
be proud."

The group voted. One by one, their hands went up. It
was unanimous, and 2112 Mockingbird Lane was named
a historic landmark. I'd get my own little circular black
and gold plaque to hang up on the front of the house. I
sat a little taller because I knew Coco was right. Meemaw
would be thrilled to know that I had completed what
she'd started.

After three more agenda items, the meeting was ad-
journed. It was now or never. I summoned up my sleuthing moxie, ready to start ferreting out the truth about
Delta's dealings with the council.

Coco had wandered off to chat with Zinnia James,
and I headed straight for Jeremy Lisle. I'd been so busy
worrying about speaking in front of the group that I
hadn't really looked closely at him. Now that I did, I saw
that he was balding, but had the cool look of Bruce Willis or Vin Diesel. Tanned skin, even on the top of his
head, slight stubble that gave him an edgy look, and one
earring in his left lobe.

Not your typical small-town Texas mayor. I wondered
if he'd win the election in the fall, or if the incumbent,
Richard Radcliffe, would.

Jeremy Lisle wore khakis and a white button-down
shirt, undone at the top. No tie. No jacket. I couldn't tell
if this state of casual cool was really authentic or if he
was trying hard to maintain his youth. I waited for an
image of him to appear in my mind, some other attire
that would help me define him, but nothing appeared.
Peculiar. Part of my Cassidy charm meant that I saw im-

ages of people in my mind wearing outfits that would bring out some latent qualities and would help them discover more of their true selves. Either I just couldn't get a read on the man, or what I saw was the true Jeremy Lisle and there wasn't anything that I could make that would fit him better.

Jeremy Lisle seemed to be an open book. No mystery. No deep wants or desires.

"Ms. Cassidy," he said, pumping my hand up and down. "Congratulations on the historical designation."

"Loretta Mae would be so happy," I said, editing *would* to *will* in my head. When I told her, I wondered if she'd become a little more corporeal for a few moments, or if she'd be so happy she'd flit around like a mad ghost, leaving just a trail of glitter in her wake.

"And do you like being back in Bliss? Loretta Mae was thrilled you were coming home."

I laughed. "I think she knew I was coming back before I did and told the whole town."

"She had a way of knowing things like that."

I looked up at him sharply, feeling even more curious than I'd been a minute ago. "Did you know her well?"

He stood straight, his cowboy boots placed firmly on the ground. "Everyone knew Loretta Mae," he said, but hesitated. He frowned slightly, then added, "As much as anybody could really know her, that is."

I considered Jeremy. He was perceptive. Loretta Mae had been affable and approachable, but he was absolutely right in his assessment. She let people see what she wanted them to see, let them know what she wanted them to know. And generally, she didn't want a whole lot of strangers knowing much about her. She had the Cassidy charm to protect, after all.

Tears pricked my eyes. Suddenly I felt a deep longing. I wanted Loretta Mae, in the flesh, back in my life. I missed her sense of humor, her voice, which I hadn't heard in so long, the zippy sound of her sewing machine as she flew through different projects. These things existed only in my memories now.

I took a deep breath and blinked hard to clear my eyes. "Such a shame about Delta Mobley," I said, changing the subject. Not subtle, but when death struck our small town, there didn't need to be a preamble.

"Sure is. Murder, I heard."

I watched him closely, looking for a twitch, a fidget, or anything that might make me think he carried a little guilt in him. But his expression held steady, he stayed rooted to the ground, and he stood tall.

"That's what I heard, too. She's my . . . I mean, she *was* my neighbor. I still can't believe it. Poor Jessie Pearl. There can't be anything worse than losing a child, and violently to boot."

We both paused for an automatic beat of silence. When Jeremy spoke again, there was a hint of sympathy in his tone. "I feel for her mother."

"Do you have any ideas on who could have done this to her?" I asked.

He shook his head. "I didn't know her well."

I frowned, letting my confusion show. "I thought she was on the council with you."

"Well, sure. But so are a lot of people. This is work, though, not social hour."

"Oh, I know. Important work. Loretta Mae taught me early how important preserving history is," I said.

He nodded solemnly. "Not everyone thinks so, but you're right."

"I love that both my house and the Mobley house are designated historical landmarks," I said.

Instead of agreeing, like I thought he would, he pursed his lips.

"Is something wrong?" I asked.

He looked around, then lowered his voice. "Look, between you and me, Delta was on the council and even had the house designated, but she didn't really believe in preserving history."

I hadn't had to work hard to get him to talk, which was *not* what I'd expected. "What do you mean? Isn't wanting to preserve history sort of a requirement of being part of the council?"

He glanced around again before speaking. I followed his lead, looking at the people milling around after the meeting. Will stood nearby, talking to an old cowboy with silvery white hair and a lanky figure. He could talk to anyone, and everyone loved to chat him up.

He caught my eye, and I knew he was giving me space to talk to Jeremy, but I was also one hundred percent confident that, at the same time, he was listening to our conversation with one ear. "Delta liked to bend the rules, shall we say? There was a lot of gray area when it came to right and wrong."

That was interesting. Over the years, I'd come to realize that people almost always acted in their own self-interest. If Delta bent the rules, my guess was that it benefited her somehow. "You mean when she was on the council here?"

"Definitely." He lowered his voice. "Between you and me, there are people in this town who don't see things the way you and I do. When I'm mayor, I'll make our Historic District and the preservation of our town's history a priority."

I wasn't sure how he knew what my personal perspective was, since we'd just met, but I assumed it was based on my application for the historic designation. I went with it, aligning myself with him for the sake of Jessie Pearl. "I know what you mean. Too many people don't seem to care about the Historic District or the history of Bliss."

"Right! They'd be perfectly happy if Bliss looked like Any Town, USA. I'll fight that till my dying breath. We've had to fight the city over tearing down some of the old houses in the area. They'd be happy to demolish them and build parking garages. Fair warning, Ms. Cassidy, the Historic District'll turn into a cement city if the restrictions are lifted."

"But Delta didn't feel that way, did she? I mean, she just had her house designated as historic, so . . ."

I left the sentence hanging there so he could expand on it and tell me what he knew. As Meemaw had taught me long ago, when you leave empty space for people to fill, they will talk. Jeremy Lisle was no exception.

"It's Jessie Pearl's house," he said, "and she did the work," he said. "If it had been up to Delta, I'd bet money that she would have bulldozed that house and sold the lot for a commercial property."

"I didn't know that," I said, surprised. "So she didn't submit the application?"

"She's in real estate, right? So she knows the value of property, but she's not ... I mean, she wasn't a home owner." He leaned closer, lowing his voice. "Between you and me, I think she didn't want the old house designated, so that when she inherited it, she wouldn't have had to jump through hoops to do what she wanted with it."

Which, if I believed Jeremy Lisle, was to tear it down and build something that could make her money.

Jeremy continued. "The difference was that your great-grandmother *wanted* your house to be a historic landmark, while Delta wanted to block her mother's application."

"But she was *on* the council," I said, not understanding. How could she not support something she was part of?

"Sometimes I think she was only on it to play devil's advocate. She didn't value the past like the rest of us do."

All along, I'd thought Delta and I had at least one thing in common—love for our history-filled homes. She had all those antiques! Or at least Megan did. But it seemed as though I'd been wrong. I wondered whether Coco and Sherri knew that their sister had tried to thwart their mother's efforts. They hadn't said anything, so either they were protecting their family—trying to keep their dirty laundry from airing—or they didn't know.

My money was on the latter.

"Reality is harsh," Jeremy said, one corner of his mouth lifting in a slight smile. It was as if he were proud to have been the one to take Delta down a notch in my eyes. He needn't have worried. There was no love lost between Delta and me, and her death didn't change that fact. We hadn't gotten to the point where we'd really put our past behind us. We may have gotten there had she lived, but now that possibility was gone. My goal in nosing around was to alleviate some of Jessie Pearl's suffering at having lost her daughter. Nothing more, nothing less. But this manipulative side of Delta came as a surprise.

"It can be," I agreed. "I was over there the other day—"

"At their house?"

"Yes. I'm making aprons for the Red Hat group Delta was part of."

His gaze darted over my shoulder, and I started to get the feeling he was scoping the place out for campaigning. Looking to see whether someone more worthy of his time had moseyed in with an ear to bend. If I wasn't careful, I'd lose his attention. But I needed more information. I waved away the words I'd just uttered, continuing with, "I saw the plaque in the entryway."

His attention came back to me. "What do you mean? Inside?"

I nodded. "On a table in the hallway."

The muscles of his face tightened. "She never put it up?"

"Um, I guess not."

"I dug around in the basement for that plaque," he said, clearly disgruntled.

"The basement?"

"Of the city offices here. We'd run out of them up here, but Delta said that her mother would be beside herself if she didn't get that plaque. She said Jessie Pearl wanted it so badly. Todd and Megan had been here helping sort some things in the basement, and Todd told Delta he'd seen one down there. Damned if he wasn't right. I searched with them and actually found one." He shook his head. "But they never put it up. That just beats all."

"I'm sure they probably just didn't get to it yet, and now—"

But his mild head shake had turned almost violent. "Oh, that's not it at all. Delta intentionally didn't put it up. I did everything possible to make that designation happen, despite her trying to stop it at every turn. She voted against it at the meeting, did you know that?"

"Against what, the designation of her own house?"

"Her mother's house," he corrected, "and yes. And then, when she lost, she was a poor sport. I shouldn't say it, but I'm glad—"

He stopped suddenly, as if he remembered where he was and whom he was talking to. "You're glad about . . . ?" I prompted. I felt pretty certain he'd been about to say that he was glad she was dead, but I secretly hoped I was wrong.

He swallowed, his Adam's apple bobbing up and down. "I'm glad the designation is done. I'm going to give Todd a call so he can put the plaque up for Jessie Pearl. That sweet woman needs something positive in her life. The plaque isn't much, but it's something." He held out his hand for me to shake. "Great meeting you,

Ms. Cassidy. Congratulations on the house. I could use your vote come election time," he added.

I nodded noncommittally. "It'll be a tough race."

"But one I intend to win." He gave me a small smile, but it didn't reach his eyes. "Stop by my office anytime to pick up the plaque for *your* house. And I certainly hope you'll hang it up."

"I will, Mr. Lisle. Thank you."

He walked away, leaving me wondering why Delta would vote against a historical designation for her mother's house, why she'd been voted off the Historic Council, and just what lengths Jeremy Lisle would go to to win the mayoral election. There had clearly been animosity between him and Delta, but I didn't feel as if I fully understood why they hadn't gotten along.

Was it possible that Delta had been an even bigger thorn in someone else's side—and had that person stooped to murder?

Unfortunately that was a question that I wasn't anywhere closer to answering.

Chapter 8

Aprons were a completely different beast compared to garment design. It was like playing with Play-Doh verses making brioche. The former was simplistic, while the latter was complex and multilayered.

Or at least that's what I'd thought before I started trying to create the perfect apron for each woman in the Red Hat group. Turns out my charm only seemed to conjure up images of full outfits, and aprons were more like accessories. I was going to have to rely on what I knew of the women to come up with the best designs. Not an easy task, since I didn't know them very well at all.

I'd whipped up Delta's apron in record time, and she'd ended up in the bottom of a freshly dug grave. Not a confidence booster. I had a vision for Georgia's apron, but part of me wondered if some ill fate would come to her if I made the apron I envisioned. Surely Delta's death had nothing to do with the charmed apron I'd made for her . . . had it?

That thought circled around my brain for a good long while, until finally, gathering up my wherewithal, I chased it away. I couldn't let my doubts get the better of me. Sure, Delta had had the apron with her when she died, but the two things weren't related. Coincidence, pure and simple. I likened my sudden insecurity to falling off a horse. I was reluctant to try again for fear of the same result, but I knew I had to get back in the saddle. The Cassidy women were made of strong stuff, and giving in to fear wasn't an option.

I had an idea for Georgia's apron, so I went with it. I'd been debating the half apron verses the full apron for her. Thinking again about the design I'd envisioned, I decided to go with the full apron.

I searched my fabric stash, wondering if I had anything remotely close to what I'd pictured. I knew a trip to the fabric store was going to be necessary for the rest, but if I could get started on Georgia's today, I felt as if it would help me get back in the saddle.

As it turned out, the perfect fabrics—or a close enough approximation—were already in my possession. I got to work cutting out the contrasting fabrics, using a base design pattern I'd created, adapting it for the ruffles and accent pieces. The pale green cotton with bright pink flowers became the skirt, the dropped band that fell mid-thigh, and the neck ties. I used a bright pink and white polka-dot fabric for the contrasting bands and decorative pocket on the apron bodice. I'd create a large flower out of fabric last, attaching it to the left seam connecting the skirt to the big ruffle.

I set to work, and in a matter of hours, I had the apron

complete. There was only one way to describe the finished product: adorably whimsical. Pretty, yet quirky and fun at the same time. It was a little more fanciful than I imagined Georgia to be, but I wanted to push her boundaries a little bit. Make her stretch and summon up some part of herself that she didn't normally access.

I couldn't predict how she'd respond to the design, but I called her up and invited her over to take a look at the finished apron. I was hoping she'd adore it and that it would help her see something in herself. I also wanted a chance to visit with her one-on-one. People often possessed information they didn't realize they had.

She was as excited to see it as I was to show it to her. Forty-five minutes later, Georgia glided into Buttons & Bows, the grosgrain strand of bells hanging from the door handle jingling softly as she opened and closed the door. Not for the first time, I saw the beauty queen quality in her. She kept her figure in perfect shape, her hair had the sheen and volume of someone much younger, and she looked as if she could have been on a hit television show twenty-five years ago.

I invited her into the shop, ushering her to the small sitting area. She took the red velvet settee. Most people opted for the sofa or loveseat. The settee required someone with feline posture and presence, and few had those qualities. But Georgia did. I often debated if I should keep it or get rid of it, but it had belonged to Loretta Mae and I couldn't bear to part with it.

"I should have asked this before I made your apron," I said as I sat across from her, "but nothing's changed, has it? Is the progressive dinner still on?"

She waved away my concern. "Oh heavens, yes, it's still on. We won't cancel it, Harlow. It's a tragedy, what happened to Delta, but like we said the other day, she'd be the first to say that she'd want us to go on. Life doesn't stop. I wouldn't say that was her motto, but if one of us had unexpectedly passed on, she would have insisted the dinner go on as planned."

"So the aprons . . . ?" I trailed off, but let my voice lilt at the end.

"Proceeding was the right thing to do," she said, answering my unspoken question.

I sighed in relief, partly because I wanted her to love the apron I'd made for her, but also because I wanted the excuse of meeting with the other Red Hatters in case any of them could shed some light on Delta's untimely death and who might be behind it.

"I made her apron first," I said. "Brought it to her the morning she died. It's a small thing, but if it gave her any bit of pleasure, then I'm glad she was able to see it."

"And mine was next on your list? Hope that means I'm not next to die." She laughed, playing off the comment as innocuous, but it cut through me like a knife nonetheless. Because of course, I'd just wondered the very same thing.

I hopped up, scurrying to my workroom behind the French doors. I'd left the apron neatly folded on the worktable in the center of the room, but now it was hanging from a hook on the old wooden screen I'd used to create a makeshift dressing room. The apron was filled out, as if someone were wearing it. I stopped short, peering more closely at it, and at the space around it. The air rippled—Meemaw was playing her games. In her ghostly incarnation, she'd reverted to her childhood sensibilities, pulling pranks just for a good, otherworldly chuckle. Her passing had shaved seventy-plus years off her mental age.

"Loretta Mae Cassidy, I need that," I said, scolding her as if she actually *were* a young child, and not a ghost with arrested development.

In the blink of an eye, the apron lost its shape and the rippling air settled back to normal again. A pipe in the ceiling groaned, but it was a happy sound, almost like laughter, and I knew Meemaw was going to move on to some other parlor trick. I took the apron from the hook she'd somehow gotten it on (I had no idea how she managed to maneuver tangible items to and fro in the house, but she did), carrying it out to Georgia.

She'd been running her index finger over the cuticles on her left hand, but looked up as I came toward her. "Is that it?" she asked, her eyes narrowing, and for just a moment, I saw a crack in Georgia's perfect veneer. Could she have had a grudge against Delta? And if so, was it enough for her to have killed over?

I nodded and handed the apron to her, tucking the thought aside for now. As I pushed my glasses up the bridge of my nose, I could see the uncertainty on her face. She took it from me, gently spreading it out across her lap.

Instantly, I felt the need to defend my design and fabric choice, but inside I was kicking myself. I was off my game. I'd gotten it wrong. Oh God, these aprons might well do me in. "Ms. Emmons, let me start by saying that

I don't know you well, but from what I've seen of you, you're a sophis—"

"Harlow," she said, cutting me off. "Is this how you see me? Flowers and polka dots?"

"Not exactly," I said, wanting to explain, and not at all sure that I could, "but that's the point. You're a sophisticated woman with style and poise. I wanted to create something that honored those things about you, but I also wanted to offer you something a little bit out of your comfort zone. The flowers in the main fabric are classic and traditional, while the polka dots are just fun. They're meant to channel something whimsical within you, if that makes sense."

She sat up on the settee, her back straight, and gazed at the apron in her lap. Slowly, she lifted her chin and met my gaze. "You do realize this is not something I would ever choose on my own?"

It wasn't a question, but a statement of fact. All I could do was nod. I opened my mouth, ready to apologize for misjudging things, but I heard Meemaw's voice in my head telling me to never apologize for what I believed. So I stopped myself from defending my choices. This was the apron I'd seen for Georgia Emmons. This was how my charm worked, and I couldn't second-guess myself now. I had to stand by my creativity and my designs, as well as my pattern choices. "If you wanted something you'd simply choose on your own, you never would have come to me to make something. You could have gone to a big-box store, or a kitchen store, or shopped online. You and your friends wanted something different. You wanted something individualistic. You wanted something only I could envision for you. And that's what I've given you, Ms. Emmons. If it's not to your liking—"

"Whoa!" Her stern expression cracked as she smiled. "I didn't say I didn't like it, only that it wasn't what I pictured for myself. It reminds me of something I might have wanted in my twenties or thirties if things had been different." Her voice grew quiet. Contemplative. "I just wonder ..."

She trailed off, looking out the front window. I remained quiet, waiting for her to finish her thought. Finally, she did.

"When did I lose the fun side of myself?" she mused.

"I don't think you've lost it," I said, answering her even though I knew it was more of a rhetorical question. "I think sometimes we just have to be reminded that there's more to us than we sometimes realize or permit the world to see."

Her lips drew together and she nodded. "Truer words were never spoken, Harlow. I love it. I absolutely love it!"

I heaved a silent sigh of relief. Despite my attempt at being strong and determined to be true to my charm, my insides had been coiled up in a knot. "I'm so glad."

"The girls aren't going to believe it. It's so unlike me, yet it's completely perfect in every way."

"The girls?"

"Randi, Cynthia, Sherri, Bennie, Coco," she said, naming the Red Hatters.

"How long have y'all been together?" I asked.

"Going on six years now, give or take, as a group, but of course we've known each other much longer than that." She tapped the pads of her fingers with her thumb, counting. "Yes, that's right, this is the sixth year. Time goes too quickly." We fell into a moment of silence, recognizing Delta's passing without saying a word. Time went too fast, and life was unpredictable. Death, and especially murder, had a way of putting a pall over a room.

"Who's next?" she asked after the moment passed.

"I haven't decided yet. Maybe Randi." Randi Martin taught yoga, was as skinny as a summer day was long, and I had no idea what her apron should look like or what magic I'd be sewing into the seams. "I'm going to take a class from her tomorrow. Thought that might help me learn something about her, so I can come up with the right design."

"I've taken her yoga classes. She's good. A little earthy, if you know what I mean, but I'm sure you'll like it."

I'd never taken a yoga class, so I didn't know what to expect, but I was excited, both for the sun salutations and for the chance to learn about Randi. If I learned anything about Delta in the process, all the better.

Georgia Emmons stood, folding her apron over her arm. "Can we pay you when all the aprons are finished?" she asked.

"Oh, definitely. I know where to find you," I with a smile.

"I guess you do. I don't think I realized you lived right next door to Delta. She rarely, if ever, had us over to her house, you see."

"Why is that?" They'd been friends for such a long

time, so why wouldn't they spend time at one another's homes?

She thought for a moment, as if contemplating how to answer. "Delta knew everyone in town. If you met her, you'd feel as if you'd known her forever."

I thought about that. Delta and the Cassidy women had never been close, but it was true that, even within the framework of a feud, there was something about her that made it feel like we had history that went beyond our ridiculous argument.

"So you're saying she wasn't as friendly as people thought?" Once again, I came back to the idea that people wore masks, presenting what they wanted others to see. Delta was in real estate and a visible member of the community, as was Coco. With their connections to the university and the people they'd worked with, everyone seemed to know them.

But was the friendly persona Delta showed people the real her, or was it simply calculated? It seemed pretty clear that Delta had an agenda of her own, and that manipulation may have been part of her MO.

Georgia's voice brought me out of my thoughts. "I stopped by her house once to drop off some church receipts. She didn't invite me in, but I caught a glimpse of the interior through the open door."

"They have a lot of interesting things in there, don't they?"

But Georgia shook her head. "They do," she agreed. "Delta's always been into antiques, but it's not that. I mean, it is, but it's more than that. I saw some things that

I'm not sure . . ." She trailed off, letting the sentence drift away.

"You can tell me," I said, encouraging her to share her observation.

She hesitated for another minute, then nodded. "There was a sideboard that I *know* I'd seen in the church basement. And on top of that, there was a lamp that I'm almost positive belonged to Cynthia. She'd donated it to a church tag sale last year."

"Maybe Delta bought it at the sale?" I suggested, not quite following what she was trying to say.

"Maybe," she said, but I could hear the doubt in her voice. "But the thing is, something just didn't feel right, so I checked. There was no receipt for it, and no one remembers selling it. We all just chalked it up to shoddy record keeping with the sale, but when I saw it through the door, and when Delta didn't let me in, well, I wondered."

"Do you think she stole the lamp?" I asked, trying to get to the root of Georgia's suspicions.

She shrugged. "I never wanted to believe that, but maybe . . . I guess so."

"The sideboard, too?" Logistically, how would Delta steal a piece of furniture from the church basement? That was one question, but the more obvious question was why. Why steal it when the theft could easily be found out? What would her motive have been?

"Anything's possible," she said.

I knew that was utterly true. I'd seen it proven over and over.

Georgia Emmons departed with her apron, leaving a

slew of questions in her wake. Delta Lea Mobley as a kleptomaniac or a straight-out thief hadn't ever crossed my mind, but then again, the best thieves seem above suspicion. I didn't know how this information translated to making her a victim of murder, but I filed it away in the back of my head to consider at another time.

Chapter 9

Walking into Bliss's yoga center, I felt an immediate sense of peace settle over me. The perimeter of the small lobby was lined with slatted wooden benches, multiple pairs of sandals and shoes lined up beneath them. A poster on the wall illustrated a whole range of yoga poses that I'd never achieve, even if I practiced for a million years. Pose number seventy-eight, a man balancing on one arm, his legs twisted above him like a pretzel, his other arm stretched above his head, made me want to turn and run. I didn't see how that particular position was humanly possible.

Randi Martin's singsong voice wafted to the lobby from the studio space behind the blue cloth curtains that separated the two rooms. She was the reason I was here, not the contortionist pictures on the wall. I slipped my shoes off, pushed them under one of the benches, and poked my head between the two curtain panels. The wood floor stretched out before me, the small lobby opening up to a large studio. Three people were early birds. They had their yoga mats laid out, blankets tri-folded and placed at the back end of the mats, foam blocks and off-white canvas straps set to the side, and were sitting cross-legged and ready for class.

"Harlow?" Randi called to me from the front of the room where she'd been lighting a candle. She padded over barefoot, her long black yoga pants accentuating her leg muscles, her thin orange cotton T-shirt long and fitted at the waist. She looked the part of a yoga teacher. I closed my eyes for the briefest moment, hoping to get a vision of an apron, but my mind was blank. Randi as a yogi and Randi in the kitchen at the planned progressive dinner weren't meshing. I needed to give it time. Maybe by the end of the class I'd have a better idea of what made her tick.

"I thought I'd take your class," I said, smiling at her.

She chuckled, her smile breaking up her long face. "To get an idea of what my perfect apron might be like?"

I felt myself blush. "How'd you know?"

"Everyone in town knows how you work, Harlow. You get to know a person and that helps you form a vision of whatever you're making for them. You think tak-ing my class will help you understand me."

I just managed to stop my jaw from dropping. I'd had no idea I was so transparent with how my charm worked. Likely everyone chalked it up to my process, rather than magic, but still, I was stunned. "I didn't know everyone knew that about my work."

"You're a novelty. A small-town girl who went to the big city and came back intact. You're like a child star who didn't get sucked into fame and drugs, instead figuring out how to become a quality actor."

"No Miley Cyrus syndrome for me," I said with a laugh. I'd worked in New York and had returned to Bliss without any scars. I was both small town and big city, and that's exactly what my designs represented.

"Grab two blocks and a strap," Randi said, pointing to the corner where all the supplies were neatly stacked.

She took a mat and blanket and padded back across the room. I followed, setting down my things next to the mat she laid out. "Have you done yoga before?" she asked.

"Never."

She folded the blanket, set it at the back of the mat like the others, and told me to sit, legs crossed.

I slipped off my sweat jacket, tossing it aside, straightened the waistband of the yoga pants I'd worn, pulled down the hem of the stretchy workout top, and did as Randi said. My spine instantly straightened when I put my sitting bones on the blanket.

"Now just breathe," Randi said before gliding across the floor to speak with someone else.

In my limited experience, people were often killed by someone they knew, and often by someone they knew well. Everyone was a suspect. I watched Randi from the corner of my eye. Could *she* have killed Delta Lea Mobley? She was thin and lithe, but with small, firm muscles evident on her arms. But Delta had been plus-sized. Could Randi have lured her into the cemetery, picked up a big rock, and crashed it against the back of her head, all without Delta putting up a fight?

I couldn't see it.

My eyes fluttered closed and I tried to clear my mind, but a familiar voice greeting Randi interrupted my yoga peace. Megan Mobley. And by her side was Rebecca Masters. They both looked like they knew their way around a yoga studio. Rebecca wore stretchy capri pants and a tank top. Megan had on steel blue pants that flared below the knee and had a split in the back up to the top of the calves. She wore a cream-colored cami under a black long-sleeve burnout tee.

When Megan walked into the studio, the air in the room grew still, as if everyone was holding their breath. She didn't seem to notice that all eyes were on her as she walked toward me with Rebecca, slipping her yoga mat from the black cylindrical bag slung over her shoulder.

"So good to see you here, Megan," Randi called.

Megan smiled wanly, giving a half wave, but otherwise didn't make eye contact. She kept her head down as she laid out her mat. My heart ached for her. Grief was a heavy burden.

"Hi," I said to them both.

Megan glanced at me, that same sad smile on her face. "Hi."

"Good to see you again," Rebecca said.

Before I could even think of something more to say to Megan, Randi started class. We brought our hands together in front of our chests and chanted "Om" three times. Randi led the class in a series of stretches, gradually moving into downward dog and into poses that forced my body into positions I didn't know it was capable of. Randi pushed us, moving us through sun salutations, balancing poses, and floor poses. I concentrated on my breath, my muscles quivering with each new move.

Randi flowed through each one, demonstrating with ease, her biceps strong, her glutes even stronger, and I reconsidered my earlier question as to whether she could have heaved a rock and hit Delta in the back of the head. It was clear that she had the strength for it, but I couldn't think of any possible motivation for her to have done such a thing.

There wasn't any chance to talk to Randi or Megan during class, but I stuck around after the closing relaxation, slowly rolling up my mat to stall for time. I snuck a look at Megan. Her eyes glistened. The yoga class had relaxed me, given me time to reflect about how to talk to Megan, and made me aware of muscles I didn't know I had. But for Megan, the class seemed to have heightened her sorrow. Her chin quivered. Rebecca stayed by her side, her hand on her friend's back.

"Are you okay?" I asked, everything else I'd wanted to ask her going out of my head.

"That's kind of a loaded question, isn't it?" she said.

"I guess it is."

"It's okay," Rebecca whispered. "Just take it one breath at a time."

Megan nodded, breathing in and out, slowly. Audibly. As if class were still going on and we were focusing on our breath. Then, finally, she said, "It's complicated. I just can't wrap my head around the fact that my mother was killed. And not just, like, passively killed in an accident, or something. That's not premeditated, is it? I mean, does a person plan a murder and say to themself, I think I'll kill her with a rock to the head?"

She'd put so succinctly what I'd been thinking all along. Delta's demise likely hadn't been planned, it had been a heat-of-the-moment killing. One thing about that scenario bothered me, though. I'd found Delta, and while she'd looked a little disheveled lying faceup in the grave, she didn't look like she'd just fought off an attacker. The blow to the head had come from behind. Would she have had a heated argument with someone and then turned her back?

It didn't seem like a smart move to me. Unless she was used to arguing with her killer, hadn't thought anything about turning around, and never saw the attack coming.

Instead of returning my yoga mat to the stack Randi had taken it from, I set it back down, flattened the soft wool blanket, and sat face to face with Megan and Rebecca. "Who do you think might have done this, Megan?"

It was a brutal question, but I knew it was something that had to be preoccupying her thoughts. I knew I wouldn't have been able to think about anything else if the same thing had happened to someone I loved. In fact I probably would have suspected every person I passed on the street. The idea that someone she knew could be responsible for her mother's death had to feel deeply unsettling. The sympathy I felt toward Megan suddenly filled me with a determination to help her. She could never undo the fact that her mother had been murdered. She could never erase the painful tragedy that was sure to haunt her. But she could have some closure in knowing who was responsible, and knowing that justice had prevailed.

She leaned toward me, chin down, but there was a new sparkle in her eyes. "That's the thing Harlow, I have no idea. She didn't do much to endear herself to the people around her, but murder? I can't imagine who would have been capable of doing that to my mother."

I thought about Jeremy Lisle and what else was behind their hostile relationship, but mostly, I wondered how Delta got along with others in the community. I needed to understand Delta better if I had any hope of figuring out what had happened to her. "Can I ask you about her Red Hat group? They've been friends for a long time, right?"

She glanced over at Randi. "They used to be close."

A red flag went up in my head. "What happened?"

"Most of them still are, I think," she said, "but not my mother. A few months ago, she started to withdraw from the group. Stopped inviting the other women over or returning their calls. It was like she put up a wall and there was no tearing it down. She used to"—she lowered her voice before uttering the last word—"care. She cared about everyone. About Granny. About me. About Todd. About Auntie Sherri and Auntie Coco."

"But she was still part of the group. I bet she still cared about the people close to her, but maybe she didn't know how to show it."

But Megan shook her head. "I don't know. She was so involved in town business, from her real estate work, it's like she gathered up information about people, then turned it against them. Auntie Coco couldn't work with her anymore."

"They used to work together?"

She nodded. "Shared an office. Coco, my mom, and my dad. But my mom made things tough. She thought Auntie Coco let a big client go, and she never forgave her. Her own sister. What if I . . . ?"

She trailed off, but the question was clear. What if Megan had done something to upset her mother? Would she have been written off, too?

We left the yoga studio together, and the peace that had flowed through me during the class was all but gone. Megan had to carry the uncertainty over how much her mother had loved her, and whether there were any limitations on that love, for the rest of her life. I, on the other hand, kept coming back to three questions: What had happened three months ago to warrant such a change in Delta? Who else had Delta shut out? And was that person responsible for her death?

Chapter 10

As a seamstress, my reaction to entering a fabric store was akin to how most of the men I'd known in my life reacted to a hardware store. My brother, Red, could spend hours trailing up and down the aisles in Jury's Hardware, the large local store. Since Will and I had started dating, I'd spent countless hours there myself — but give me the quilt shop on the square or one of the big fabric stores in Granbury or Fort Worth any day. The rows of stacked bolts of fabric, the notions and patterns, the lace and tulle and burlap all filled me with contentment. And joy.

Yet right at this particular moment, I felt like a mama duck, trailing her brood of ducklings behind her. Only the ducklings were Randi Martin, Bennie Cranford, and Cynthia Homer. We'd met at the store so I could figure out designs for the rest of the aprons. "Do y'all like to cook?" I asked, slipping into Southern speak in hopes that they'd open up to me

Cynthia scoffed. "My kitchen has never seen a turkey in the oven."

"It's never seen anything in the oven, has it?" Bennie said with a laugh.

"I tried a ham once, but otherwise, no. The oven is just eye candy."

"You and Coco." She nudged me. "She has one of those super expensive numbers. All stainless steel with red knobs. And she barely boils water."

"I can make hard-boiled eggs," Cynthia said, "but that's about it. I prefer takeout. Have y'all tried the little teahouse on the square? They cater now."

"So I guess you'll be using them for your stop on the progressive dinner?" Bennie asked.

Cynthia met Bennie's challenge head-on. "I haven't decided. I imagine *you'll* be cooking all week so you can put us all to shame." It wasn't a question, but a loaded statement. And more than a little bit accusatory.

"I have no intention of putting you to shame," Bennie responded, "but I do have *my* part of the menu planned. And I'm working with Todd and Megan about theirs. Delta had been on the schedule for dessert, and they're going to host it now."

"Is Todd a good cook?"

"Oh yes. He went to cooking school."

"Megan said she's gained ten pounds in the few years they've been together. Poor thing, he's pretty critical of her weight, but then he turns around and makes all this great food for her."

"I thought he went to law school," Bennie said.

"Right. At College Station, but he's a renaissance

man. He helps Megan with all those flea markets and antique shows. Another Anson, if you ask me."

My heart still ached for Megan, but having Todd as support was something, at least. For all of Delta's distaste for the Cassidy family, Megan had always been the opposite. She liked Nana's goats, had come over to meet Earl Grey, my teacup pig, and had even looked at my rack of prêt-à-porter clothes, buying a high-low skirt that I'd made one rainy Sunday afternoon. I'd realized after she left with it that I'd actually had her in mind when I'd made it. The Cassidy charm at work.

Bennie sucked in an audible breath, a sudden thought occurring to her. "Most people are killed by loved ones, aren't they?"

"Did you see that on one of your crime shows?" Cynthia asked.

Bennie didn't bat an eyelash. "Maybe, but it's true, right?"

"What are you saying?"

"Well, what about Delta's family? Megan? Todd?" She drew in another breath. "Jessie Pearl? Could one of them have done it?"

We all stared at her. "Jessie Pearl hit her own daughter on the head with a big rock?"

"She's strong for an old lady," Randi said. "She takes my senior class once a week. Or she did until she hurt her leg."

Cynthia shook her head, frustrated, staring them both down. "Why not Coco or Sherri? Do you think one of them might have killed her, too?"

"The thought did cross my mind," Bennie said.

Cynthia's eyes narrowed to thin slits. "Oh for Pete's sake, Bennie, how can you even begin to think it was one of Delta's own family?"

Bennie shrugged. "Someone gave her her due?"

"Her due? Do you think she deserved to die, Bennie?" Randi asked, showing her own mortification.

A spatter of red spread from Bennie's chest, up her throat, and to her cheeks. She fiddled with the headband in her hair, readjusting it. "That's not what I meant. All I'm saying is that I don't believe any of her own family was to blame."

"I don't, either," Cynthia said.

Bennie leveled her gaze at her friend. "If you had to say, then who do you think could have done it, Cyn?"

She shrugged nonchalantly. "I'd put my money on Jeremy Lisle."

We all stepped back, pressing ourselves against the bolts of fabric shelved in the knit section, as a woman pushed her cart past us. "I talked with him the other night at the Historic Council meeting," I said. "He didn't strike me as a murderer." Which didn't really mean a thing. I'd met several people who'd turned out to be murderers, and not a single one of them had seemed off to me at first. Which made me take a sidestep. Of all the people I'd met in relation to Delta's death, the women around me, as well as Georgia Emmons, seemed the least likely murderers. It was definitely possible that one of them had attacked Delta, leaving her for dead.

I looked at each one in turn, trying to imagine the scene in the graveyard, each in the starring role as murderess. Randi, the yoga teacher, was strong enough. Bennie looked like she'd have enough spunk. Cynthia was the only one who didn't seem to have the gumption. She was too proper. Too put together. I couldn't even imagine her traipsing through a graveyard, let alone killing a woman who had been a friend.

"Megan said something happened a few months back and that Delta changed. Did any of you notice that?"

"I remember this one conversation we had a while back," Cynthia said. "It might have been two or three months ago. We'd been reorganizing the personnel files at the church, and we were getting ready to break for lunch. Then out of the blue, she says, *You ought to be able to trust your husband, right?*"

The other women stared at Cynthia, Georgia gasping. "Surely she didn't think Anson was up to something?"

Cynthia shrugged. "She wouldn't say any more than that, but I wondered."

"She started spending more time talking about the mayoral campaign," Bennie said. "And helping Megan and Todd with the antiques and the cooking."

"It was as if she was reprioritizing things in her life," Randi said, her voice calm and contemplative. "Almost as if she knew her time here was limited."

We all pondered that in silence for a moment until another woman, this one with a baby in the front section of the shopping cart and a toddler holding fast to her hand, passed us. We stepped back as far as we could to let them by, but the woman frowned. We were clearly blocking the fabric selection from her curious eyes. "Let's look around," I said, clapping my hands and making my voice cheerful. "The progressive dinner must go on, which means we need aprons. We'll try the cottons first," I said, and led them to the next row to get out of the woman's way.

"Do they make nice aprons, then?" Bennie asked.

"The best," I said. Adding fancier fabrics and embellishments made them more interesting, but a cotton base made the most sense. "Let me know if you see something you like." I watched them as they wandered up and down the aisles, hiding a smile behind my hand at the delight on their faces. I knew just what they were experiencing.

I remembered my very first trip to a fabric store. Meemaw had been the mama duck and I'd trailed behind her, skimming my hand along the bolts of fabric as if they were made of spun gold. Eventually, she'd led me to the flannel section and asked me which one I liked. I scanned the patterns, zeroing in on one. It had a teal background and scattered over it were chubby pink and gray elephants, umbrellas clutched in their trunks. As an imaginative five-year-old, I had wondered if I had something made from the fabric, would I float away like the elephants?

Meemaw had taken the bolt up to the counter and had the clerk cut a length of it. *Is this for you?* she'd asked, handing it to me all folded into a neat square.

I'd looked up at Meemaw, who'd nodded. *Every girl needs floating elephant pajamas,* she'd answered.

"Harlow?" Bennie's voice pulled me out of the happy memory.

I swiped away the pools of tears that had gathered in my eyes. "Did you find something?" I asked, noticing right away what an understatement that question was.

What she'd found was a shopping cart, and it was already piled high with bolts of mismatched cotton. Cherries, graphic birds and flowers, denim with embroidered daisies, and a brown and pink collection with cupcakes and coffee cups. "Oh yeah," she exclaimed, "Take a look!"

I dug through the rest of the cart, trying to envision an apron that I could design which could combine a few of the fabrics. None of them quite fit Bennie in my mind. But then again, what did I really know about her? Her short, curly dark hair was always perfect. She often wore fun headbands that made her look younger than her sixty-some-odd years. She wore pastel-colored capris and cute, matching tops. She looked like she could have appeared in one of the iconic ads from the 1950s, pushing a vacuum with one hand, reading a book in the other.

She was Bennie the Homemaker.

And none of the fabrics in her cart really worked for her, in my opinion. "What's your favorite color, Bennie?"

"Yellow," she answered immediately. "Definitely yellow. And red. Happy colors."

I guided her back through the aisles, replacing a few of the bolts, choosing another cherry pattern instead of the one she'd selected, and adding red and yellow ribbon and a package of green pompoms. "Not sure what we'll do with these, but I can't pass them up."

She looked skeptically at the miniature pastel green puffs, but nodded. "You're the expert."

The moment I smiled back at her in encouragement, a vision of her in an apron finally came to me. A retro cocktail number with ruffles. "Perfect!"

Bennie transferred her skeptical gaze from the pom-poms to me. "What's perfect?"

"I know what your apron's going to look like," I answered, "and I think you'll love it."

She looked at the shopping cart. "So which fabrics?"

"None of them."

Her smile drooped. "None?"

"Well, maybe one. This green one, I think. I have just what I need at home for the rest of it."

She frowned, and I could see the question plain on her face. She'd just told me she adored yellow and red, so why would I choose a green fabric? And none of the others she'd liked?

"You'll love it, I promise."

"If you say so," she said, but she didn't sound convinced. She pushed her cart, wandering off, and I went in search of Randi and Cynthia. I had a feeling that getting them all together again would be like herding cats.

They hadn't had as much success as Bennie, but Randi had found a selection of tie-dyed and naturally dyed fabrics. I helped her choose a few that I could work with.

Cynthia, on the other hand, looked to be stymied by the entire process. "Can I help?" I asked her. She hadn't selected a single bolt and seemed to have stopped looking.

"I'm not going to bother with an apron."

Uh-oh. So Bennie had gotten to her. "Cynthia, of course you are! You've all been looking forward to this dinner. You can't be the only one to not have an apron."

She fluttered a hand in front of her. "It's not like I'm cooking. Why would I need one?"

It was a good question, but I'd done a bit of research on the history of aprons, and one of the things I'd realized is that the utilitarian purpose they'd had in the past was long gone. Their resurgence wasn't about protecting the clothing underneath. It wasn't about actually cooking. "The way you all are using them," I said, "for this progressive dinner? It's more of a fashion accessory. It's retro-chic. You have to have one."

I had expected my pep talk to sway her, but Cynthia looked at me, her eyes flashing and determined. "I don't need an apron, Harlow, and I don't want one. You go on and make the others, but don't waste your time on me. Delta's not here to—"

She trailed off, her voice cracking. Losing Delta must have opened a floodgate of emotions, and those feelings didn't just evaporate overnight. Dealing with the grief of losing a friend was a long endeavor.

To my mind, despite her protests, Cynthia deserved an apron made just for her. She might say she didn't want one, but I was going to make her one anyway, and if my charm held true, it would help her realize whatever dream she held close in her heart and was afraid to let free.

Chapter 11

A church tag sale in a small town could always be depended on to bring the people out in droves. Mama, Nana, and I had signed up to volunteer together during the late afternoon shift that Saturday, which had given me the morning to work on aprons.

I had started with a pattern I found in the attic once I got home from the fabric store. It was a retro cocktail apron with three ruffles, and I dubbed it the Susie Homemaker. It was perfect for Bennie, who I knew made her husband dinner every night and who thrived in the kitchen, loved throwing parties, had a classic Victorian house, and couldn't wait to host her part of the progressive dinner.

She was a homemaker through and through, and this apron was going to be perfect for her. I'd also considered the stack of vintage fabric from my great-great-grandmother's youth and ended up picking two coordinating fabrics, one from my stash, and the second one the cherries we'd ended up buying the day before. There was a vintage cooking theme with the cherries, teakettles, dishes, stoves, and pies. The background of the vintage selection was white, while the primary colors were red and a vibrant green. "This'll be the top ruffle," I told Gracie, who'd come over to help me sew.

She held up the green print Bennie and I had agreed on the day before. "How about this one in the middle? Maybe with those little green pompoms hanging from the hem?"

I nodded in approval. She had a real knack for color and design. She was a natural. "Bennie loves yellow," I said, remembering what she'd told me. I held up the last fabric, another from my own collection. The background was lemon yellow with a white pattern scattered through it, softening the color. "We'll need to tie in the red from the first piece," I said, "and bring the yellow up to the top. I think I'll make the waistband with this, and maybe appliqué a few of the flowerpots from this one." I tapped the vintage piece that would be the top ruffle.

We laid it all out on the cutting table in my workroom, and thirty minutes later, all the pieces were cut and we were ready to sew. I could do it myself in less than an hour, but Gracie was rubbing her hands together and bouncing up and down on the balls of her feet. She wasn't saying, but she wanted to do this project on her own. I handed her the three main pieces, put my hands on her shoulders, and directed her to the sewing machine. "You take this one," I said. "I have an idea for Randi Martin's."

"Really? Are you sure?"

Her grin was infectious. "Oh yes, one hundred percent. I'm right here if you need me," I added, but I knew she wouldn't. She'd made most of her own homecoming dress, and had tackled a slew of other projects. An apron would be easy for her.

She set to work, and I pulled out the fabrics Randi had selected at the store. I'd had an inspiration during the night: the perfect apron to compliment her earthy style. The background fabric would be muslin. Three short ruffles, one in a fabric I'd found that had writing on it and looked like newsprint, the next in muslin, and the third in a natural green color. A teal piece of ribbon would sit above the ruffles. I'd use appliqué to form the stems sprouting from the teal ribbon, with fabric appliquéd flowers sitting on top of each stem. Finally, I'd use small rectangles of muslin, embellished in fabric pens with inspirational words like "creative," "inspire," "evolution," "vision," "empower," and "believe," sewing them on to make the apron complete.

I spent the next two hours cutting and hand sewing the flowers from some of the colorful fabrics Randi had chosen. I used embroidery floss and simple braiding to form the stems. After my stint at the tag sale, I'd construct the apron itself and begin attaching the appliqués to the muslin. The inspirational words would come last, but they'd be the final touch that would make the apron perfect for Randi.

At two o'clock, I left Gracie working on her project and headed to the church. The front parking lot was full, and there wasn't a single space along the street. I drove around the lot behind the cemetery, a feeling of déjà vu coming over me as I walked through it and past the very spot where I'd found Delta Lea Mobley's body. There had been a small funeral ceremony with family only. I wondered whether they'd been afraid that no one would show up if they'd opened it up to the community.

At that thought, a feeling of sadness came over me. Everyone's life had value and should be honored, and Delta's had been cut short. I had enough time before my shift to scout the cemetery and look for her final resting place. I found it not far from where she'd died. There was no marker yet, but I knew it was hers by the bouquet, an assortment of bluebonnets, gladiolus, and other native Texas buds lying at the top of the grave. Jessie Pearl often puttered around the front yard taking care of the flower garden, and I knew these had come from the Mobleys' front yard.

I stopped to pay my respects, speaking to her in a soft voice. "Delta, I won't stop until I learn the truth and your mama has some peace."

"I can't tell you how relieved I am to hear you say that, Harlow."

I jumped, startled at the voice. Coco came up behind me, Megan and Todd trailing after her on the path. Rebecca Masters ran up behind them, panting as she handed Megan a wad of tissue.

"I'm sorry. I didn't know you were here," I said. "I'll leave you—"

"Of course you're not going anywhere," Coco said, putting her hand on my arm. "I'm touched that you would come to pay your respects, especially knowing how Delta treated y'all after the goat incidents."

"Well," I said, "she certainly could hold a grudge."

Beside me, Megan nodded. "Yes she could."

"You can say that again," Todd said, his arms folded over his chest. "A personal grudge against me for making enchiladas."

Megan lightly knocked the back of her hand against Todd's arm. "But she loved your pasta puttanesca, right?" She kissed her fingertips, fanning them out in front of her. "*Delicioso*."

"True," he said, smiling. "She had seconds every time."

"Thirds, probably," Coco said. "Cook her things she liked and she could forgive anything—"

"Almost anything . . ." Todd said, grinning.

"Which is why she'd never forgive me," Coco finished. "You couldn't pay me to prepare a meal for her."

"She can probably hear you, you know," Rebecca said. "And she wouldn't like that you're talking about her."

She said it jokingly, but I glanced behind me, looking for rustling trees and listening for howling wind. Because of Meemaw, I knew ghosts existed, but all was quiet here in the cemetery.

"I'm heading to the church," I said. People often had to deal with their grief in their own ways, and I didn't want to intrude on their time at the gravesite.

"You don't have to go," Coco said, but Todd stepped closer to Megan, wrapping his arm around her, nodding a thank-you to me.

"I'm late for my shift at the tag sale. Are you stopping by?"

"We're not buying anything at the sale. I hauled so

many boxes of stuff from the house over here for her the day before she passed," Todd said.

"Nice of you to contribute given your antique business," I said to Megan.

Megan shrugged. "I sell what I buy and collect, but the stuff Mother donated to the tag sale was mostly Granny's."

"Your grandmother didn't want you to sell it for her instead?"

Rebecca laughed as Megan said, "Oh no. Granny doesn't get the whole eBay–flea market thing. She thinks it's a dumb job. Mother would give me something of Granny's every now and then, but she'd swear me to secrecy. *Your grandmother would not want this sold,* she'd say, *so just keep this between us.*"

Coco drew in a sharp breath. "Mother's things were not hers to get rid of. How dare she?"

The color drained from Megan's face. "I thought you knew."

Coco used the back of her hand to nudge her glasses back into place, then put her hands on her hips. "You thought I knew that Delta was getting rid of my mother's things, bit by bit, without telling me or Sherri?"

I asked my own question. "Why would Delta send some of Jessie Pearl's things to the church tag sale?" I asked. If Delta was trying to be underhanded about it, it seemed easier to have Megan sell the things she'd taken from Jessie Pearl.

Coco rolled her eyes. "Oh, I'll tell you why. Mother is forgetful. Easier to convince her that she forgot she'd donated something for the church versus giving it to Megan to sell for profit."

"But why?" I asked. "Why would she give away Jessie Pearl's things in the first place?"

Coco's expression grew indignant. "So she could stop Sherri and me from having any of it," she said matter-of-factly.

We all stared at her. Todd spoke first. "Why would she want to do that? You're all three her children."

Coco adjusted her glasses again. "Sibling rivalry, I guess," she said.

I shook my head, still trying to understand, and wondering if this was a recent change in Delta. Randi's words about her knowing her time was limited came back to me. But no, that didn't make sense. I'd spoken with the sheriff, and he hadn't mentioned anything to indicate that Delta was unwell. "But does taking Jessie Pearl's things and getting rid of them accomplish that?"

"That I don't know," Coco said, "but mark my words, that's what it was about."

Todd cleared his throat, getting our attention. "We're standing next to her grave," he said. "Maybe we should talk about this some other time."

Rebecca coughed, turning away, and Megan dabbed her eyes with the tissue in her hand. Coco turned to look at Delta's burial spot. "She's probably in there listening and laughing," she said. "Delta would be the first to admit that charity was not something she believed in. Get up and help yourself, that was her motto, wouldn't you say, Megan?"

Megan's brown eyes were wide as quarters. She stole a quick glance at the grave, but nodded. "She kicked me out of the house once, all because I didn't want to go to a college readiness class she signed me up for. I told her I didn't want to go to her alma mater, and that I wanted to be a police officer. And what's wrong with that, anyway? But she got so mad, I thought she was literally going to explode." She turned to Todd, tears spilling from her eyes. "I don't think you ever saw her like that. She was clenching her fists, and her neck turned bright red. If she'd been in a cartoon, the top of her head would have popped open and steam would have poured out."

Her lips quivered, and the quiet sobs she'd been holding in turned to a slight giggle, then a full-on laugh. "She was always mad at me, I think. More often than she wasn't, anyway, but . . . but . . ."

"But she loved you," Todd said, pulling her close.

"She should still be here," Rebecca said, taking Megan's hand. "It's not right. But Todd's right. She loved you more than anything, and I bet that you were the last person to cross her mind before she died. She was willing to go to the mat for you, Megs, whatever it took."

Coco reached over to take Megan's hand. "She didn't always know how to show it, Meg, but she did love you. No mother in her right mind would cheer at her only daughter becoming a police officer. There are crazy people in the world."

The statement hung there over Delta's grave like a dark cloud. Someone had been crazy enough to kill her, and we all wanted answers. But right now I had nothing but a few hypotheses, and none of them seemed any good. If I believed Coco, Delta had something against her own sisters, and there was some strife between her and Megan, too. None of the relationships in Delta's life seemed to have been easy or conflict-free. But I thought Coco was right. Delta had loved Megan, and the poor girl needed to understand that or she'd carry the weight of disappointment her whole life.

In the distance, I could see people swarming around the tent, moving up and down the aisles. In the church itself, the pastor peered out the window, taking in the fund-raising efforts of the congregation. It was a sight he had to be proud of.

Something Delta had said that very first day when the Red Hat ladies had cornered me about the aprons suddenly came back to me. The town leaked like a sieve, she'd said. I'd forgotten about it, but now I couldn't get it out of my mind. What church incident? And did the pastor know about it?

Seize the moment, that was my motto. With the pastor alone inside the church, this was my opportunity to see what he might know about any incidents in Delta's life.

I checked my watch and edged toward the pathway that led to the church. "I'll see you at the tag sale?" I asked.

"In a little while," Todd said. He took Megan's hand and guided her closer to the grave. They needed their own moment of silence and time to grieve privately. Another reason for me to take my leave.

I hurried off, leaving the cemetery, and minutes later I was skirting my way through the tent. Before I made it past the first aisle, someone called my name. Make that

two people. Mama and Nana stood at the end of the next
row over, a mess of trinkets covering every square inch
of their table. Vases, bowls, salt and pepper shakers, figurines. I'd never seen so many knickknacks in one place.
They seemed to have quadrupled since I was here last.
And there wasn't anything I was inclined to bring home.

"Darlin'," Mama said, waving, "over here. Come over
here."

I waved back. "Coming."

I headed toward her but stopped in my tracks when I
caught sight of a sparkling pocket on a rectangle of blue
denim. I'd never been attracted to the bling so many
Texas women adored. But there was something about
this particular pair of jeans that drew my eye. I just didn't
know what it was. I picked them up, checked the tag.
They were my size. Meant to be, I reckoned. And they
looked as if they'd fit me perfectly. Tucking them under
my arm, I scanned the rest of the table. Another pair
jumped out at me. Not jeans, I realized. Overalls. They
weren't my size. They weren't particularly stylish. The
faded color. The soft denim. The oversized pocket on the
front panel.

I passed them by, but backtracked a moment later.
There was something about them that I liked. They'd
been worn, but that didn't mean they had no use left in
them. Deconstruction was always an experiment in creativity, and what better tool to start a deconstruction
project with than a pair of denim overalls? I had no idea
what I'd make with them, or whom I'd make it for, but I
knew I had to have them.

I grabbed them before heading down the aisle, stopping again when something else caught my eye. It was a Lladró figurine, and it looked exactly like the one I'd seen in Delta Lea Mobley's house the week before. I'd looked it up when I'd gotten home that night. It was a retired design. A woman in a long dress with a coat, a sewing basket over her arm, and a pink umbrella. I'd been right about her being a dressmaker.

Delta hadn't mentioned that it was coming to the tag sale, and neither had Jessie Pearl. And from what I'd seen online, it was worth several hundred dollars. I snatched it up in case it was a mistake. I wanted to check with Jessie Pearl to make sure she'd meant to donate it—if it did, indeed, belong to her. I checked the price tag. Ten dollars. That *had* to be a mistake.

I glanced around, quickly spotting three more of the figurines I'd seen in the curio cabinet at Delta's house. I cradled them all, very carefully, finally making my way over to Mama and Nana.

"What in heaven's name do you want with all those things?" Mama asked. She was all about nature and flowers. She collected clay pots and had some stained glass in her greenhouse, but ceramic collectibles were outside her comfort level.

"I love them," I told her, "but they're not really for me." I filled them both in on where I'd seen the figurines and carefully handed them over. Then I pulled out my cell phone and dialed Jessie Pearl. When there was no answer, I debated calling Coco or Sherri. Their relationships with Delta seemed to have been complicated, love and scorn all wound up into one tangled ball of yarn. But I didn't actually have Sherri's number, and I'd only just left Coco at her sister's grave and she might still be there. If she was, I didn't want to disturb her.

I needn't have worried. Once again I heard my name being called from the opposite end of the tent. I turned to see Coco waving at me. "I have a question for you!"

"I have one for you, too," I said when she came up alongside me. But before I could ask it, she'd grabbed one of the figurines I'd rescued, clutching it in her white-knuckled hand.

"Where did you get this?" Her voice had gathered a hard edge to it. She swept her hand over the rest of them, then looked in turn at Mama, Nana, and then me. "All of these. Where did they come from?"

"They were on the table over there," I said, pointing to the aisle behind us. "I thought they looked a lot like your mother's. Do you think they're hers?"

She pursed her lips, looking like she was trying hard not to explode with anger. "Oh, there is not a doubt in my mind. I *know* they are. And I know just how they got here, too. Damn her."

"Darlin'," Mama said to Coco, "you've been through a horrible shock, losing your sister. Maybe you ought to sit down here." She pulled up a stool that was marked for sale at thirteen dollars. It didn't escape my attention that the stool had a higher asking price than the collectible figurines.

Coco waved it away. "I prefer to stand." Her spine had stiffened, and she lifted her chin in defiance, her short blond curls bobbing around her head. "In fact, what I really need to do, right this very minute, is go have a word with Pastor Kyle."

"What about the figurines?" I asked, catching her by the arm. "I'm sure we can say they were donated by mistake."

"Of course we can't say that, Harlow. They're here and they're for sale. I doubt my mother even knows they're gone. But she'd be horrified ... *horrified* ... to know that her precious Lladró collectibles were at the church tag sale priced at—"

She stopped short and backtracked a few steps, picking the Dressmaker up and flipping it over. "Ten dollars?! That's just ... I can't believe ... Delta would rather *give* away mother's things than let me or Sherri have them."

"Do you really think that's why she donated them? But why upset your mother by taking them?" This was a side to Delta I hadn't seen. Our feud over the goats was based on the herd chowing down on the flowers in Delta's yard, so even if I didn't understand the degree to which Delta was disgruntled, I understood why she was upset and how that frustration transferred to the other Cassidy women.

But if Coco was right, Delta had taken their mother's precious collectibles and donated them just to spite her sisters.

"Absolutely," she said. "Everything with Delta was always a competition. She needed Mother to love her more than she loved Sherri and me."

"But why take your mother's things?" I asked. "If Jessie Pearl discovered that she was giving away her treasures, that whole idea of being loved best would have backfired, wouldn't it?"

"Mother's forgetful. I'm sure Delta could have convinced her that she'd been the one to donate something, or that she'd misplaced something. Whenever Sherri or I noticed something was missing, Delta always had a story. Mother gave it to Megan to sell. She donated it to the women's shelter. She gave it away to the church."

"But why?"

Coco's nostrils flared and her fists clenched. "To make us crazy. She wanted us to think that she was closer to our mother." She looked around, making sure the coast was clear, then turned back to me and continued. "No one would believe it, of course. We saw her true colors, but most folks only ever saw what Delta wanted them to. She was good at pretending."

If what Coco was saying was true, I was awfully glad I hadn't been able to reach Jessie Pearl. She didn't need to hear more grief about her murdered daughter. "You can buy them back, Coco."

Coco's chin quivered, her emotions getting the better of her. "I can. You're right, I definitely can." She opened up her billfold and pulled out a wad of cash, handing it over to me. "Thank you, Harlow. Now I need to go talk to the pastor."

With that she marched out of the tent and into the church.

And I followed.

Chapter 12

Will caught up with me at the entrance to the church. I'd left the money, the figurines, and my overalls and blinged-out jeans with Mama before I'd hurried away after Coco.

"Where are you off to in such a hurry?" Will asked.

I answered as I pulled him into the church. "To talk to the pastor about . . . about . . ."

"About what?" he prodded.

I stopped long enough to furrow my brow. "About Delta Mobley."

"Ah, I see," he said, nodding as if everything was suddenly crystal clear.

I straightened my glasses, shoving my hair behind my ears. At my temple, the streak of blond that was common to all the Cassidy women tingled. I'd come to use this as a touchstone, almost like a sixth sense. But at the moment, I was puzzled. "You do?" I asked Will, definitely surprised, because things were far from clear in my mind.

I had no clear suspects in Delta's death, and now I'd learned she had a vengeful streak against her sisters. Were they the only ones she targeted, or had she rubbed someone else the wrong way, sending them into a murderous rage against her?

I'd always thought she was a pillar of the community, but the deeper I dug into her death, the more I realized that she was on weaker social footing in Bliss than she'd made it seem. So who was the real Delta Lea Mobley?

"Not really," Will admitted, "but I bet I'll understand in another fifteen minutes after you figure it out and explain it to me."

I had to laugh at that. And bat him on the arm. "Fifteen minutes, huh? We'd better get moving, then."

It had been more than ten minutes since I'd seen the pastor through the window, but I assumed he was still upstairs. I bypassed the main hall that led to the sanctuary, instead heading down the central hall that led to the back staircase. "Coco?" I called her name as loudly as I dared. I always felt a sense of reverence in a church, and that meant no yelling. It was also ingrained in me since, as a child, I'd had my ear pulled by Meemaw more than once for inappropriate church behavior. Sitting in the pew during service meant being quiet, staying still, and being contemplative. I could *think* about sewing, or flowers, or tipping cows, or climbing water towers. She hadn't cared what wayward thoughts raced through my mind, just so long as I was silent.

There were footsteps on the stairs. Which stopped suddenly. I took another tentative step, Will right on my heels. "Why are you tiptoeing?" he asked. "Is the church closed?"

"Do churches close?" I whispered back.

"Don't think so."

I guess I didn't really need to be sneaking around like a cat burglar. So why was I? The only explanation was that all the murder investigations I'd been involved in since I'd been back in Bliss had me questioning everyone.

"Coco?" I said again, louder this time.

"Upstairs," she answered.

"After you, Sherlock," Will said. He put his hand on my lower back, urging me forward.

I started tiptoeing up the stairs before I remembered that Coco knew I was coming and that it didn't have to be a secret that I was in the church. I shifted to a normal walk as Will's hand brushed my side. "I like the view from down here." When I turned, blushing, he gave me a wink and a grin.

I smiled right back, challenging him. "Play your cards right, and I'll let you take me home after church."

"Promises, promises."

I turned, flashing him another coy grin. "What, you don't believe me?"

"Not for a second, Cassidy. I think whatever you learn here is going to set you off investigating somewhere and then I won't see you, unless it's to talk about murder, for the next two days or however long it takes you to crack the case." He took hold of my wrist and pulled me down until our lips met. "So I'll take my kiss now."

"Ah, William Flores, you know me too well, I fear."

"Like the back of my hand, darlin', like the back of my hand."

Coco was leaning against the wall at the landing at the top of the stairs when we made it up there. "Good grief, and I thought *I* took the steps slowly. You two are like turtles." She lifted her hand in a slight wave. "Howdy, Mr. Flores."

"Just Will is fine."

She nodded and waited.

After a moment, I realized that she was waiting for me. "I wanted to talk to the pastor, too, so I thought I'd come along."

She looked from me to Will and back to me. "You want to talk to Pastor Kyle?"

"We do," Will said, joining in. He'd been by my side since I'd moved back to Bliss, and I took comfort from his support.

"Do you think he's involved?" she asked, surprised.

I waved my hands in front of me. "No. Not at all." I told her about the sideboard and the lamp Cynthia had mentioned to me, and how she thought they'd come from the church. "I thought the pastor could shed some light on it."

Coco stared at me, speechless.

"I don't know that Cynthia's suspicions are right," I said, "but it's worth asking about."

"So the plot thickens." She turned to head down the hall. "Right this way, kids."

We found Pastor Kyle Maguire in his office, the same room where I'd spotted him at the window. He was tall and reedy, his hair thinning on top. He sported a goatee much like Will's. The difference, though, was notable right away. Will's very slightly salt-and-pepper goatee made him look just a little bit dangerous, in an outlaw country singer kind of way, while Pastor Kyle's completely gray growth made him look more haggard than anything else. His button-down cowboy shirt with the mother-of-pearl-covered snaps and pale blue plaid pattern hung loosely on his bony shoulders. With his sunken cheeks and lanky body, I thought he might blow away if a strong wind came through town.

"Sorry to bother you," I said, after we'd already barged in.

"No, no, not at all. No bother. Thank you ladies for all you're doing for the tag sale." He gestured toward the window. "It looks like a great success."

We all nodded in agreement, and I said, "There are a lot of people coming through."

After a bit more chatter about the tag sale, he pointed to the sofa and chair against the side wall of the room. "Please, have a seat." Will and I sat on the sofa, side by side, while Coco took the chair.

"What can I do for you?" the pastor asked us.

I looked to Coco, who so far hadn't uttered a word. She was perched on the edge of her seat, staring out the window. The cat had her tongue, which was something I hadn't seen before. Usually she was bright with spirit and conversation. She was stymied, so I took the lead. "Pastor, we're trying to figure out what might have happened to Delta. Her family is really upset. I'm sure you can imagine."

He nodded. "Horrible business," he said. "Just horrible."

"You didn't see or hear anything that morning?" I asked. I knew the sheriff would have already asked him this, but I hadn't yet finagled my way into Hoss McClaine's office on a fact-gathering mission, so I had to start from the beginning with the pastor.

He shook his head. "Delta came in early sometimes. She liked to help out, and get an early start before her day really began."

"Did she usually go through the cemetery?"

He ran his thumb over his goatee, thinking. "Everyone parks in the parking lot over there. With the tag sale, we wanted the shoppers to be able to use the front spaces. I don't know if she always cut through the cemetery, but we all did sometimes."

"Did you see her that morning?"

He shook his head. "No. And I still can't believe she was killed right outside. I parked in the upper lot and walked through the perimeter of the cemetery because the John Deere digger was sitting there, blocking the path." He lowered his chin to his chest. "I must have walked right past her and never saw. If I had, I might have been able to save her. . . ."

He trailed off, his guilt settling in the room like a wave of humidity. How many other people had walked near the cemetery that morning, never dreaming that Delta lay in an open grave?

Coco had been listening, but now she leaned forward in her chair. "Who would she have met out there, Pastor?"

"I've wondered that myself, but I don't know."

"What time did you get here?" I asked. "Were there other cars in the parking lot?"

He gazed at the ceiling, looking as if he were replaying that morning in his mind. "There were a few cars. I think seven? Or maybe eight? Cynthia was here. She's the project manager for the tag sale, so of course she's always present. Sherri was here. Georgia Emmons, too, and a few other volunteers." He fell silent for a moment. "I passed a few cars as I drove up to the back lot. Delta's daughter's, I think." He hesitated, his eyes clouding. "And Anson's," he said. "I recognized his Jeep."

She looked up at the pastor. "Did you tell the sheriff all this?"

He nodded his head but looked sheepish. "I did, but I might have downplayed it. I can't believe any of my parishioners would be involved in Delta's death."

I wanted to keep the pastor talking, in case he had other important information tucked away in his memory. "You've been at the church here for some time. Five or six years, is that right?"

"Seven, actually," he said, leaning his bony backside against the edge of his desk. "Aside from what happened to Delta, Bliss is a nice little town."

Something in his tone made me look up sharply. He'd said the words, but I got the impression he didn't fully believe it was a nice little town. "I don't think I'd want to live anywhere else," I said. "It's home."

"What about Manhattan? Isn't that where you were before you came back?"

So he knew my background, too. There were very few

secrets in a small town. Cynthia, Georgia, Sherri, Megan, and Anson had all been around the church the morning Delta had died. Each of them had opportunity, but did any of them have a motive warranting murder?

"Yes, but there's no comparison. My mama always says you can take the girl out of the small town, but you can't take the small town out of the girl. That's one hundred percent true, at least in my case."

He nodded, but remained silent. He'd probably learned, as I had, that if you left a silence alone, someone would rush to fill it. Usually it was me keeping quiet, but this time I filled the space with a question. The pastor, I realized, was also here that morning. Opportunity. But did he have a motive? "What brought you to Bliss?" I asked.

He tilted his head to one side, studying me. I couldn't tell what he was thinking, but my gut said he was wondering why I was asking him personal questions.

"I'd been a youth pastor for a lot of years, but I was ready for a church of my own," he said, his arms folded over his chest. He stared out the window as he spoke, as if he were slipping into the memory. "There was an opening here, and I applied. Came down from Colbert, Oklahoma," he added, as if we'd know that particular small town. "Heard of it? No? Not surprising," he said when we shook our heads. "About eleven hundred people from edge to edge is all. Not much to see or do. Which is why I jumped at the chance to come to Bliss. But this murder business . . ." He trailed off and shook his head. "I don't understand it."

"Neither do we, Pastor," I said. "We're trying to figure out who would have done this to her."

Coco flung her hand up and got our attention. "I want to know about the things she donated to the tag sale," she said, leaving out the part that the figurines we'd found actually belonged to Jessie Pearl.

Pastor Kyle stroked his goatee as he shook his head. "That's Cynthia's domain. To tell you the truth, I didn't know Delta brought anything to donate. After she quit volunteering in the office, she didn't come around much. I never was sure what happened and why she turned her back on us."

Coco waved his words away, going back to the donations. "We found some of my mother's very precious collectibles right down there on one of the tables. I know Mother didn't bring them. She'd never part with them, or even if she'd decided to, she doesn't drive, so she'd have needed me or Sherri or Delta to bring them. She didn't ask me. I called Sherri on my way up to see you, and she didn't know a thing about it. Which means it had to be Delta, which would be just like her."

"Didn't Todd say he brought some boxes over for her?" I said. "Maybe Delta asked him to."

The pastor nodded. "I do recollect seeing Megan come through with a box the other day. Didn't see her husband, but that's not to say he didn't drop things off. People have been coming and going for weeks."

Coco fell silent for a beat. Maybe she wanted to give Delta the benefit of the doubt. I thought we needed to go to Jessie Pearl and simply ask her. For all we knew, she'd given the items herself and we were throwing Delta under the bus without cause.

Pastor Kyle had lowered his hand back to his side. "I'm sorry for your loss," he said to Coco. "If there's anything I can do—"

"I have one more question, Pastor," I said, interrupting him. Coco, Will, and Pastor Kyle all turned expectantly to me, and I went on. "Someone mentioned to me that a piece of furniture at Delta's house had been in the church basement at one time."

"An old sideboard?" the pastor asked.

"Yes," I said. "Exactly."

"It was falling apart. I'd left it in the basement during last year's tag sale. That, and a few other bigger items. Delta's daughter bought it," he said. "She said her husband could fix it up. They moved it out of here last summer. I thought they were going to sell it. They didn't?"

"Not yet," I said. "But I don't know their plans for it." I thought back to what Cynthia had told me. She'd made it sound as if Delta had kept her and the other Red Hatters out of her house to hide stolen goods, but according to the pastor, the sideboard wasn't stolen at all. Had Cynthia known Megan had bought it, and had she been leading me astray for some reason?

I drew in a sharp breath as I realized something else. She'd steered me toward Jeremy Lisle. To throw me off the trail by painting him as a possible suspect? After all, she'd been at the church the morning Delta died. She could have intercepted her at the cemetery, cornering her at the open grave.

But why? That was the unanswered question.

Will cleared his throat. "Pastor, could I talk to you for a minute?" He flashed a meaningful look my way, silently communicating to the pastor that I couldn't hear whatever it was he needed to speak about. "Privately."

The pastor nodded, and they stepped into the hallway. As soon as Will closed the door behind him, I leaned forward on the sofa, meeting Coco's gaze. "Are you okay?"

"I don't understand, Harlow. What did that old sideboard have to do with anything?"

"I'm not sure. Maybe nothing. But is Cynthia in charge of all the tag sales?" I asked. If she didn't have anything to do with the last one, she might not have known that Megan had bought the furniture from the basement. That still wouldn't explain why she'd been so quick to implicate Delta as a thief, but it was a start.

But Coco nodded, and my heart lodged in my throat. "She's been in charge of the tag sales for as long as I can remember. She runs the office."

"And Delta used to volunteer here at the church?"

"For about three years or so. I don't know why she stopped."

From what the pastor had said, he didn't know, either. Which meant I needed to find out from the one person who seemed to know a lot more than she was letting on. Cynthia Homer.

Will and the pastor came back in looking a touch conspiratorial, which had me wondering just what they'd been discussing. They shook hands, and Will waited by the door. "Ready?" he asked us.

I was. I had a new theory swimming in my head, and I needed time to think about it.

Chapter 13

Half an hour later, Coco had gone to work, and Will and I had left Mama and Nana to their volunteer time at the tag sale. As we were walking back through the cemetery, passing by Delta's gravesite, the figurines, overalls, and jeans packaged up in a bag strung over my forearm, I asked, "What was the powwow with the pastor about?"

Will held my free hand, pulling me along at a quick clip. "Just giving you time to talk with Coco and poke around the office."

I stared at him. Oh Lord, I'd missed a perfect opportunity to snoop! "I might need to go back," I said sheepishly.

"You didn't poke around?" he asked, an amused tone in his voice.

I hung my head, thinking that a real detective would never have missed such a prime opportunity. "Not even a little bit. I was preoccupied thinking about how Cynthia Homer might be involved. Snooping wasn't even on my mind."

"You probably wouldn't have found anything, anyway. The pastor seems like a stand-up guy to me. Not the type to resort to murdering anyone. I didn't get any hint of a motive, either."

I had to agree with him. I hadn't gotten the impression that the pastor and Delta had been close, or even friends, but I also hadn't sensed any animosity toward her from him. More than anything, he'd seemed genuinely concerned about Coco, wanting to help her cope with his counsel.

"Who else could have done it?" Will asked as we entered the parking lot.

I was going to keep the idea of Cynthia as a suspect to myself until I could give her more consideration. "Jeremy Lisle," I said, revisiting the candidate for mayor and the president of the Historic Council.

He leveled his gaze at me. "I've known Jeremy for a long time," he said.

"Do you think he has it in him?"

He shrugged. "Anybody probably has it in them if they're pushed enough and something snaps. But that doesn't mean either of those things happened with Jeremy."

"They argued about something," I said, before I remembered that Cynthia had been my source for that information. Had Jeremy and Delta really argued, or was that something Cynthia had said to throw the scent away from her?

"They had a difference of opinion," Will said. "She never should have been on the council in the first place."

"But she was voted off."

Will opened the driver's door of Buttercup for me, but we both stood alongside it, not ready to end our speculations. "Which means *he* had *her* voted off the council," he said. "That gave her reason to do *him* in, not the other way around."

That was a very good point. "But there could be more to the story. They didn't get along. She supported Radcliffe for mayor. Donated money to Radcliffe's campaign, even. She didn't believe in preserving the history of the town."

"Jeremy may be a lot of things—driven, a hard-ass, and competitive—but a murderer? I don't know about that, Harlow."

He'd used my given name, which meant he was serious. "Maybe you're right, but he had a motive. We already know that it doesn't take much to bring a person to murder in the heat of the moment. If Jeremy Lisle has any violent tendencies, Delta might have pushed too far, and he might have unleashed on her."

Will didn't look convinced, and frankly neither was I, but we couldn't rule him out. The motive was there. It was early enough in the morning—or late enough at night—that surely he'd had the opportunity, even if the pastor hadn't identified his car as one he'd seen that morning. Maybe he'd called Delta, asking her to meet him to talk things out. He might have chosen the cemetery as a secluded location, knowing she wouldn't be found until much later.

"He has my historical landmark plaque at his office. He said to stop by anytime. We could go get it."

His expression was grim. "You need to be careful, Cassidy. Someone killed Delta. You poking around and asking questions could get the killer, whoever it is, pretty riled up."

"Only if I ask the *right* questions," I said. "And I'm always careful, Will."

He gave my hand a squeeze before I got into Buttercup and headed to the city offices to pay a visit to Jeremy Lisle, Will right behind me in his truck.

Chapter 14

We found the mayoral hopeful in his office in between meetings. He was dressed just like he'd been when I'd met him at the Historic Council. Khakis and a button-down shirt made him seem approachable, but there was something about him that put me on edge. It very likely could have been that I suspected he might be a suspect in Delta Lea's murder . . . or it could have been my imagination. I just wasn't sure.

"Thanks for seeing us," I said, after he ushered us into his office. The space was masculine yet minimalistic in décor. The furniture felt vaguely old and utilitarian. It fit what I knew about Jeremy and his love for the history of Bliss. A framed map of the town, circa 1890, hung on the wall behind his desk. In the corner of the office were boxes of files. All historic information, I imagined.

"Here for your plaque?"

I clapped my hands. "Yes! Will's going to put it up for me. Meemaw's dream come true."

He rifled through a drawer, emerging a moment later with a black box. He opened it to reveal a round bronze and gold plaque. It was about five inches in diameter with an HL in the center. Around the perimeter, it read: PRESERVING THE PAST FOR THE FUTURE. "Here you go," he said, presenting it to me.

I thanked him, admired it, and tucked it into my shoulder bag. "Are you already campaigning?" I asked, gesturing to the yard signs toward the back of the office.

"A politician is always campaigning. Look at Hillary Clinton. She didn't have to announce her candidacy, yet she led the race as the democratic candidate. Her entire existence is in the spotlight. There's no distinction between her public and private life. Everything is part of her campaign, even when she's not running for anything. That's the life of a politician."

"That sounds intense," I said.

He sat behind his desk and steepled his fingers under his chin. "That's what it takes to win."

"Would you like me to take an election sign for my yard?" I asked, glancing at the signs again.

"It's a little early, but hell's bells, if Delta Mobley can have one in her yard even after she's gone from us, then you can have one in yours." He ambled over to the stack and brought one back for me, the red, white, and blue design subtle yet effective. Jeremy Lisle was a patriot, and that message came across loud and clear.

Ever the Southern gentleman, Will took the sign for me.

"Have you been in Delta's house?" I asked, fishing for more information.

"Once upon a time, she was my Realtor. Drove me around the Historic District and pointed out her place."

So their relationship extended beyond the Historic Council. Interesting.

"Look," he said. "I know you're trying to find out what happened to Delta. She was a lot of things, but she sure wasn't subtle. If she didn't like you, she went out of her way to show you just how deep her dislike ran. If she thought she knew something about you but couldn't prove it, she found a way. If she wanted something, she took it whether it belonged to her or not. She had everyone fooled, but the truth is, she only followed her own rules."

I let this sink in. So far, only Delta's family had made me question who Delta really was, but Jeremy Lisle had some pretty firm beliefs about her character, too. "What do you mean she'd find a way to prove something?"

He clasped his hands in front of him, looking calm, but I wasn't fooled. His left eye twitched, just barely, and inside, I suspected that his emotions were going haywire. "Let me preface this by saying that I didn't kill Delta Lea Mobley. We weren't friends, but I'm not a murderer."

Will and I shot a glance at each other. Unless Jeremy was a master manipulator and was using reverse psychology on us to throw us off the trail, I suspected that whatever he was about to say was the truth.

"Okay," I said, nodding reassuringly.

He took a deep breath, and then said, "She didn't just switch to the Radcliffe camp. She wanted to discredit me."

"How?" I pressed, wondering to myself if he would be

willing to discuss with us something that could possibly be perceived as a motive for murder.

"I think she wanted to get some dirt on me. Help the Radcliffe campaign. For about a week, I know I was being followed. Everywhere I went, this silver Monte Carlo would show up. It'd be driving behind me, or parked across from my house. It was everywhere."

I leaned forward in my chair, fascinated. I thought people in Bliss were much more transparent than they apparently were. My neighbor had been a total and complete mystery to me. Vengefulness. Secrecy. Detective work. What else would I discover about her? "And you're sure it was her?"

"She wasn't actually in the car, if that's what you mean, but there isn't a doubt in my mind that she hired someone to do her dirty work."

"But why are you so sure? What was she hoping to discover?"

He shrugged. "Who knows? I'm sure she wanted to catch me in an impropriety of some sort. Discredit me in the election." One corner of his mouth went up in a satisfied smile. "Like the pot calling the kettle black, if you ask me."

I inched closer to his desk, certain some big revelation was coming. "How d'you mean?"

"There aren't many secrets 'round here."

That seemed to be a running theme. No one thought anything could be kept on the down low in Bliss. "No?"

"No. She thought nobody knew why she stopped volunteering at the church."

"But people did?" I asked, thinking back to Coco and

the pastor. Neither one had seemed to know. Or at least they hadn't offered up the information.

He paused, seeming to consider how to respond. "Even a pastor has to have someone to talk to," he finally said. "He's a good guy. Came to me knowing I worked with Delta and needing advice."

Will and I sneaked another surreptitious glance at each other. The pastor hadn't mentioned that he knew Jeremy Lisle, let alone that he'd gone to him for counsel. "What kind of advice?"

"He felt bad for her, about her husband's affair, but she used her place at the church to snoop into other people's business."

My jaw dropped. "Her husband was having an affair?" I asked.

"You're going to catch a fly like that, Ms. Cassidy," he said, the fine lines around his eyes crinkling. My blatant surprise seemed to amuse him.

"I just . . . I never suspected . . . I'm stunned is all," I finally said, but as the words left my mouth, something Cynthia had said came back to me. Delta had told her that you should be able to trust your husband. "So she knew?" I asked after a beat.

"From what I gather, she told Pastor Kyle that not all husbands could be trusted, and that she'd get her proof delivered to her by a private investigator. I do believe she was inherently untrusting of all the people around her."

"But why?"

"That I do not know," he said, frowning. "I thought about hiring a PI myself. Prove that Delta was up to no good. Catch her on the wrong side of the law, but she was a pro. She manipulated people, but didn't actually cross any lines, you know?"

"What would you have done with the information if you'd gotten it?" Will asked.

Jeremy shrugged. "Use it as leverage. Get her to back off on the election sabotage. She was ready and willing to take the campaign negative on behalf of Radcliffe. And he was ready and willing to let her do the dirty work. I wanted to stop her at the gate. But," he added, wagging his finger at us as if he realized the implication of what he was saying, "I didn't kill her. I didn't like her, I'll admit that, but I'm not about to ruin my political career for some meddling woman who couldn't keep her nose out of other people's business."

We said our good-byes and thanked Jeremy for the plaque. On the way home, Will carried the election sign while I carried the unease of knowing that the man we'd just spoken to had a pretty clear motive for killing Delta Lea Mobley. I wanted to believe him when he said he didn't kill her. He seemed on the up and up, and his political aspirations were great. He'd handed us his own motive, for heaven's sake. How much damage could Delta have done when she didn't have anything on him?

But there was a new concern that really had me worried after Will and I parted and I drove home—the fact that if Delta had confronted her husband about him having an affair, then it was very possible that Anson Mobley may have killed his wife.

Chapter 15

I loved everything vintage, including the rounded fenders and domed cab of the old Ford truck that I had inherited from Meemaw, and if I had my way, I'd drive it forever. Will and I had gone our separate ways from the church's parking lot. The town was building a new library, and he was the architect in charge of the project. I, on the other hand, still had aprons to make and only four days until the progressive dinner.

I drove through town, unable to escape the unease settling in me. One murder and too many suspects. So far Cynthia Homer, Jeremy Lisle, and Anson Mobley were neck and neck to my thinking in terms of motive, means, and opportunity. With the exception of Cynthia, they each could have had their own reasons for wanting Delta dead. Again, with the possible exception of Cynthia, they each would have had the strength to wield the rock that killed her. And they each could have easily created the opportunity. They all lived in town, plus she died in the early hours of the morning when few people were out and about, especially at the cemetery, so truly, it could have been any of them.

And then there were the rest of the Red Hat ladies. I didn't want to believe it could be any one of them, but I also couldn't rule them out.

The one person whose name had come up quite a few times but I hadn't yet met with was Mayor Radcliffe. I couldn't summon up a motive for him—after all, Delta had been on his side in the election antics—but who knew what lay beneath the surface? I added him to my mental list of people I wanted to pay a visit to.

I pulled onto the pebble driveway of my house under the possumwood trees. Mama's much newer, but still old, truck was parked there, too. I glanced through the yard. Sure enough, she sat on one of the white rocking chairs on the front porch, gently moving back and forth. The chair next to her swayed, too. Meemaw was right there beside her.

Mama had taken to coming over daily. It used to be that she'd come just to see me, but I'd begun to suspect that now she came just to be in the presence of her grandmother. As a ghost, my great-grandmother hadn't mastered the art of communication, but the Cassidy women all felt her around us. Unless she was playing parlor tricks, being in her presence was like being enveloped in a cocoon of warmth, bolstering us up and lifting our spirits.

I threw the truck into park, and in seconds, I'd joined Mama on the porch, leaning against the railing so as not to disturb Meemaw. Having the three of us, or better yet, the four of us (when Nana was here) in the same place was always a treasured moment. "Where have you been?" Mama asked. "Out sleuthin'?"

"Guilty as charged."

She kept both cowboy-booted feet on the ground, pushing with her toes to move the chair back and forth. "And?"

Mama made a good show of looking chagrined that I was involved in yet another murder investigation, but I knew she was just as curious about the crime as I was, and the mother in her had untold sympathy for Jessie Pearl's loss. I filled her in on my thoughts, including my suspicions about Cynthia Homer, Jeremy Lisle, Mayor Radcliffe, and the newly discovered information about Anson Mobley.

"Maybe you need to go have a little chat with Jessie Pearl."

"Yes, but under what pretense?"

A gust of wind suddenly swirled around us, rustling the plastic shopping bag I'd set on a little red table next to me. It held the jeans and figurines from the tag sale.

We both looked at the bag, then at each other, finally both turning to the empty rocking chair. Meemaw was a smart cookie.

"I can return these to Jessie Pearl," I said, taking up the bag. And there was no time like the present. I paused at the bottom of the porch stairs. "Are you coming?"

Mama stopped rocking and practically jumping off the chair like a child from a swing. "Sure am." She winked. "When I said *you*, you know I really meant *we*. And I reckon it's time I paid my condolences to Jessie Pearl."

I stifled a smile as she threaded her arm through mine, and together—feeling a little bit like Dorothy and the Scarecrow from *The Wizard of Oz* as we walked arm in arm up the brick path in my front yard—we went next door to the Mobley house. Although I had seen Todd pulling weeds and mowing the small lawn since Delta's death, their yard looked sad somehow. As if the garden could sense the mourning happening inside the house and responded. The colors of the grass and flowers seemed muted, and the stems of the shrubs had grown leggy and drooped in a way they hadn't just a week ago.

As we walked to the front door, I looked back over my shoulder, knowing that Mama's charm had kicked in. The colors were brighter. The flowers bloomed, petals opening wide to reveal vibrant reds, yellows, and purples. Even the grass was greener.

"Nice, Mama," I said, nudging her with my elbow.

She grinned and gave a small shrug. "It's the least I can do."

Todd opened the door after we knocked. He greeted us, stepping aside so we could enter. He glanced past us at the yard, then did a double take, his brows knitting together. "What the . . . ?" he muttered.

"Sorry to come by unannounced," I said quickly. "Is Jessie Pearl here?"

He shook his head, as if he were clearing away cobwebs, looked one more time at the yard, then focused on me. "No problem, she's here."

We stepped inside, and he shut the door behind us. I knew the way, so I wove through the furniture, moving toward the kitchen. Behind me, I heard the sharp intake of Mama's breath as she took in the array of knickknacks and antiques. I hadn't prepared her for what to expect in the house. She murmured under her breath, in awe. She wasn't a collector, but Nana was. Mama had grown up in a house where every piece of furniture, every vase, picture frame, and trinket had a story.

Todd led us inside to the dining table where Jessie Pearl sat, her crutches leaning against her chair. She was looking at a sketch of their front yard. We offered our condolences to her before Todd continued. "I was thinking of putting paper lanterns out for the progressive dinner," he said. "Make it more festive."

Jessie Pearl patted his hand as he sat down at the table next to her. "It's a fine idea, Todd. It'll be a nice way to honor Delta."

He slid the sketch toward me. "This is what I was thinking. White lights in the trees. The lanterns along the walkway. And if I have time after work this week, Megs and I thought we'd plant some flowers in the pots by the front porch."

Now Jessie Pearl's chin quivered in earnest. She squeezed her hands tighter together to control the shaking. "Lovely," she said, but her voice was tight. "Delta would have enjoyed that."

"I can't wait to see it," I said to Todd.

He grinned, turning the gold band on his finger. He was shy, I realized, and self-conscious from the praise. "Should have skipped law school and gotten into landscape architecture instead."

Just then, Megan came out of the kitchen. She wound a white and red ticking dishcloth in her hands. She came up next to him, rubbing her hand on his back. "You can do both."

"And a chef, right? A man of many talents," I said.

Mama ran her fingers over the yellowed leaves of a neglected houseplant. "Do you work in Bliss?"

He shrugged modestly. "Bliss already has its fair share of attorneys. I would have to consider working in Fort Worth. Maybe as far as Dallas. But that would mean moving, and Megs is settled here. So, no, I've given up on the law."

"You just have to put your resume out there," Megan said. "Something'll turn up." She looked at us. "In the meantime, he keeps busy around here, and he's doing some special projects for the church. Plus he's cooking Friday night. The array of desserts will be awesome!"

"I thought Bennie was helping y'all with that," I said, thinking maybe I'd misunderstood Bennie at the fabric store.

"She wanted to. In fact she asked me to show her how I made my cream puff pastry. Said she could make those for the dinner to help me out."

Megan laughed. "He told her it was a trade secret."

He put his hands out, palms up. "It is. And I don't need any help, thank you very much." He turned back to Mama and me. "I told her I could handle it."

"Where did you go to cooking school?" I asked, but he was already out of his chair. He disappeared into the kitchen and returned a few seconds later with five coffee mugs. He disappeared again, this time returning with a coffee pot, and started pouring.

"He went to the culinary institute in Chicago," Megan

said, answering for him. "Then to law school here in Texas. That was all before I met him, can you imagine?"

"But none of it meant anything till I met you," he said, squeezing her hand.

"But your true calling is landscape architecture?" I glanced again at the sketch he'd done of the front yard. It looked like something out of *Southern Living* magazine. If he could pull it off in a matter of days *and* make cream puffs, I'd be impressed.

Megan ran her hand up his arm, beaming. "He's amazing. You can just show him a picture of something you want built, and he'll build it. Just like that," she added, snapping her fingers. "Show him a picture of some fancy meal, and he can make that, too."

"I'm sure the yard will look great and the desserts will be delicious," I said, wanting to get back to the reason for my visit.

Mama perked up, suddenly finding a way to jump into the conversation. "If y'all need any help with the flowers, I can get most anythin' to grow."

My gaze instantly flew to the plant she'd been touching. The yellow leaves had turned a vibrant green, perking up as if they'd just had a much-needed drink of water. They looked plump and renewed. I quickly pushed the plant out of the way, blocking it from view before any of them noticed. People might not be able to keep secrets in Bliss, but we could still try.

Todd considered her, a little twinkle in his brown eyes. "I've heard that about you, Mrs. McClaine."

The words were barely out of his mouth when Mama scooted back on her chair, looking for all the world like she'd been struck across the cheek. "I don't know who you think you're talkin' to, but there ain't no Mrs. Mc-Claine around here—"

"Mama!" What had gotten into her?

Todd's eyes flew open wide, and he looked shell-shocked. "I—I'm sorry? I'd heard you were married to the sheriff."

"She is," I said, just as Mama sat up straight in her chair and said, "Oh, I'm his wife. But I will always be Tessa Parker Cassidy. I did not take the sheriff's name, but I sure welcome him to take mine."

I stared at my mother, flummoxed. She wasn't usually so combative with folks she didn't know well. She saved that particular personality trait for her loved ones. Her name was clearly a sensitive subject.

"You're one of those feminists, aren't you?" Jessie Pearl asked, narrowing her eyes as she looked at Mama.

"No," Mama said. "I'm a Cassidy."

Jessie Pearl seemed to consider this for a moment before responding. "Taking your husband's name doesn't make you less of a Cassidy. I took my husband's name proudly. He passed goin' on twenty years now, but I kept his name just as surely as I kept my own. The name doesn't define me, Tessa."

"Maybe not," Mama said, "but we've got a strong and unique family history. Butch left us a legacy that is part of who we are. I carry his name because it is a daily reminder of the love he and Texana shared. The love that survived, against all odds, and resulted in our family line."

Jessie Pearl shrugged her hunched shoulders, waving

away Mama's defense. "A name is just a name. Cassidy wasn't even that man's real name. It don't mean anything. Hell's bells, I could call Megan by her middle name, but it don't change who she is. Would it, Isabel?"

Megan and Todd looked at each other, hiding smiles.

Jessie Pearl continued. "I could up and decide to call Todd, I don't know, Zachary, but he's the same young man he was before, isn't that right, Zachary? Er, I mean Todd?"

"Call him George, like Rebecca always does," Megan said with a laugh. "She thinks he looks like a blond-haired George Clooney."

Todd rolled his eyes, but nodded. "That's right. Call me Zach or Michael or George. I can be someone different every day, if you like."

Mama grinned, and suddenly I saw through her. She might well believe everything she was saying, but more than anything, she was getting Jessie Pearl to talk and think about something besides her dead daughter. I caught her eye and winked.

"There you have it," Jessie Pearl said. "You can call a zebra a horse, and we might all believe it, but the truth of the matter is that a zebra can't change his stripes. He's still a zebra at the end of the day. I can call you Mc-Claine, but you'll still be a Cassidy. I just don't know what difference it makes, but there you go."

She struggled to stand, nodding to the bag I held. "What do you have there?" Todd hurried forward, helping her into the nearest chair, an antique American arm-chair. It rested on three turned, button-footed legs, and one front cabriole leg with a pad-style foot. She collapsed again, the effort at the short walk taking its toll.

Coco might have wanted to handle it differently, but she also wanted me to find out the truth, so I went with my gut. "Ma'am," I said, lifting the sack I carried. "I found these at the tag sale. They looked like the ones you collect," I said, pointing to the curio cabinet. "I thought maybe they were added to your donation by mistake?"

I snuck a look at the figurines on the glass shelves as I unwrapped the first one from the church sale. The Dressmaker that had been in Jessie Pearl's collection a week ago was gone. A layer of dust covered the shelves, several clean spots evident where figurines had recently been. I hesitated handing it over, not wanting to upset her.

"Give it here," she said, her gnarled hand reaching for the Dressmaker. She was elderly and looked frail, but she was a spitfire. "You got this at the tag sale, you said?"

"Yes," I said, nodding as I handed her the bag.

She took it, her shoulders hunched, and then patted the chair seat next to her. "Harlow, sit."

This chair was black framed with black-and-white floral fabric on the back and seat cushions. I sat, watching her hands tremble slightly as she unwrapped the next figurine. One by one, she examined the five Lladró figurines I'd brought back with me from the church, and then she raised her head and turned to look at me. "I knew they were missing," she said to Todd, "But I don't understand. Todd?"

Todd raked his fingers through his dark blond hair, the ends standing up. "She gave me the boxes to donate. I asked her if there was anything Megan could sell. She said there wasn't, that this was all a bunch of junk, so I took them."

"A bunch of junk," Jessie Pearl repeated, her head low. "Doesn't that beat all?"

She handed me the Dressmaker. "Would you put them back on the shelves for me?"

"Of course." I took it, admiring it once more before standing. I ran my finger over the delicate lines of the woman's dress, over the base. The ceramic was cool to the touch and smooth . . . until my thumb brushed over something barely poking out of the bottom of the figurine. I turned the Dressmaker over to see what looked like a bit of white paper tucked into the small hole there. My mind raced. Surely Delta hadn't left a message in the figurine. Or had she?

I turned to Megan. "There's something in here. Do you have a pair of tweezers?"

The color drained from Megan's face, and she looked as if she'd seen a ghost, but she nodded, popped up, and ran down the hallway, returning a few seconds later with the tool. Everyone seemed to hold their breath as I poked the end of the tweezers into the opening, emerging a moment later with a scrap of paper rolled tightly like a cigarette.

Jessie Pearl peered at me, then at the note in my hand. "Oh my stars, don't tell me . . ."

"Mother," Megan said, her voice scarcely more than a whisper.

Mama and I looked at each other, then at Megan. "Are you okay?" I asked.

Megan ran the back of her hand under her nose, her face close to collapsing. "Ever since I was a little girl, my mother would leave little notes for me."

"I did the same for her and her sisters," Jessie Pearl said, her own voice quiet as she recalled the memory. "I'd put notes in their lunches every once in a while, but they squealed in delight when I got creative. I'd put them in their pillow cases, tape them to their mirrors, I'd roll them around the handle of their toothbrushes."

"Mother did the same thing," Megan said. "The best was the time she came on campus after school was out for the day. When I came to school the next day and went to my locker, there was a note taped to the inside of the slats. *Hail or storm, rain or shine, I'll protect you always, because you're mine.* I still have that note," she said.

I went back to the chair next to Jessie Pearl and unrolled the paper, holding it so we could both see the message scribbled there.

Collins College. No record. Alias?

Jessie Pearl's snapped her gaze at me. "That's Delta's handwriting, but what kind of note is that?"

Not a sweet endearment, I thought.

"Delta packed up the last box for the tag sale after you left that night," Jessie Pearl said to me. "She must have added the Lladrós, but why?"

A chill crept up my spine. Was the note a clue? Had she suspected harm might come to her? If so, why not simply tell someone?

Megan voiced the same question. "Why would she

leave notes in figurines she gave away? If she wanted me—or someone—to find them, why not put them somewhere obvious?"

If the note was discovered and she was fine, she could laugh it off. Or she could have bought back the Lladrós herself. But if something *did* happen to her, there was a chance the note would be discovered by whoever purchased them at the tag sale. Was it a bread-crumb trail?

There was no guarantee of discovery, but on the other hand, if she'd been hypothesizing, hiding the cryptic message was the safest way not to draw undesirable attention.

"Notes," I repeated, realizing that Megan had spoken in the plural. "Oh mercy, I bet there are others." I grabbed the bag and withdrew the other four figurines I'd found at the tag sale. One by one, I pried scraps of paper from the hollow insides of the Lladrós, handing them to Jessie Pearl. Each had a different message.

No history. No past.

Regret. It's useless, but I'm sorry, Megs.

Friendships are not what they seem. Ask Rebecca.

The cemetery, five a.m. I will know the whole truth.

Tears flowed down Megan's cheeks as she read the brief notes. She looked to the ceiling. "I don't understand, Mother. What about Collins College? What are you sorry for?"

"Delta didn't beat around the bush with things," Jessie Pearl said. "Why in the devil would she be so cryptic?"

"Someone killed her, Jessie Pearl," Todd said. "She must have been scared and trying to tell us something."

"Why not just call us into the kitchen and say whatever was on her mind? For pity's sake, how are we supposed to know what all this means?"

"She met her killer at the cemetery," I mused aloud. "Why not go to the sheriff? Why would she risk her life?"

"She wasn't sure about whatever she knew," Mama said matter-of-factly. "But she was taking precautions. Just in case it went badly. If she wasn't sure, she couldn't just come out and accuse someone of whatever it was they'd done wrong—Delta had more integrity than that."

I had to agree. She'd driven me crazy with the goat feud, but Delta wasn't generally unreasonable.

"We need to show these to Hoss," Mama said.

Everyone nodded in agreement, and Mama pulled out her cell phone, making the call. "He'll be here lickety-split," she said a minute later.

"Put the figurines back," Jessie Pearl said, handing me the Dressmaker.

I stood, carefully turning the tasseled key and opening the door to the hutch, and put the Dressmaker back where it had been. Todd handed me another Lladró and took the last three himself. "That one goes there," he said to me, pointing to an empty space on the glass shelf. After he placed the three he held in their spots, I started to close the door, but stopped. There were at least nine other figurines in the curio cabinet, as well as three mini teapots and a few other knickknacks. Could there be messages in any of the others?

Quickly, I picked up each figurine, turned it over, and

felt along the base for evidence of anything hidden inside. Nothing. I moved to the teapots, half listening to the chatter behind me about how Delta and Coco had created a system for communicating and passing notes to each other, excluding poor Sherri. "She was five years younger than Coco, seven years younger than Delta," Jessie Pearl said. "The poor thing idolized her older sisters, and they tortured her."

"That's the benefit of being an only child," Megan said, "but I still wish I had a brother or sister."

I lifted the lid off one of the small teapots, tilted the base, and peered inside. Once again, I came up empty. I wasn't holding my breath that I'd find anything more. *Wishful thinking*, I thought, but when I lifted the lid of the last one and looked inside, I saw a folded-up sheet of paper. My pulse kicked up a notch at the discovery. "There's something here," I said, poking two fingers inside of the opening to withdraw the potential clue.

"Let me see that," Jessie Pearl said before I had a chance to unfold it myself. I'd wanted the first look, but instead, I handed it over to her. Her arthritic fingers slowly maneuvered the paper, undoing the folds. Finally, she had it spread out on her lap, and as she peered at it, she drew in a sharp breath. "Good Lord," she muttered under her breath.

From where I stood, the half sheet looked worn and faded. "What is it, Granny?" Megan asked.

"Sherri wrote this one," Jessie Pearl said, looking up at Megan, her eyes glassy. "To your mother. Let's see, you've been married, what, going on six months now, is that right?"

"Right." Todd nodded. "Love at first sight," he added, winking at Megan.

She smiled faintly, turning to Mama and me with an explanation. "We fell in love practically overnight. Todd asked me to marry him on our one-month anniversary."

"Wow, that's incredible," I said.

Will and I were taking our time getting to know each other, and I preferred it that way. I wanted to know just what I was getting before I made a lifelong commitment, and he did, too. But part of me admired people like Todd and Megan, who knew just what they wanted and didn't wait before they went for it.

"What's the note say?" Mama asked, circling back to Jessie Pearl.

"This must have been when they had that falling out, do you remember that?" Jessie Pearl asked. To us, she said, "Sherri and Delta were a bit like oil and water. Sherri was always trying to impress her big sister, but Delta wasn't easily impressed. Sherri had told Delta about some antique show she'd been at over in Plano and some of the people she'd met there. Someone she thought Delta knew or something. Do you remember that?" she asked Megan.

But Megan shook her head. "Not at all. They didn't talk for a while, right? Sherri almost didn't come to the wedding, remember that?" she asked Todd. He nodded, and she continued. "She told me that my mother was too mule-headed to listen, but I talked her into it. I told her it was my day, and that I wanted her there. I don't think she wanted to come and see Mother, but she did anyway."

"She stayed at a back table the whole reception,"

Todd said, shaking his head at the memory. "What was the point? She just sat there, wouldn't talk to anyone, hardly ate."

We all turned back to the half sheet of paper Jessie Pearl had in front of her. "What does it say?" I asked.

Jessie Pearl cleared her throat and read aloud.

> *Will you ever listen to me, Delta? I'm right, and I hope that whenever you realize it, there isn't a trail of broken hearts along the way because it was too late. You'll always be my sister and I love you, but good God, you're stubborn. I've hidden this note, as you and Coco used to do. Someday, when you find it, you'll remember how I tried to warn you.*
>
> *~Sherri*

We stood in silence, processing the message from Sherri to Delta, hidden away. I didn't understand the family's penchant for note writing and note hiding. Why not simply say these things to one another? Why leave a note so well hidden that it might never be found? "It's like a purging of the soul," I said under my breath. Maybe, as Sherri indicated, she'd tried to say what she'd wanted to in person, but it had fallen on deaf ears. Writing the note was a way to rid herself of the worry she couldn't get her sister to listen to.

Were Delta's notes the same? Maybe she didn't care if they were ever found. Maybe they were more of a touchstone for herself. A way of getting her thoughts out without committing them to a diary or some other form of writing that could be found and misinterpreted.

I sighed. Too many questions and no way to answer them.

"It doesn't matter," Jessie Pearl said. "Sherri and Delta were fine. They picked at each other their whole lives, but sisters do that."

"Sherri doesn't much like conflict," Todd said. "Maybe she was just unloading in a safe way."

"Just what I was thinking," I said.

Todd helped Jessie Pearl to her feet again, holding her by the wrist and elbow of one arm as he carefully guided her upright and handed her the crutches. "At least it wasn't out of spite," Jessie Pearl said, so softly I almost didn't hear. The cryptic messages aside, it was a comfort to her that one of Delta's last acts hadn't been one of bitterness and sibling rivalry.

Megan dried her eyes as I looked at each of the notes again. After a moment, she sat us straighter. "What did it say about Rebecca?"

"Friendship is not what it seems. Ask Rebecca," I said, repeating what was on the slip of paper.

"Ask Rebecca what?" She clasped her hands to the sides of her head, pressing, her fingers curling until her fingernails clawed into her scalp.

"Call her," Todd said, handing her his cell phone. "Ask her to come over."

Megan shook her head. "I've been calling her since yesterday, but she's not answering, and she hasn't called me back."

"Try again," he prompted, handing her his cell phone.

Megan took it and stepped out of the way, letting Todd and Jessie Pearl lead the way back into the kitchen. Mama and I followed. "Still no answer. I left a message,"

she said when she came in a minute later. She went back
to the counter, sliding cookies off a tray and putting
them on a plate. The kitchen held an array of aluminum
casserole dishes, Styrofoam containers, a CorningWare
dish filled with what looked like banana pudding, a few
bottles of wine, and a variety of other things people had
brought over. Feed a cold, starve a fever, and stuff grief.

She brought the plate to the kitchen table, setting it in
the middle, then poured more coffee into the mugs we'd
brought with us. Her eyes were vacant and unfocused,
and my heart ached for her. She didn't know what was
going on any more than the rest of us, and it had been
her mother. The notes, the apology, the reference to her
friend. It was all puzzling, and Megan looked as if she
was going to crack any second.

After the coffee was poured, she perched on her husband's lap. Todd rested one hand on her hip. Despite
their loss and the drama of the last half hour, they
seemed close. A happy, young married couple with their
future in front of them. I closed my eyes for a second, a
glimpse of an apron for Megan coming to my mind. It
was flirty with a gathered band across the chest, a wide
waistband, and a flared and ruffled skirt. Youthful and
playful in a way the ones for the Red Hat ladies weren't.

A quick image of a black, traditional apron flashed
through my head. Todd wore it, a metal spatula in his
hand. If I had time, I'd make one for him, too. I added it
to my mental list.

Hoss McClaine would be here soon, and he'd start
asking his own questions. In the meantime, I asked another of my own. "How's your dad doing?"

Megan wiped away the last of her tears and said, "He's still shaken up. We had the memorial for the family, and he couldn't say good-bye. Wouldn't go up to the casket. Wouldn't look at her." She squeezed Todd's hand for strength.

"He disappears," Todd said. "He doesn't like to be here."

I thought back to the tag sale that morning. *Anson can barely get through the day without her*, Coco had said. *He isn't showing up to work. He's standing up clients. That's what happens after so many years of marriage, do you know? There are good times and bad times, but you're more of a unit than you're not, and when the unit is ripped apart, well, what do you do?*

I hadn't really thought of marriage in quite those terms, but she was right. Mama and Hoss McClaine had been hitched only a few months, but they were like peas and carrots. I could hardly remember what Mama was like before she had Hoss, and I was pretty sure she couldn't, either. The Mobleys weren't wealthy and didn't have a lake house in Granbury or a second residence anywhere that I'd ever heard of. "Where does he go off to?" I asked.

Todd shrugged. "No idea."

"Does he have a friend he can lean on?" I thought about my conversation with Jeremy Lisle. Even if it were true that Anson was having an affair—and right now there was no proof that he was—he was still mourning the loss of his wife. "Someone who maybe y'all don't know about, perhaps?"

Jessie Pearl considered me for a good long beat, and then blew a burst of air through her lips. "Now why in heaven's name would you say that?"

I felt my cheeks turn warm. "Just a thought."

Jessie Pearl considered me, her lips thin and tight. Right now it looked as if she were ready to shut down. "You know, don't you?"

The color drained from Megan's face. "Know what? What does she know?"

I cursed under my breath. Had I been that transparent? Jessie Pearl was a perceptive old woman, and she called things as she saw them. She was a lot like Meemaw in that respect. "I heard someone say that your dad might have been having an affair," I finally said.

Jessie Pearl nodded, her eyes narrowing, but I got the feeling I'd at least earned a new measure of respect in her eyes for being straightforward.

But Megan drew in a sharp breath. "No, he's not—"

"Let's listen to what she heard," Jessie Pearl said, shushing Megan with her hand. "The sheriff is on his way, remember? It'll all come out in the wash, anyway."

Megan closed her mouth, swallowing whatever she'd been about to say. "How did you find out?" she asked after a beat.

I didn't want to say that Pastor Kyle had told Jeremy who'd told me, so instead of giving her a straight answer, I asked my own question. "I heard she hired someone to follow your dad. Did you know that?"

I didn't know if my theory was true, but if she'd hired someone to follow Jeremy Lisle, why not do the same to learn the truth about her husband—assuming she'd suspected? I'd planted the seed. Now I just needed to see if it would take root.

Todd shook his head and started to say no, but once

again Jessie Pearl beat everyone to the punch. "She most certainly did. Probably as short, bald, and stocky as the day is long, but I guess he'd be good at his job."

She said it as if most short, bald, stocky men weren't. "What did he find out, exactly?" I prodded.

"Not much, unfortunately, but she gave the whole kit 'n' caboodle to Todd." Jessie Pearl rolled her eyes. "Said she couldn't stand to look at it for one more second."

I didn't blame Delta for not wanting to have the file to look at. It would be akin to having a pint of Ben & Jerry's in the freezer, calling to you. How could you not succumb and take a bite? Or eat the whole thing? Or in the case of Delta, read and reread the report about her husband's infidelity? Giving it to Megan wasn't an option. What mother would burden her daughter with that kind of evidence about her father? Giving it to Jessie Pearl was out, too. More fodder for her to hate her son-in-law. No, Todd was the logical choice. He was one step removed from the family, so he was safe.

"I thought about burning it," Todd said. "Or taking anything incriminating out to protect them."

"But there wasn't much there," Megan said.

My heart raced with excitement. "So you still have it?"

I looked at each of them in turn. Megan fought back tears, her chin quivering. Todd was beaten down, as if he couldn't believe he was mixed up in such a sordid tale, and Jessie Pearl looked triumphant, as if she'd just won a bet. "Todd, go on and get it."

"It's private," he said, lacing his fingers together and staying put. "Personal family business."

"Harlow's involved, and if she can help figure out what happened to Delta, then we can't hold anything back. We all know Harlow has a gift for crime solving," she said, shooting me a quick conspiratorial look, "and if the report can help her, then who are we to hide our dirty laundry? We need to hand it over to the sheriff, too. Should've already done that, don't y'all think?"

Megan turned her back on us, leaning close to Jessie Pearl. "Do we have to?"

"Yes," I said. "Definitely. If it'll help them, they need to see it."

"But the report is inconclusive," she said between sobs. "It doesn't actually prove Daddy's seeing anyone."

"Megan, I know this is hard," I said, "but if he is, and if your mother found out, do you think he could have killed her?" I asked, cutting to the chase.

Megan let out a loud, angry sob. "No!"

Jessie Pearl sighed. "Megs, I've lived a lot of years, and one thing I've learned is that people can snap. If she pushed him too far, who knows?" She looked at Todd. "Go on. Get the report."

He hesitated, but finally got up and headed down the hall to the bedrooms.

"I told him to hide it," Megan said to me after Todd had been gone a few minutes. She'd dried her tears, but from where I sat, it looked like she'd break down again any second. "I didn't want it just lying around, you know?"

"It could be evidence," I said. "The sheriff might be able to get to the truth if he has more information."

"But it doesn't prove anything one way or another," Megan said.

"Are you sure?" I laid my hand on hers and tried to reason with her. She didn't want her father to be guilty, but I agreed with Jessie Pearl. People didn't always behave rationally. "Don't you want to know the truth, whatever it is?"

Before she could answer, the doorbell rang. Jessie Pearl nodded to Megan, who jumped up, looking relieved to escape answering my question. She scurried off to the front of the house, returning a moment later with Sheriff McClaine and his son, Gavin, the deputy sheriff, in tow. "Evenin', y'all," Hoss said, tipping his white cowboy hat. He looked at Mama, and I could have sworn he winked, but it happened so fast that I wondered if I'd imagined it.

He gave a slow nod to Jessie Pearl, in particular. "Ma'am."

Jessie Pearl dipped her chin in return. "Sheriff."

Hoss McClaine, with his salt-and-pepper soul patch and iron gray hair, was as weathered a lawman as you were likely to find in Texas. He looked like he'd just as easily wrangle a mess of wild horses as catch a posse of bad guys in Bliss. He sat down next to Jessie Pearl and got right to it, looking at the messages I'd pulled out of the figurines. "What would have possessed your daughter to hide these?" he asked her. "The likelihood of them being found by someone who might think they're important was slim."

Jessie Pearl shrugged. "And yet, they *were* found . . . right here in this house, just days after Delta's murder."

"You're right about that, ma'am. Still, not a surefire way to communicate something."

"Isn't it? Sheriff," I said, addressing him formally, since this wasn't our family gathering. "The family wrote notes to each other, and donating these figurines meant someone would be examining them. I think it's a great way for the notes to have been found."

"She's right about the note writing. Mother still does it," Megan said before catching herself. "I mean, she still did it up until . . ."

"It's okay, darlin'," Jessie Pearl said, patting Megan's hand. "What she means is that Delta never stopped. She left notes for Megs all the time."

"Do you have any of them?" the deputy asked.

She nodded. "Do you want me to get them?"

"Yes, ma'am," Gavin said. "You can bring them to me."

I hid a smile. Gavin would never abide my being involved in crime solving in Bliss. He saw it as an intrusion into his domain, and I didn't disagree. But I wouldn't say no to a friend—not if I could help. By now, he knew that about me, too.

Todd returned just as Megan went to get the notes her mother had left her. He clutched a goldenrod envelope in his hand, stopping short as he reentered the kitchen, looking unsure of where to go with the investigator's report.

"Mr. Bettincourt," Hoss said, nodding at Todd.

"Sheriff."

Hoss nodded to the envelope. "What d'ya have there?"

Todd hesitated, looking to Jessie Pearl for help. She jerked her head toward Hoss. "Hand it over, son."

I had the feeling that, just like Meemaw, whatever Jessie Pearl wanted, she got. I suddenly saw where Delta may have gotten her straightforward mentality. Jessie Pearl might look frail, but they were two strong personalities.

As Hoss took the envelope, I was able to catch a glimpse of a company logo in the upper right-hand corner. Boyd Investigations. I couldn't make out the address, but with the company's name, I'd be able to find it and dig a little deeper into what had been in Delta's mind when she'd hired them.

At least I hoped I could.

"What's this?" Hoss asked as he slid the report from the envelope and perused it. He had only one speed: slow.

Megan spoke up, anger tingeing her voice. "My mother hired this Boyd guy to follow my dad. It's all right there," she said, nodding at the file in his hand.

I angled my neck, stretching to see what Hoss was looking at. It was a typed document with random dates, times, and what I presumed were Anson's actions.

"I never would have guessed that he had it in him," Jessie Pearl said with a frown. "He was sly, I'll give him that."

Hoss pulled out a handful of photos, taking in the details in each picture. I was able to catch glimpses of a few. His Jeep at what looked to be a hotel. The same car parked in front of the church tag sale tent, and at a few other locations around Bliss, but not a single one showing a woman he might have cheated on Delta with. "No idea who he might have been cavorting with?" Hoss asked.

Megan, Todd, and Jessie Pearl all shook their heads. "Delta die—was kill—" Jessie Pearl broke off, collecting herself. "She fired the investigator just before she passed, so she never got a name," she finally said. "Guess she decided she didn't want one."

"How'd she know there was an affair in the first place?" I asked, ignoring Gavin's low, guttural growl.

They looked at each other, but none of them seemed to have the answer to that. Megan shrugged. "She didn't ever say. I was making cookies, and she just walked into the kitchen and dropped the envelope on the table. She started muttering about Auntie Coco and Auntie Sherri. She said she wasn't going to be made a fool, and then she told me that he couldn't be trusted. She said to give it to Todd."

"And that's what you did?" Gavin asked.

"My mother left, and I called Todd. I was afraid to look at what was in the envelope until he was with me."

"I was at the church doing some projects in the garden, but I came right home when Megs called. I looked at it all first, and then we sat around the table—pretty shocked, I must say."

"Speechless," Megan said, reaching toward Todd.

"She came back then, and I asked her what she was going to do about Anson," Jessie Pearl said. "She looked at me like I'd lost my mind, and then she laughed and said, *Anson? Bah. I've got bigger fish to fry*."

Jessie Pearl looked to Megan and Todd, who were both nodding. "That's exactly what she said," Megan confirmed. "*Bigger fish to fry*. Whatever that meant."

"That was the night you left her apron on the front

porch," Jessie Pearl said to me, "and the next morning, her body was found."

"Your dad still lives here?" I asked. They were a family of SUVs, and I saw him pretty regularly pulling in and out of the driveway in his Jeep, but rarely saw him out in the yard.

Megan nodded, but Todd answered. "They didn't talk much. At least not since I've been part of the family. I wouldn't say it was a very good marriage."

Megan glared at him. He threw his hands up defensively. "It's true, babe."

I pondered this. Despite whatever their marriage had become, presumably they'd loved each other once upon a time, but if Delta and Anson's marriage was on the rocks, why would she hire a private investigator to catch him in an affair? There seemed to be one of two reasons. Either she still loved him and desperately wanted to be wrong, or she wanted to use the information against him in a divorce.

I looked on as Hoss flipped through the stack of glossies. Had Delta seen something in these pictures to clue her in to the mystery woman Anson Mobley had been with?

The close-ups of the car obliterated any excess scenery. The next set showed the Jeep at a distance. In one, a hotel sign was clearly visible. Had Anson just left, was he arriving, or was he just passing by? There was no way to know. In another, just on the edge of the frame, was a flash of white. Beyond the car was a blur of trees and a dark brown barn that looked like any other barn across North Central Texas. It was nondescript and didn't give a single clue about where the picture might have been taken. The next shot showed the back of the car as it drove through the square in town, the back of Anson's head above the seat back. I peered, looking more closely, gasping suddenly. "Look," I said, pointing at the picture. "Right there through the window, do you think that could be a *red hat*?"

Hoss held it up close to examine it, then handed it off to Todd. "I don't know. It's pretty hard to tell."

Megan looked over his shoulder, her eyes narrowing to slits. "It might be, though. In fact, it kind of looks like *hers.*" She thrust the picture at Jessie Pearl. "Doesn't it?"

"You mean Delta's?" I asked.

Megan nodded. " 'Course they all sort of look the same. Red. Feathers or flowers. But, I don't know, there's something . . ."

"Maybe," Jessie Pearl said, "but why would she be in the car with him when she was having him followed to prove he was having an affair?"

That was a very good question.

I mulled over the fact that Delta had gotten this packet of information from the PI, but then had fired him, telling her family that she had bigger fish to fry. What was bigger than discovering your husband was having an affair? And why would she stop the investigation into that affair, unless . . .

"Oh my God," I said breathlessly. "She knew who it was."

Six pairs of eyes swiveled to look at me, each wide with surprise. "You think she knew whoever my dad was having an affair with?" Megan asked, her eyes bugging as she sank back down on the kitchen chair.

"It makes sense, doesn't it? She had the report from the investigator but wasn't pursuing anything more with him. Why would she do that? Wouldn't you want to know who the affair was with after going to the trouble of having him followed in the first place?"

"Maybe she just blamed Anson and not the woman," Todd said. "Right? He's the one who's married and didn't keep his pants zipped."

I couldn't argue with that, but I wasn't convinced. "How do we know she wasn't married, too?" I shook my head. "No, there's more to it. Delta may have blamed your dad for having the affair in the first place," I said to Megan, "but if she somehow recognized someone in these photos, or put something together and figured out who he was having the affair with, and *if* the woman was a friend of hers, wouldn't that be worse in her eyes? Wouldn't the woman be the bigger fish she had to fry? Women are betrayed by their husbands all the time." Mama and Megan both frowned at me, and I hurried on before they could interrupt. "I don't mean it's not horrible and that adultery isn't a betrayal, but I wonder if she would have seen the betrayal by a friend as *worse*. Especially if it was one of the Red Hat ladies. Those were her closest confidants, right? She'd known them forever, so it would have been a shock to have been betrayed by one of them with her own husband."

They all sat silently, taking in what I'd said. Mama had the pictures now. "You can't make heads or tails of the woman in these," Mama said. She scrutinized them, shaking her head and muttering under her breath. "Some detective. He didn't get a single clear shot of her."

"She may have recognized the red hat," I suggested. "They all look similar to you, Megan, but maybe not to her."

Jessie Pearl snatched the picture in question from Mama and gave it a good long gander. "You reckon? I can't hardly make out that it's red, let alone any details."

We flipped through the pictures one more time, looking for any other identifiers. Hoss started asking more questions.

"Tell me more about Delta," he said, and they were off and running.

"She loved money," Jessie Pearl said. "It always came down to money. Even as little girls, Delta, Coco, and Sherri would pool their money to buy a bag of cookies and split it between the three of them. But if she put in even two cents more than the others, Delta got a bigger piece of the split."

While they continued to talk about Delta and her love of money, I ran through the list of Red Hat ladies in my head, wondering which of them might betray Delta by cheating with her husband. Georgia Emmons seemed too proper and ladylike. I couldn't picture her mussing up her life with an affair. Randi Martin, on the other hand, was very free spirited. She might have a *seize the moment* attitude, figuring that if it was true love, why squander it?

Cynthia Homer struck me as opportunistic. If something benefited her, then I suspected she might go for it. An affair for love? I wasn't sure that would be a motivator for her, but what if Anson promised her something she wanted, or what if, pure and simple, she wanted revenge on Delta for some reason? I discounted Sherri

Wynblad and Coco Jones out of hand. They were Delta's sisters, after all, and this wasn't a Shakespeare play where family betrayal was front and center. Sure, Sherri and Coco had had their issues with Delta, but family was still family, and I couldn't imagine either one of them betraying their sister on that deep a level.

Lastly, I considered Bennie Cranford. She, like Georgia, was on the prim and proper side. A homemaker who took pride in her work. I'd been in her house, and it was night and day compared to Delta's. Bennie kept a neat, orderly home. Her taste was traditional and went with the period of her Victorian house. She had special pieces of furniture, and she herself looked like she was cut from a 1950s cloth. Very different from Delta and her abrasive in-your-face attitude. Could Anson have been drawn to her, someone so opposite from Delta? And would Bennie betray her own family, as well as her friend, for an affair with a married man?

"There she goes, a-woolgathering," Mama said. She rubbed her hand on my upper arm, shaking me out of my thoughts. "Darlin', you have a brainstorm?"

I gave a vague smile. "No, just thinking," I said. I didn't have anything worth sharing, and continuing to talk down and dirty about Megan's parents and their marital issues in front of her didn't feel right. Megan was older than Gracie by a good chunk, but Gracie was my barometer. I imagined how she'd take a conversation like this if it had been her family instead of Megan's we were discussing. Not well, I reckoned.

"Jessie Pearl was just askin' if you're still making her an apron," Mama said.

"That dinner thing's just a few days off now," Jessie Pearl said, "but if you can swing it, I'd sure love to have one for myself. I feel like I need to do my part for Delta. Be the hostess, do you know?"

Jessie Pearl needed something fresh and vibrant to boost her spirits. She needed color and style. She needed something uniquely hers. "I can definitely swing it," I said to her.

Three days until the progressive dinner, where I had every intention of figuring out just which Red Hat lady had been with Anson Mobley and betrayed Delta. And that meant I needed to get sewing. And I needed to do it right quick.

Chapter 16

In between the hours I spent that day working on my apron projects, I convinced Madelyn Brighton to come with me to the mayor's office under the pretense of taking some photographs for the city Web site. "Shouldn't that wait until after the election next fall?" his secretary had asked when I'd called to schedule an appointment.

Good question. I thought quickly, saying, "That's the point. This photo op could actually help with the election. We plan to put it on the Web site now, with a brief interview with the mayor to help him get his message out."

His secretary started singing a different tune. "He's free at one o'clock," she said.

At one o'clock sharp, we stood in Mayor Radcliffe's office, the man himself sitting behind his big mahogany desk. In appearance he was the polar opposite of his election opponent. Where Jeremy Lisle looked like an older man trying to stay young and relevant, Mayor Radcliffe looked like the leader of the good-ol'-boy network. A brown cowboy hat hung from a coat rack in the corner, alongside a rust-colored shearling-lined boar suede jacket. He wore cowboy boots under his brown slacks and a white button-down shirt. He could easily transition from the mayor's office to Buckeye's, a local bar where a lot of businessmen held court, to the Masons meeting at the Grange.

"I'd like to shoot outside," Madelyn said, taking charge. Even if the photo shoot was a ruse, she took her job seriously. "The light's not great, but I believe it'll be better than inside shots."

"Sure thing," he said. "You ladies are in charge."

She set to work, getting him up from his chair, having him don his jacket and hat. As we left his office, he stopped at his secretary's desk. "I missed a call from Lou."

She nodded, glancing at a pink message slip. "He said the resume didn't check out."

Madelyn and I waited at the door while the mayor finished his conversation. As he walked out, he donned his cowboy hat and muttered, "Interesting," under his breath.

"Everything okay?" I asked him.

He snapped out of the daze he'd slipped into for a second, blinking hard then nodding his head. " 'Course. Just the intrigues of a small town," he said.

We went outside to the front of the old church that now served as the city offices. Madelyn got him settled against a tree and started fiddling with her camera settings, changing the aperture and the shutter speed.

"Morning light is definitely better for taking pictures outside," she grumbled to me.

"In a perfect world, sure, but this is what we have. This light has to be good enough. Work with me, Madelyn," I pleaded.

She winked. "For the sake of investigation, absolutely, but whenever you and that darling man of yours decided to take some pictures together for, oh, I don't know, an engagement announcement, for example, it'll have to be in the early morning. Got it?"

I couldn't help but roll my eyes. So Madelyn had joined the cause. Mama, Nana, Meemaw, my good friends Orphie and Josie, and now Madelyn were all determined to get Will and me hitched, and right quick. "If that happens, it'll be in its own time," I said, "but I'll pencil early morning in."

"You mean *when* it happens."

"You gals about ready to get this horse saddled up?" the mayor called.

Madelyn waved. "Yes, sir!" She snapped a series of pictures, checking them on her screen before moving on to the next pose.

"Sir," I said, trying to get his attention. He was comfortable in front of the camera, that much was clear. He could have been a model in some past life if he weren't quite so soft around the middle. He had the moves down pat. "Sir?"

"Questions, right? Shoot."

"Again, thank you for taking the time to meet with us. I'll be quick. I know you're a busy man. Sir, people are wondering where you stand on the Historic Council's issues in town. Preservation or moving to the future instead of focusing on the past?"

The easy expression on his face tensed. "I am not opposed to honoring the past, Ms. Cassidy. Like you, I have a storied family. My great-grandpappy was a barber here in Bliss. Ran the first integrated shop in town back in a time when there was still plenty of segregation. Then there was my mother's granddad. He worked the oil fields up in the Panhandle. Used ranch and barbershop equipment as collateral for loans. Couldn't do that nowadays, could you?"

"I reckon not."

Madelyn continued snapping pictures as the mayor went off on his rabbit trail about his family's origins in town. "My great-grandpappy, he had his share of notoriety. Caused a good ruckus when he opened up his barbershop to everyone in town. I don't want to forget about any of that, but does that mean I want to relive it all the time and never move forward? All those houses in the Historic District, should the folks who own them really not be allowed to change things about them if they see fit?"

I waited for him to continue, but he moved to a new pose without saying anything further, all the while keeping his gaze on me as if he were waiting for my response. Finally, I spoke up. "I think the Historic Council serves a good purpose, though. If they didn't provide a little oversight, we might end up with some pretty horrible monstrosities on Mockingbird Lane and all the streets surrounding the square."

"Good God, you're one of them," he said, his voice

light and laughing, but his smile tight. "I'm not saying lift all the policies and let it become a free-for-all. Someone I know, er, knew, enlightened me about the need for regulations."

My heartbeat kicked up a notch. Could that someone be Delta? "Is that right?"

"She agreed with you. Said that the policies were in place to protect the homeowners, and that we needed the council to help monitor things. But, she also said— and this is what I wholeheartedly agree with—she also said that too much oversight could stifle the growth of a place. She said we need to be able to change with the times. Honor the past, sure, but always be movin' forward."

According to Jeremy Lisle, that's not at all what Delta believed, so it sounded like it could be a lot of double-talk. But I went with it. "That sounds just like something my neighbor would say. 'Course she recently passed." I held my breath, waiting for his response.

"You live, er, lived by Delta Mobley?"

"Is that who you were just talking about?" I asked with a big smile. I almost slapped my thigh, but Madelyn whipped her head around and frowned at me. Her message was clear. I was laying it on too thick. "I live right next door to the Mobley house. Well, I guess it's actually the Lea house, seeing as Jessie Pearl actually owns it, but regardless. Such a tragedy about Delta."

"It sure is. I'll miss her support during my campaign. She could get things done. No lollygaggin' around with her. Donated to my campaign, you know. Quite a substantial amount, between the group of 'em. Brought in her whole family to help. Her husband, her daughter and son-in-law, her mother, her sisters. Had my team running around getting their paperwork filled out and processed in no time. The whole gang, she called them. Said she had pull with each of them and that if she wanted them to help, they would. And they did."

I kept quiet, hoping he'd continue. He did. "She could read people like nobody's business. Do you know, she could spot a liar from miles away? Why do you think she signed on to help with my campaign? *Can't tolerate liars*, she said. God knows we didn't see eye to eye on everything, but I'm as honest as the day is long, and she knew it."

I wondered if Jeremy Lisle would say the same. And if the implication was that he wasn't as upstanding as the mayor.

Madelyn beckoned the mayor to another area in front of the building, this time wanting to capture some of the architectural components of the old church. Even if these shots were just a pretense to get some face time with the mayor, Madelyn was a professional . . . and a perfectionist. She'd never take subpar pictures if she could help it.

"And your opponent, Mr. . . . ."

"Lisle. Jeremy Lisle," he finished for me.

"Right. Mr. Lisle isn't quite as honest as you?"

Mayor Radcliffe did a quick scan of the area. Lucky for me, there wasn't another soul in sight. "She wouldn't ever give me any particulars, in case I wanted to use them against him. She wasn't as unethical as all that. But she was plenty clear about her intentions. *I'm gonna flush out the liars*, she said. *No matter what it takes.* Let me tell you, I believed her. I didn't want to get on her bad side."

"But she never said what he lied about?" Madelyn asked as she took him by the arm and escorted him to yet another area, positioning him about a foot away from the building's wall.

"Pretty sure it had to do with his schoolin'."

Madelyn and I both stared. "What do you mean? You think he lied about going to school?"

He adjusted his cowboy hat. "Not necessarily if, but where. Do people check where folks go to school, or is it all the honor system? Me, I'm a Red Raider, and damn proud of it. But Lisle, where's his school pride? Was he a Longhorn? An Aggie? Hell, if he didn't go to a top Texas school, more's the pity for him, but he went somewhere, right? So where's the pride?"

Madelyn turned her back on the mayor, fiddling with her camera, but she shot me a puzzled look.

All I could do was shrug. I don't know if absence of college spirit in a man of Jeremy Lisle's age meant you'd lied about your academic history. Seemed a stretch to me.

"So you don't know where he went to college?" I asked, wondering if he'd ever just bothered to make an official query to Jeremy Lisle.

"No idea. We're not exactly on friendly terms," he said. "Delta said she was finding out, but she died before she reported back to me. Not that it would've mattered, anyhow. I run clean campaigns."

By that point Madelyn had snapped a few more pictures and declared the photo shoot complete. "Got enough for the Web site?" the mayor asked.

We both nodded. Madelyn put her camera gear away in the Epiphanie bag she always carried, and I shook the mayor's hand. "More than enough," I said, thanking him and wondering if Delta would have called *me* out as a liar.

As soon as I got home, I called Boyd Investigations. It was my third attempt to reach someone there, and this time, a woman actually picked up. "Boyd Investigations."

I learned three things right off the bat:

1) Apparently Kristina Boyd was the licensed investigator, and the business was all hers—no male gumshoes anywhere to be found;

2) She was tight-lipped about her clients, even those who fell into the deceased category like Delta Mobley; and

3) She did have a heart, even if it went against her better judgment.

"Your mother never shared the report with you?" she said slowly, after I'd given a fake story about being Delta's daughter and needing a duplicate of the report she did for Delta.

"No, she died before—"

I broke off, hoping she would fill in the blanks. "If she didn't give them to you, I'm afraid I can't help you, Mrs. Bettincourt," she said. "Your mother's passing is a tragedy, but the investigation I did was for her use, not anyone else's."

She'd used Megan's married name, so she'd done her homework on the family. I went on, summoning the feelings I knew Megan was experiencing as I went fishing for information, wondering whether Boyd Investigations had been the ones trailing Jeremy Lisle, too. "It's just . . . I just want to know what my mother found out about Mr. Lisle, that's all. I'm trying to hold on to her, you know? Figure out what she was thinking all the way to her very last breath."

"Mr. Lisle . . . ?" She sounded genuinely puzzled. So maybe she hadn't been following Lisle.

"And my daddy. I know you were investigatin' him, but she *had* to be wrong. He couldn't have been having an affair. It has to be a mistake. I don't want to lose him, too, and I don't know how I can forgive him if he was. But he wasn't," I added. "He couldn't have been!"

There was a heavy pause on the other end of the line, as if she was thinking hard about how to answer. "I'm awfully sorry for your loss, Mrs. Bettincourt," she finally said, "but even though your mother passed, our dealings were and are confidential."

My frustration was real, coming out in a heavy sigh just like I knew Megan's would have if she'd actually been making the call. "Please," I said. "Just tell me about my father."

"There's nothing to tell about either of those men," she finally said. "I will say that I found no evidence that your father was having an affair."

I drew in a sharp breath, startled that she'd given me anything, and even more startled that she'd just completely discounted the idea that Anson was an adulterer.

So much for the Red Hat lady in the car with him. "Thank you!" I gushed, truly thrilled that I could alleviate some of Megan's current pain. "Oh, Ms. Boyd, thank you so much. And Mr. Lisle?"

"I'm sorry," she said, "I don't know a Mr. Lisle."

"Jeremy Lisle? I was sure De—my mother asked you to look into his background."

If she heard my slip, she didn't let on, but her tone became more short and to the point. "I'm not familiar with that name. Now, if there's nothing else . . . ?"

Huh. So maybe Delta had only had Anson investigated after all, and Jeremy had imagined a car following him. "Was there anyone else she had you looking into for her?" I asked, hoping I wasn't pushing too far. If it wasn't Jeremy Lisle, maybe the mayor had misunderstood and he wasn't a liar. Maybe, I thought, it was Pastor Kyle who wasn't who he said he was. Or maybe it was one of her oldest friends, one of the Red Hat ladies. For all I knew, Delta was paranoid and had ignored Kristina Boyd's findings that Anson wasn't seeing anyone. After all, she'd come home with the report and had told Megan that he couldn't be trusted.

"Mrs. Bettincourt, I'm afraid I can't help you anymore than I already have. I'm sorry for your loss, truly."

I thanked her and hung up, but deep down, I felt pretty certain that she actually had helped me quite a bit. I just hadn't figured out how quite yet.

Chapter 17

The next two days were a blur of sewing and contemplation. I had told Megan, Todd, and Jessie Pearl what Kristina Boyd had told me. "Then why would she have told us that he was cheating?" Jessie Pearl asked, voicing the same question I had.

The possible answers were that Kristina Boyd was a horrible investigator and Delta had figured that out, or that she was so angry she just couldn't turn off her suspicions. I'd seen it happen. People had been known to convince themselves that lies were the truth, despite the evidence.

Now it was the day before the progressive dinner. Taking stock of what I'd created and what still needed to be done, I laid the completed aprons out on the sofa and loveseat next to a curled up Earl Grey, who was fast asleep. I still had Jessie Pearl's apron to make, plus Cynthia's. Of anyone wrapped up in the sordid mess of Delta's death, her mother was the most distraught and needed peace. A tea towel apron made from one I'd found in the stack of runners she'd given me would be the perfect distraction. We were all still reeling from the murder, trying to figure out who else might have wanted Delta dead.

I'd already given Georgia Emmons her apron. Bennie's was complete and had been delivered. I'd just finished Sherri Wynblad's. It was the most traditional of the group. I didn't know Sherri well, but she'd always struck me as a straight arrow. She loved her family, but she also didn't put up with anything. She, Coco, and Delta were the same in that respect, they just manifested it differently. Sherri and Coco had restraint, honor, and a sense of boundaries that Delta hadn't had, but they were cut from the same cloth. Direct and single-minded.

Coco had asked me to help figure out what had happened to Delta, and she wouldn't rest until we had answers. She'd called every day since I'd seen her last to check my progress. I'd filled her in on the private investigator, the affair that wasn't, and my uncertainty at where to go next in the investigation.

She jumped to a different conclusion than I had. "She sacked the PI because she's wrong. Oh, he was having an affair. He had to have been."

"I've been thinking about that," I said. "What if it was Delta in the car with Anson? The investigator captured them together. That would explain why Delta stopped having Anson followed."

"But what's the bigger fish she had to fry?" Coco asked. I'd told her everything, even about the notes in the Lladrós and the one from Sherri that had been hidden in the teapot.

"Good question."

"There wasn't any love lost between Delta and Jeremy. Maybe she was after him. He thought she was having him followed. Was she?"

"The investigator wouldn't give me anything on Jeremy."

"But that means nothing!" Coco exclaimed so loudly, I had to yank the phone away from my ear. "She told you about confidentiality, right? So she couldn't very well say anything specific about Jeremy. That would be defamation if it got back to him. I'm surprised she gave you as much as she did, frankly."

I'd thought the same thing. "He's ambitious. And if she was trying to thwart his run for mayor, that might have been enough for him."

"So basically, we still don't know," she said. "You're not giving up, are you?"

"The sheriff is investigating, Coco. They have better resources than I do—"

"What do they have so far?" I imagined her shaking her head in frustration on the other end of the line. "Don't stop now, Harlow. We've got to get to the bottom of this."

I didn't know what more I could do, but Delta hadn't deserved to die, so I promised I'd keep my ear to the ground.

Coco had agreed to pick up the aprons I'd made and deliver them to their owners, so I could finish Jessie

Pearl's. "It's good of you to make one for Mother," she said when I told her my plan.

"An apron isn't going to make her forget anything, but taking Delta's place at the dinner might help her get some peace."

"Go on then," Coco said. "I'll be by in a while to collect the aprons."

We'd hung up, and I went back to the workroom. I put Sherri's apron aside and took another look at Randi's. I had to admit that it was my favorite of the bunch. It was reminiscent of Donna Downey and her mixed-media art, the inspiring words strategically placed on the skirt panel completing the artsy look of the apron. Part of me desperately wanted to keep it for myself, but I'd made it for Randi. I'd create another in the same style for myself when I had a lull in business. Which at the rate Buttons & Bows was growing would be never. I already had Bliss's version of the upcoming Fashion's Night Out on my calendar, and that would take a good two months to orchestrate and sew for. My own apron would have to wait.

But all this was good. I could live without my own special apron, just as long as I could keep creating and doing what I loved.

I went back to the collection I'd finished. Figuring out what to make for Coco had been tough, but it had come to me after we'd paid a visit to Pastor Kyle. She was all about family. She was loyal and would always be there for Megan and Todd, would do whatever it took to make things right for Jessie Pearl, and she and Sherri would bend over backward for each other. I picked up her apron, knowing that her deepest wish was that Delta's murderer would be brought to justice. So many people around me were suffering. I wanted to sew a design for each one of them, help them all, and ease their pain.

I would have to go about it one garment at a time.

For Coco's apron, I'd ended up taking the overalls I'd bought at the tag sale, deconstructing them to create an apron using the bodice of the overalls and about twelve inches of the denim from the waist down. I'd cut the legs off the overalls, changing the neck strap to a teal patterned fabric I'd bought at the fabric store, no idea at the time what I'd do with it. Now it was obvious. Teal and denim went together like cornmeal and okra. I used the same teal cotton to create a contrasting waistband to thread through the already existing denim belt loops.

The final touch was the vintage doily I sewed to the large front pocket on the bodice, giving it a strong feminine touch. I added a little crocheted flower to the center. It was subtle, but the teal tied it all together.

I wanted to keep this one for myself, too, and I knew without a doubt that I had to make something similar for Nana to wear while she worked making her goat cheese.

At the rate I was going, if I managed to make versions of all the aprons I loved, I'd have myself an abundant collection before I was through.

I laid Coco's next to the others on the couch and moved on to examine Megan's. I loved it as much as Randi's and Coco's. This one was a homespun antique white cotton. It had a muslin-like finish, but was sturdier than the typical limp variety found at the chain fabric stores. It was similar in style to the cocktail apron I'd made for Bennie, but the fabric and extra gathering in the ruffles made this one more youthful and flirty than the vintage, yet colorful, version I'd done for the older woman.

If I closed my eyes, I could see Megan in her half apron, walking through a field of grass, her husband by her side, a basket full of wildflowers over one arm. The appliqué of a muted, handmade fabric flower on the left side just above the top ruffle added to the flirtatious look of the piece. I hoped Megan would love it, and just like with the other women, I believed it would help her greatest wish come true.

The aprons looked impressive lying there side by side. Each was unique and truly spoke about the person it belonged to. Suddenly the bottom hems fluttered as if a door had opened and a breeze had blown in. But it wasn't a waft of fresh air blowing in from outside. It was Meemaw. The window behind me in the workroom suddenly opened. Loose fabric pieces lifted from the cutting table and fluttered around the room. "Meemaw!" I hurried to the workroom, catching the pattern pieces before reaching up to close the window.

Through the window, I could see my grandmother's goats milling around. Staying out of trouble for a change. But it wasn't the goats that had caught my eye, it was the fence creating a barrier between Nana and Granddad's place and mine. The dark wood panels were rustic and worn. I envisioned the aprons I'd made hanging from the top, a row of color and whimsy in the Texas yard.

Had Meemaw known what I'd see and think when I looked out the window? She was a spitfire of a ghost, and intuitive to boot. I scooped up the aprons, wishing I had the full apron I'd done for Georgia. But I didn't, and I couldn't cry over spilled milk. I took my camera and headed out the back door to arrange my creations and snap some pictures for my developing Web site and lookbook. Granted, aprons weren't something a fashion designer would normally put in her design collection, but I was no ordinary fashion designer, and this was not New York.

It took about fifteen minutes and some rearranging before I had the aprons in the order I wanted, with the colors complementing one another and the balance between half and full designs working together as a whole collection. The waist ties hung down on either side of each apron, moving gently with the breeze.

It took another few minutes to adjust the settings on my camera to work with the fading light outside, and then, with my eye at the viewfinder, I framed the picture and shot. It took ten tries before the breeze, the light, and Thelma Louise, the granddam of Nana's goat herd, who'd decided to poke her head through a gap in the fence, cooperated. I ended up with the perfect picture of the aprons hanging from the fence, and in fact, the one with Thelma Louise was my favorite. She was a rascal of a goat, but she had personality and spunk, and I had to admit that I liked her.

"Harlow!"

The Dutch door from my kitchen banged closed as I turned to see Coco waving at me from my back porch. She held on to the railing as she came down the stairs and walked across the yard. "I saw you from the window," she said, as she got closer. "Look at those! They're beautiful." Her eye caught the camera I held, and she smiled. "Are our aprons going to go on your Web site? Will they be up on that corkboard you have in the shop?"

The bulletin board hung on the eastern wall in Buttons & Bows, behind the rack of ready-to-wear clothing. It held my latest designs, sketches, printed pages from my lookbook, and swatches of fabrics. It was my design board and was something I continually updated. "It just might," I said.

But she'd already zeroed in on one apron and headed straight toward it. "This is it, isn't it? I hope this one is for me!" She fingered the ruffle on the bottom of the denim and teal creation.

I smiled jubilantly, nodding. "How'd you know?"

She looked down the fence line, her brow furrowing as she considered the question. "I'm not rightly sure," she said finally. "I just knew. The others are lovely, but this one . . . this one *speaks* to me. Does that even make a lick of sense?"

"It does," I said. "It spoke to me before I made it, and I knew, *one hundred percent knew*, that it was right for you."

"You've got a God-given talent, Harlow, you know that? I'm sure I'm not the only person to ask you this, but why in heaven's name did you come back to Bliss? Surely you could have made it in Manhattan. Seems to me you have a unique style. 'Course, what do I know?"

"The New York City fashion world isn't for the faint-hearted," I said, nodding. "But no, that's not really it. I missed Mama and Nana and Meemaw when I was away.

It was good for a while, but I kept feeling like I'd made the wrong choice. I was meant to be here." I shrugged. "I don't know. It's hard to explain. All I know is that when I came back, I just couldn't leave again. Meemaw was right to bring me back home."

"I think I understand," she said. "Bliss is a special place. I was born and raised here. And I'm not leavin' Bliss till I'm horizontal." She gave a bitter laugh. "Guess me and Delta have that in common."

"I'm starting to feel the same way," I said. There was something about Bliss that drew you in and didn't want to let you go. It wasn't the frenzied energy of a big city, but a cocoon of comforting warmth. It was a place to settle down in, a place to raise kids, and a place to call home.

"Very clever of you to have found those notes," she said as she helped me gather the aprons. She gave a nostalgic laugh. "I didn't realize Delta and Sherri still wrote them." She shook her head, the soft light of the fading sun heightening her melancholy expression. I could almost see her mind going back in time as she imagined herself as a girl, writing notes and playing games with her sisters.

I'd called Sherri three times, wanting to find out more about whatever she'd been talking about in the message she'd left in the teapot, but so far, she hadn't called me back. I'd follow up on it later, but for now, I went back to the aprons.

"All I have left before the progressive dinner is finishing Cynthia's apron and making your mother's," I told her. "Then I'll be done."

"They're incredible," Coco said, but by this point, I could see she was done thinking about aprons and was back to pondering Delta's murder. "I've been wondering about something," she began.

"Wondering what?"

"I heard about the private investigator's report. Do you know Sherri and I hadn't seen that? Mother filled us in on every last detail. Because the sheriff has it now, of course," she added.

"I'm sure he'll return it as soon as he can."

She waved that idea away. "I don't need it. Mother told me about the picture of the car and that you thought there was a woman wearing a red hat."

"But if the investigator said Anson wasn't having an affair, then it doesn't matter anyway."

"Maybe not, but it still needs explaining."

She had a point. "What if that was Delta in the car with him? What if they were trying to rediscover their love?" Stranger things had happened. Why not Anson and Delta falling for each other again? That could explain why she suddenly knew there was no affair, and why she dropped the investigation. She was the person Anson was seeing, and it had been captured in one of the photographs.

But that didn't explain Delta's comments in the kitchen about not being able to trust her husband, and about having a bigger fish to fry.

Coco threw up her hands. "It's possible. I've always liked Anson, and let me tell you, I have a no-good ex-husband. It was a low time in my life, to be sure, but would I trade it? Heavens, no. If I did, I wouldn't have my children, and I wouldn't be as strong as I am. Because I *am* strong. I *had* to survive—for my kids, even when I just wanted to give up. It was three of them against one of me, and let me tell you, there were plenty of times I wanted to raise a white flag and just say, *I quit. You win.*

"But of course I didn't do that. I *couldn't* do that because I was all they had, and they were all I had. They are the best things that ever happened to me, and I wouldn't change all the horrible times for anything if it meant I'd have to give them up. Now I have the best husband in the world, I have them, and let me tell you, I know Delta would be saying the very same thing about Anson and her and Megan. She would have done it all again if it meant she'd have her daughter. So they may have had problems. What marriage doesn't? But I can't see her giving up on it."

Coco's story brought my own father to mind. Mama had been crushed after my daddy, Tristan Walker, left her. He found out about our magical charms and had turned tail and run, never looking back. But Mama couldn't give in to her sorrow. She couldn't lie down and give up. She had Red and me to worry about. And as hard as those days had been on her, I knew she wouldn't change it for the world. She'd raised us well, and now she had Hoss. Things were as they were meant to be.

"Have you talked to Anson?" I asked.

"Not since the memorial, and not much during it, in fact. He's a man of few words, anyway. Now, with his grief, he's mostly silent."

A car drove by outside. I glanced through the front

window in time to see a Jeep Wrangler roll past, stopping in front of Jessie Pearl's house. "Speak of the devil," I said, cracking the front door open wide enough to take a closer look. "I'm going to go talk to him," I said, suddenly making up my mind. I knew Hoss and Gavin had to have already spoken to him, but maybe I could get something from him.

"I'll stay here," Coco said. She sat down on the loveseat, one elbow resting on the armrest, and planted her feet on the ground.

"Are you sure?" I asked, but I was glad. Coco was a presence to be reckoned with, and at the moment, I thought I'd do better talking to Anson Mobley on my own.

She waved me on. "One hundred percent."

I looked around, quickly coming up with an excuse to go next door. The mail was stacked in the center of the dining room table. Under the bills were three or four catalogs. One, I knew, was home and garden décor. I snatched the catalog, thumbing through it. In a series of pictures at the end of the publication, a yard done up with twinkle lights and lanterns was showcased. It was an awful lot like what Todd had described for the dinner party. This would do as a pretense for stopping by.

"I'll be back," I said to Coco as I hurried out the front door, down the porch steps, and out to the sidewalk. I was just in time. Anson Mobley came out the front door, a suitcase in one hand, a duffle bag in the other, and a deep frown on his face.

I slowed my pace, stalling until he got to the curb, and

then as he approached his Jeep, I sped up and plowed right into him. "Oh!"

"Watch it!" he barked, but he dropped his bags and grabbed my shoulders, keeping me upright.

"I'm s-so sorry," I said. "I was just stopping by to show this catalog to Todd and I didn't see you there. Mr. Mobley, right? I'm Harlow Cassidy." I pointed to my house. "I live next door."

His scowl faded, but he remained silent.

"Todd's been working in the yard, getting it ready for the progressive dinner tomorrow night, and I thought he might like to see this," I continued, holding up the catalog. "There are some good ideas in here."

He glanced back at the yard. "Should have tried harder when Delta was here. He blows with the wind, passionate about one thing today, and something else tomorrow. But, yeah, he's doing a good job now."

Maybe everyone should have tried a little harder when Delta was here, I thought, but I kept it to myself.

"I'm awfully sorry for your loss, Mr. Mobley."

He made a gruff sound and swallowed, his Adam's apple sliding up and down in his throat. Anson wasn't Hollywood gorgeous, but he was attractive. He was on the short side, probably about five foot eight. With the low heels of my boots, we were at eye level with each other. He had a wide mouth, which threw off the equilibrium of his face, and with his persistent frown, he looked ready to bite off someone's head. The breeze rustled his dark hair, a healthy spattering of gray at the temples making him look older than he might have otherwise. He had to be in his mid-fifties, but the weariness around his eyes added ten years.

I nodded to the suitcase and duffle bag. "Are you going out of town?"

His whole face tensed. "No. I just need space. Time alone. My wife, she wasn't always easy to live with, but God almighty, I . . . I . . . I loved her."

Emotion laced his words, and I felt his anger, loss, and frustration as if they were heavy clouds pressing down on us. I wasn't sure what to make of his emotions. My guess was that Delta and Anson, like most couples, had a complicated relationship. At one time she thought he was cheating on her, after all. I imagined saying Delta wasn't easy to live with was akin to saying Texas has a couple of snakes. The truth is, I suspected that, at times, Delta had been at least a Category Four hurricane, and Texas has sixty-eight species of snakes, fifteen of them venomous.

I didn't know how to respond, so I didn't. True to human nature, he filled in the empty space. "Do you know that my wife hired a private investigator to follow me? She thought she'd uncovered some deep, dark secret. An affair." He raked one hand through his hair, making it stand on end. "Horseshit."

Denial, straight from his mouth. "So you didn't have an affair? You're *not* having one?" I asked.

He leveled his fiery gaze at me. "An affair? No way, nohow."

A second passed and he seemed to come back to his right mind, blinking heavily. His neck and ears turned red, and he backed away. "I need to apologize, Ms. Cassidy. I don't know what came over me, telling you all that. Please forgive me."

He loaded up his bags and sped off, leaving me staring after him.

I'd forgive him, all right. In fact, I thought I could discount him as a suspect in Delta's murder, which filled me with relief. But eliminating Anson didn't point me in the direction of anyone else. Delta's killer was out there, and as of now, I was still completely in the dark.

Chapter 18

I'd spent the night contemplating every possible motive for Delta's murder. Anson wasn't having an affair, which meant none of the Red Hat ladies were mistresses. That eliminated their possible motives. Jeremy Lisle still seemed like the strongest suspect. There had been no love lost between him and Delta, and whether it was true or not, he thought she'd been trying to undermine his run for mayor.

I hadn't rustled up any viable motives for Pastor Kyle or Mayor Radcliffe, but that didn't mean they didn't exist. A new idea niggled in the back of my mind. Could it have been Sherri who killed Delta? I ticked off the possible reasons on my fingers.

1) Coco and Delta had been thick as thieves as kids, leaving Sherri on the outs. She could have harbored a lot of old bitterness that had finally erupted;

2) Whatever discovery Sherri had made, causing her to leave that message in the teapot, could have caused a huge rift. Again, Sherri may have sought revenge or restitution;

3) Sherri's grief, given her distant relationship with her sister, seemed almost over the top. Guilty conscience?

I hadn't been able to discern any other motives for the Red Hat ladies. They all seemed fond of Delta, and their friendships spanned decades. The rest of Delta's family was hell-bent on finding out the truth, led by Coco, so I saw no motive there.

I sighed, defeated. I'd finished the last two aprons, the progressive dinner was set to begin, and I was no closer to the truth.

"Don't take it personally, Cassidy," Will said. Coco had told me I could bring a guest, and I'd roped Will into it. He'd given in pretty willingly, though. *Free food and an evening with you? Wouldn't miss it,* he had said.

He looked dapper in his dark jeans, cowboy boots, and white button-down shirt. He'd left his cowboy hat at home so that his dark hair and swarthy skin shimmering in the moonlight. "The sheriff'll find whoever killed Delta. You did everything you could. It's better this way, anyway. You can get back to your dressmaking."

I *had* done everything I could, but I still felt as if I'd failed. There had been so few clues to follow that I felt as if I'd flitted around without purpose or direction. I'd let Coco down. Sometimes, I realized, my best just wasn't good enough.

The first stop on the progressive dinner route was Georgia Emmons's house. "The way it works," Coco had told me the day before, "is that whoever's hosting a stop sets up their house for the course they're serving. You have to be organized so you can leave your house and go along to the other stops on the dinner."

"And if you're not organized?"

"That would defeat the whole purpose of the night. We're not showboating. Most of us, anyway," she said with a slight roll of her eyes. "It's just about spending time together with our friends and family."

"Oh, so other people outside the group are invited?" This was my first progressive dinner, and it was a brand-new experience.

"A few. Cynthia always likes to shake things up, no matter what the occasion."

"So who else is coming besides the Red Hat ladies?"

"Jeremy Lisle and the pastor."

Interesting. For a brief while, I'd forgotten that the pastor had been the one to tell Jeremy that Delta suspected Anson of having an affair. Had he known that Delta and Jeremy weren't on friendly terms? If he'd killed Delta over their differences, he may have hoped to pin it all on Anson.

"Cynthia likes to stir the pot," Coco said, interrupting my thoughts.

"There are always people who do." It made sense to me. Why else would Cynthia have invited someone Delta didn't get along with to a Red Hat event?

Just before Will had arrived to pick me up, I'd grabbed the three small brown gift bags, each tied with a strand of burgundy checkered ribbon, that contained Jessie Pearl's, Megan's, and Cynthia's aprons. Coco had delivered the rest of them. These were the last of them. For the dinner, I'd brushed my hair back, trying a new, straight style. I'd switched to my iridescent blue-framed glasses to better complement the pale periwinkle wrap dress I'd chosen for the evening. I'd made it more than a year ago, but it was a timeless piece that I could dress up or down, wear with sandals, heels, or boots, add a gold necklace or a leather strap, put my hair up or down. The possibilities were endless.

The poet sleeves were flirty and made me feel like I should be running through a field of wildflowers, and the long skirt, ending mid-calf, was feminine. I adored it, but kept it for special events. Will had never seen me in it, and my heart beat a little faster than normal in anticipation of his reaction.

I'd considered going for comfort by wearing my burnt-red harness boots, but instead, I went with the already feminine vibe I was feeling and put on strappy heels. They'd bring me closer to Will's height, and while I was still hoping I might be able to solve a murder tonight, I also planned to take full advantage of my night out with the man I loved. Come hell or high water, I'd make sure we got some time alone.

I hurried next door, turning onto the brick walkway leading up to the front door. Todd had lined the path with paper lanterns, and it looked just as magical as he'd described it. He hadn't lit them yet, but I could imagine candles flickering as the sun set in the west. Twinkle lights sparkled in the branches of the trees. They'd hung a dried hydrangea wreath on the front door. It looked warm and welcoming and not at all like a house with the pall of death still hovering over it.

I knocked on the front door, gift bags in hand. Megan answered it, her face drawn and pale. Instead of inviting me in, she stepped onto the porch, closing the door behind her. "God, you look gorgeous," she said, giving me a once-over. "Is that one of your designs?"

I smiled, resisting the urge to spin around like a princess. "It is. Megan, you have to come over to Buttons and Bows sometime."

"I can't afford custom designs, Harlow."

"You'd be surprised," I said, "but I have quite a few ready-to-wear designs. I know there are some things you'd love."

Her chin quivered. "But my mom . . ."

She trailed off, the sentence unfinished, but I could guess what she was thinking. Her mother was dead, so how could she think about fashion and pretty dresses and dinner parties?

I took her hand. "Megan, your mother would want you to be happy."

A harsh laugh escaped her lips. "She didn't always want me to be happy when she was alive, but she does from the afterlife?"

The moment the words left her lips, she broke down sobbing, big tears spilling over her cheeks. "I didn't mean that!" She turned away from me, leaning her forehead against the doorframe. "Oh God, what kind of daughter am I?"

I put my hand on her shoulder, hoping my touch could offer her a small amount of comfort in her grief. "You lost your mother," I said. "Your dad's moved out. You've got all kinds of emotions to deal with. You don't have to hold it all in, Megan."

"I know you said he didn't have an affair, but what if she was right?" She looked over her shoulder, as if someone might jump out at her and whisk her away from voicing her thoughts. "What if he's not a good man?" she asked, her voice scarcely more than a whisper.

"Whatever happened between your parents has nothing to do with how much your dad loves you," I said. "He loved your mother."

She nodded, and I could almost see her mind at work as she tried to convince herself that her mother had been wrong about her father. She swept her fingers under her eyes, whisking away her tears. "Are those the aprons?" she asked, her gaze flashing to the bags I held.

"Yes." I handed her one of them. "This one's yours."

She untied the ribbon, pulling the apron out. I took the bag from her so she could get a proper look. "Wow!" She beamed at the off-white garment, fingering the prairie ruffles and the handmade fabric flower, her whole face lighting up. "I love it, Harlow. It's exactly what I would have picked if I'd seen it in a store."

She tied it around her waist. It was a good contrast against the small flowers of her nondescript dress. I gave her arm a squeeze as I said, "You ready for tonight?"

"As much as I can be."

I handed her the bag for Jessie Pearl. "So I'll see you at Georgia's?"

She drew in a deep breath, slowly letting it out through her nose, and nodded. "We're leaving in a few minutes."

I left her with a good-bye and made my way back to my property.

The air was cool, and wearing my heels and dress, a chill wound through me. I had just made it to the front arbor separating my yard from the sidewalk when Will pulled up in his shiny white truck. I waited as he rolled to a stop right in front of the house. His eyes roved over me as he got out and moseyed around the front of the truck. "Cassidy, you are a sight to behold."

I felt the heat of a blush on my cheeks, but another chill brushed over my skin. "What, in this old thing?" I said, a flirtatious note in my voice.

"Yep, in that old thing. Which, by the way, has got to be just about the prettiest dress I've ever seen you in."

"Thank you, Mr. Flores," I said, smiling up at him.

He wrapped his arms around me, pulling me close. "Is it one of your designs?" he asked, his lips brushing mine.

I draped my arms around his neck, sinking into him. "Mmm-hmm."

"And you made it for yourself?" he asked, his voice rumbling against my mouth.

"Mmm-hmm."

"So a deep wish of yours will come true?"

My lips curved into a smile against his. "All my wishes have already come true. I have you and Gracie, Buttons and Bows is doing well, and I'm back in Bliss with my family. I don't think there's another thing I could ask for."

He smiled, too. "No?"

I shook my head. "No."

"Not even some good food tonight?"

I laughed. "I don't need my charm to ensure that'll happen. There'll be plenty of good food tonight—that's a given."

"Then what? You must have a wish."

I thought about it. "To figure out who killed Delta, and why," I said.

He nodded, one side of his mouth lifting in a mischievous grin. Which was his usual state. He always looked like he was up to something. "Then let's get going," he said, "because tonight's the night. Your wish is going to come true."

Chapter 19

Georgia Emmons and her husband lived in a modest brick and stone house in the Ranch Hills neighborhood in Bliss. The yard was trimmed and tidy, two rows of manicured hedges lining the walkway to the front door. Inside was just as neat. "Refined" was the best way to describe Georgia's taste. The sofa and chairs were covered in high-end fabrics. The coffee table and curio cabinets were made from a rich mahogany wood, polished to a high sheen, the glass cutouts crystal clear and without a single fingerprint or streak.

I tended toward rustic and old-fashioned for my own home, but I could appreciate the look Georgia had gone for. It fit her and her coiffed image. As we walked toward the dining room, I saw the other Red Hat ladies and their husbands. It looked like Will and me, and Megan, Todd, and Jessie Pearl, who hadn't yet arrived, were the stragglers. Everyone else was here, including the invited guests, Jeremy Lisle and Pastor Kyle. The whole cast of suspects in Delta's death, at least as far as I'd been able to surmise. I suddenly felt as if I were in an Agatha Christie book. I wanted to flip to the front page and see the write-ups of each person. Would it help me understand any of them any better?

Will and I passed a curio cabinet lined with trophies, brochures, sashes, and tiaras. Beauty pageant paraphernalia, courtesy of Georgia Emmons's lifetime spent in competition. I pulled Will to a stop so I could take a gander. From the looks of it, she'd competed in pageants her entire life, beginning with a Miss Texas Child when she couldn't have been more than seven or eight, and ending with the Ms. Senior Texas America Pageant just last year where she'd been first runner-up. I never watched beauty pageants on TV, so they were far outside my radar, but I couldn't help but admire Georgia for her accomplishments.

"It was quite a competition last year," a voice said from behind us. Georgia appeared, continuing to speak. "Myra Blanton's been part of the pageant behind the scenes for twenty years. She's competed before but took quite a few years off. Came back this year and took the whole shebang."

"I'm sorry you didn't win," I said.

Where most women I'd encountered might have shrugged or frowned, Georgia's smile grew. "It happens."

Something about her smile sent off a warning signal in my brain. She was practiced at hiding her true feelings.

"So you'll compete again this year?" Will asked.

She looked up at him, her smile broadening. "Without question," she said as she held her hand out to him. "I don't believe we've met. Georgia Emmons."

"Will Flores," he said, taking her hand. "I'd say you were robbed last year. I can't imagine Myra Blanton holding a candle to you."

I stifled a grin. Will was charming, and first runner-up to Ms. Senior Texas America or not, Georgia Emmons wasn't immune. She fluttered her eyelashes, glancing away coquettishly. With her dropped-ruffle apron over a solid red knit dress, she looked radiant. She was all glamour, and right now she was in top form. "You're awfully kind to say so, Mr. Flores. I learned long ago that you have to deal with ups and downs in the pageant circuit. That being said, I will admit that it's never easy to lose. If there's something I want, I'll fight for it." She winked at Will. "Myra had better watch her back."

A chill went up my spine, and for a split second, I wondered if Delta and Georgia had ever been on opposing sides of anything.

"My word, where are my manners?" she said suddenly. "You both need a glass of wine. Or would you prefer beer?" she asked Will, cocking her head slightly. She was an expert at flirtation. I was sure I could learn from her, if flirting were on my list of things to master. Flutter the eyelashes. Cock the head. Smile slightly. Brush your fingertips over the man's sleeve. All things Georgia had done in the past couple of minutes while talking with Will and me. I was included in the conversation, but Will was the focus.

"A beer would be great," he said. His smile was sincere, but he'd put a bit of restraint into it. He wasn't encouraging Georgia, harmless as she seemed.

She turned, flagging down a tall, silver-haired man sporting a thick mustache. "Wayne, be a doll and get this young man a beer."

Wayne nodded obligingly, altering his course to the dining room and heading to the kitchen instead. "Red or white?" Georgia asked me.

"Red, please," I said. She disappeared into the dining room, returning a moment later with a wineglass just as Wayne came in from the kitchen carrying a green glass bottle of beer.

Georgia led us into the living room, calling to the rest of the Red Hat ladies, their husbands, and the guests to join us. Megan, Todd, and Jessie Pearl had arrived right behind us, and when everyone had gathered and Jessie Pearl was settled in a chair, Georgia cleared her throat, garnering everyone's attention.

"I'd like to thank you all for starting this progressive dinner with us tonight. Wayne and I welcome you to our home." She paused, in what I judged to be a practiced move from her years of public speaking. "I'd like to take a moment to remember Delta," she continued.

I'd been wondering whether anyone would talk about Delta, or if her friends would want to stifle the emotions that might come from talking about someone they'd so recently lost. I'd hoped for the former. It was as if Georgia had read my mind, bringing her up right at the beginning of the evening's events.

"This dinner was her idea," she continued. "She may not be here to enjoy it with us, but I'd like to honor her by raising our glasses in her memory."

She lifted hers. One by one, like a wave, the other Red Hat ladies, and then everyone else, raised theirs. "To Delta," Georgia said.

The two words echoed in the room as everyone repeated them. "To Delta."

Eyes sparkled with newly formed tears. A few of the women sniffled, the loss suddenly fresh again. But no one said anything. Just when it felt on the verge of becoming awkward, Coco stepped forward, coming to the front of the room to stand next to Georgia. "I think it would be a lovely gesture if each of us took a moment and remembered something about Delta, and then shared it."

The group gave a collective nod. "She was a good friend," Randi said. She was divorced and had come to the dinner alone. She stood next to Jeremy Lisle, and I couldn't help but noticing they looked like they'd make the perfect couple, him with his cool Vin Diesel/Bruce Willis vibe going on, earring in one lobe, and casual shirt undone at the top, her with her spiky silver hair, three inches of jangly bracelets, and long, flowing gauzy skirt that was a throwback to the 1970s.

"You know, Delta refused to take my yoga class," she continued. "Said she was too heavy to do all those crazy bends and positions. *Everything I have will fall right out*, she told me. I thought that was an excuse, and for a while, I was offended. But then I told her I wanted to find a renter for the apartment above the studio. Before I could blink, I had a tenant. Your friend, Rebecca," she said to Megan and Todd, but then she frowned. "'Course, she moved out a few days ago, so if anyone knows someone who needs a place to stay . . ."

Megan frowned. I remembered her saying she'd been trying to get in touch with Rebecca on her cell phone, but to no avail. Now we knew the reason, but why would she have left so suddenly?

I didn't have time to ponder it. A few people laughed, and Randi blushed, continuing. "Delta didn't always know how to show it, but when it came down to it, she was a good friend."

"Hear, hear," one of the men in the room said.

Everyone raised their glasses again and drank, and then Cynthia stepped forward. "Y'all know that Delta and me, we go way back. We were in kindergarten together. Besides her family, I think I must have known her better than anyone here."

I shot glances at Coco, Sherri, who stood in the back of the room, Jessie Pearl, Megan, and Todd. There wasn't a dry eye among them. Georgia's toast to Delta and Coco's request to honor her sister were both heartfelt and healthy, but I could see the emotion flooding the people who'd loved Delta, and my heart ached for them. Losing someone you loved was hard enough. Losing someone as complicated as Delta was probably harder because your own emotions were that much more complex.

"We had a love-hate friendship," Cynthia continued. She gave a staccato laugh. "But good God, I loved that woman. She'd give you the shirt off her back, if you needed it."

Everyone in the room nodded, confirming that Delta would do anything for them.

"She was always there for me," Cynthia continued. "Sure, she might have grumbled about it, but I knew I

could count on her for anything. Anything," she repeated. She looked at the ceiling for a few seconds, her
eyes glistening. "We needed someone to fill in for Jacob
at the church when he fell ill, oh about four months ago.
Y'all remember that?"

About half the group nodded, so Cynthia seemed to
feel the need to explain further. "He does our bookkeep-
ing. Got sick, then came down with pneumonia. Almost
didn't make it. He was in the hospital for, goodness, a
month? Maybe six weeks? Well, I mentioned to Delta
that I needed someone to help out, and she didn't hesi-
tate. She sent me Todd." She paused, nodding to Megan
and her husband. Megan smiled up at him, leaning
against his arm. "He's a jack of all trades. Came right in
and took over for Jacob until Delta . . ." Cynthia's face
grew tense. Memories of a lost loved one were tricky.
They filled you with warmth and a sense of happiness on
the one hand, yet at the same time, they brought the grief
right up to the surface.

She shook her head, just barely, and then raised her
glass. "To Delta."

Once again, everyone echoed the sentiment. "To
Delta."

"You know Iris, my Golden Lab?" Bennie asked,
moving forward to take Cynthia's place at the front of
the room.

Aside from Will and me, everyone nodded.

"She's an escape artist, right? She gets up on her hind
legs and bats the latch of the back gate and gets out.
About three weeks ago now, she got out while I was at
the market. When I got home, there was no sign of her.

No one saw her. She was just gone. I called all y'all, remember?"

This time, everyone except Will, me, Jeremy Lisle, and Pastor Kyle nodded.

"Y'all came, and I appreciate that. More than you know. But it was Delta who organized things. Called Anson to help. Megan and y'all helped, too," she said, looking at the family. "But she didn't stop there. She organized the area by grids and sent people to search in specific places. We found Iris all the way down at FM 2951." Her chin quivered. "If not for Delta, I don't know if we would have found her. We all know she was going through something these last few months. She wasn't quite herself."

A low murmur of assent went through the room, and Bennie continued. "But she was still Delta, and she'd have done anything to help any one of us." She raised her glass. "To Delta."

"To Delta," the group echoed.

One by one, each person told a similar story about Delta and their friendship with her. By the time Megan and Todd spoke, my head was spinning. The stories painted such a drastically different picture of Delta than what I'd known of her for most of her life. She was loved—of that, there was no doubt.

I thought about what Meemaw had always said. People are not always what they seem. Usually, I interpreted that to mean that the goodness people showed often masked something darker. But with Delta, it seemed to be the opposite. The grumpy, cranky, irritable Delta I'd seen masked the goodness she'd clearly had in her and had showed to everyone else. She'd helped her friends in multiple ways.

I thought back to when Delta had first asked me to make the aprons. She'd been boisterous and had come close to being rude. At the time, I'd thought her friends had been frustrated with her, and maybe they had been, but they knew that to be the cantankerous side of their friend, not the *only* side of her. They also knew she had a lot of bark, especially lately, but maybe her bite wasn't all that vicious.

The question that I kept coming back to was why had she become so curmudgeonly? Bennie had said she'd been different lately. What had happened to change her? She had a husband who appeared to love her, a healthy, happily married daughter, Jessie Pearl was as fiery as ever, and she had two sisters, who, despite their differences, knew that everything always came down to family. What more could she have wanted?

Sherri had been hanging back, her eyes glistening, her lower lip trembling. She hadn't worn her apron, I noticed. I wondered how long the Cassidy magic worked in the garments I sewed. If it wasn't worn right away, would the person's dreams be realized? I had no idea, but Sherri looked like she could use a bit of help right about now.

I grabbed Will's arm as Sherri suddenly dragged her fingers under her eyes and propelled herself to the front of the room. A crazy look had come over her. "What's she doing?" I whispered, although, of course, he had no more idea than I did.

We watched as her eyes narrowed. She looked at each

and every person in the room in turn. A chill ran through me as she met my gaze, but it passed as she moved on to the next person.

"Sherri?" Coco moved toward her sister, her arms outstretched. "Come on, darlin'."

But Sherri shrunk back from Coco, shaking her head. "I'm gonna have my say," she said. She paused, as if she were garnering strength or gumption. Or maybe both. "Someone in this room," she said, her voice icy and accusatory, "killed my sister. I know it, and you know it. You'd best be scared, because"—she paused, looking at me—"we *will* bring you to justice."

The chill that had vanished came slithering back over my skin. What in tarnation had come over her? Everyone in attendance looked shocked, but not a single one revealed themselves as a killer with a sneer.

Unfortunately.

I agreed that the killer was probably in the room. Truthfully, it could be any of them.

Before I could ponder that any further, Sherri was talking again. "The dinner must go on, but I refuse to stay in the company of a killer . . . whoever you are." And then, without another word, she turned on the heels of her flats and marched out the front door.

Chapter 20

Sherri's outburst was like a big ol' white armadillo in the room. Everyone tiptoed around it as we tried to enjoy our pre-dinner drinks. After a while, we all gave up, piling into our trucks and SUVs and caravanning the five blocks to Randi's house, the second stop on the progressive dinner route. She lived alone in a small Craftsman, and while the houses on her street varied in age and style and were well kept with manicured yards, only Randi's showed any personality. Three cement gnomes stood on the porch to greet guests. Instead of a traditional wreath on the front door, she had a galvanized steel watering can filled with fresh flowers.

She had raced ahead of the rest of us in her hybrid. Now she stood at the front door, holding it open, looking like an earth goddess in her gauzy dress and half apron. "Come on in, y'all," she said. One by one, we filed inside. The interior was an eclectic mix of bright curtains and rugs, bold furniture, mellow yellow walls, and artwork.

She had a collection of miniature Buddhas on a console table and a dark blue and green woven wall hanging that looked a bit like I imagined Aladdin's magic carpet would.

The theme for the progressive dinner was favorite family foods, and from the looks of Randi's table, her family came from five different countries. She'd been in charge of appetizers and had bruschetta from Italy, seven-layer dip from Mexico, baba ghanoush from the Mediterranean, Chinese pot stickers, and meatballs simmering in a Crock-Pot. People acted like flies at a picnic, hovering around the dining table, as if filling up their plates somehow absolved them from having to address Sherri's accusations. But once the plates were laden with appetizers, the chatter couldn't be held at bay. "Y'all were her closest friends," Jessie Pearl said to the Red Hat ladies who'd circled round. "Sherri spoke outta turn. I know none of you coulda done anything like that to Delta."

Bennie squeezed Jessie Pearl's hand. "Of course not," she said, but she glanced at each person in turn, a hint of suspicion clear in her eyes. "We've known all y'all for so long. A lifetime. So why in heaven's name would she say something like that?"

My thoughts exactly. Did she know something we didn't? And if so, that sent a wave of concern through me. If she was right and one of the people at the dinner was the culprit, and she'd just called them out, it had been a challenge. The question was, would the killer react?

Another thought struck. A note in one of the the Lladró

figurines had mentioned Rebecca, and Randi had said
Rebecca had suddenly moved out of her rental. Coincidence, or was she running from someone? What did Rebecca know?

I racked my brain, trying to make a connection between Rebecca and anyone here. Megan had said they'd
met at an antique show in Granbury and had become
fast friends. She lived above Randi's studio. Neither connection sparked an idea, but I'd keep thinking.

One thing about Sherri's challenge kept me at ease.
She hadn't made it to Randi's house yet, and if she was
right and one of the people in the room now was the
killer, that meant she wasn't in immediate danger.

But where had she gone to, and was she coming back?

The women dropped their voices, appearing to offer
comfort to Megan and Jessie Pearl. Will and I circled
around to the opposite side of the table. He filled up a
plate with samplings of every appetizer. I was more
sparse in my selections, my appetite having been re-
placed by healthy curiosity. I wanted to know what
Sherri was thinking and what she might know, but since
I couldn't pick her brain, eavesdropping on the invited
guests was the next best thing.

The men and women had naturally segregated, the
women on one side of the table and the men on the opposite side in two groups. The husbands of the Red Hat
ladies stuck together. I could tell this was not their first
Red Hat rodeo. They threw back their drinks, piled their
plates high with food a second time, and spoke in deep
baritones with the familiarity of family. Not surprising.
Their wives had known each other for too many years to

count, which meant the men had, too. Will, Jeremy Lisle, Pastor Kyle, and Todd were the outsiders. They stood off to the side, each of them cradling their plates in one hand, a drink in the other. "So if I leave, they'll think I killed Delta?" I overheard Jeremy asking, sounding as if he couldn't quite believe he was mixed up in all of this.

Todd shook his head. "Sherri didn't mean it. She's grieving."

"High drama, that's what it was," Jeremy said.

"Every family has secrets," Pastor Kyle said.

"Did Delta?" Jeremy asked. He acted nonchalant, but I sensed tension in his shoulders.

Pastor Kyle offered counsel to his congregants. Had Delta gone to him, and if so, would she have told him what had put her on edge these last few months?

"Sure," Pastor Kyle said, but he immediately closed his mouth and took a step back. He seemed to realize that he'd spoken out of turn, revealing something that should have been private.

The room had grown completely silent, all eyes on him. His face clouded, and a panicked look took over. "Look, she couldn't stand that she'd been lied to. She never said who lied, or what it was about, just that she had proof and wouldn't tolerate it." He looked at me, cocked a frenzied eyebrow, and then he threw up his hands. "That's it. That's all she said."

Jessie Pearl, with her pursed, thin lips, hobbled toward the pastor, crutches under her arms. "You sure about that, Pastor? She didn't say nothin' else?"

But instead of answering, he tossed his plate on the table and headed toward the door. "Dragging Delta's name through the mud isn't going to bring her back. It doesn't matter anymore what she thought of folks. She's gone, and nothing's going to bring her back."

"No, but it could help us figure out who killed Delta," I said.

He whirled around to face me. "The truth is, folks lie every day. They lie about what they do, about what they think, about who they are." He gestured to us all. "I see the worst of people when they come to me, but I also see the best in them. They so often focus on the bad things in their lives. Delta was no different from anyone else. She felt betrayed? Well, who doesn't? She loved you and only wanted to protect you," he said, looking straight at Megan. "She loved her family and her friends, even if she didn't always know how to show it in the best way. Remember this. No family is what it seems from the outside, and everyone has secrets. I reckon Delta knew that better than most."

Megan surged forward, draping her arm through Pastor Kyle's. Her eyes glistened with a fresh layer of tears. "Thank you, Pastor. Granny, Daddy, Todd, Auntie Coco, Auntie Sherri, and me, we're all grateful to you. Whatever my mother told you, it was between you and her."

He patted Megan's hand. "She's watching down on you. She'll always be your protector. Your own personal guardian angel."

The tears she'd been holding back let go in a waterfall. She tried to say something more to him, but her words seemed to stick in her throat.

Todd had moved next to Megan, pulling her into a comforting embrace. Gently, he drew back. "It's going to be okay, Megs." He led her out of the dining room and away from everyone, bending his head toward hers. Solidarity. It was just what I imagined Will doing for me if I were ever so distraught.

The pastor headed for the door. "I'm leaving, but—"

"We all know you didn't kill Delta," Coco said, waving away his worry at Sherri's earlier accusation.

He laughed it off, but he looked relieved to have had it spoken aloud. "I'm sorry for your loss," he said to the group as a whole, and then he shut the door behind him.

I debated what to do. I had a question to ask the pastor, but I also wanted to be a fly on the wall during the dinner party. So much could be learned by sitting quietly back and listening.

I leaned over to whisper in Will's ear, deciding that the chance to speak with the pastor was more important than eavesdropping. If the killer was standing right here in the dining room, he or she wasn't going to suddenly say something to reveal the truth.

"I'll keep my ears open," Will said, reading my mind.

I squeezed his hand in thanks. "I'll be right back."

He edged his way into the group, while I dashed quietly outside to intercept the pastor. He was walking down the sidewalk, passing truck after truck. Except for Randi, the Red Hat ladies had come with their husbands, each sitting shotgun in the 4x4s their husbands drove. Even Jeremy Lisle and Will had trucks. Only one SUV was parked on the street, and it stood out like a sore thumb.

Pastor Kyle had a crossover. It was the same red as Anson Mobley's Jeep, but a different make and model.

For a second I'd entertained the idea that the vehicle in the private investigator's pictures wasn't Anson Mobley's at all, but someone else's altogether. Without a clear view of the license plate, it was possible.

"Pastor?" I called.

He stopped, his arm outstretched. His car beeped, the locks releasing. When he turned to face me, a chill danced over my skin. His nostrils flared and his jaw was tight. But it all changed in an instant, as if a pale yellow light slipped over him to soften his features, and I wondered if the streetlights and the darkness were playing tricks on me. Still, my nerves were on edge. I slowed down, staying back so I could cut and run if I needed to.

"I wish you'd stay," I said.

"Cynthia's heart was in the right place inviting me. She'd hoped to help Delta mend some of her broken fences, and I'm a peacemaker, but this night should be for her family and friends."

"Maybe," I said. "But so many of them attend your church. You offered everyone a lot of comfort. Just your presence made a difference tonight." He didn't seem to know what to say. "Pastor, are you okay?" I asked.

He stared up at the night sky. There wasn't anything to see there. The stars were obscured by a thin layer of clouds, but he was lost in it anyway. "It's always hard to bury someone in the community, especially someone who's been a fixture for as long as Mrs. Mobley was," he said finally. "People take it hard when a loved one is taken from them of natural causes, but something like this, well, it's just all the harder to make sense of it."

"Delta and I, we were neighbors. I saw her, even from a distance, nearly every day. It's such a shock that she's gone."

"She was rough around the edges, but the thing is, she admitted it when called on it. She bent the rules in her favor, and she didn't have any qualms about it. Cynthia caught her red-handed, rifling through the employee records at the church, but do you know what she said?"

I shook my head.

"Well, of course, first she gave an excuse. She'd come prepared with it. Said she was filing Megan and Todd's resumes. That she'd found them on the desk. Of course that was a lie. We don't ask for resumes, and Cynthia is an excellent office manager. She doesn't leave things lying around."

"What do you think she was really doing?"

"I never did figure that out. She said God knew all of our secrets. Every last one of them. She said that nothing was confidential to Him, and we all worked for God, didn't we?"

He laughed, shaking his head at the memory. "As if that justified breaking the rules. How in the world do you argue with logic like that?"

How indeed? "Pastor," I said, just wanting to get to the nitty-gritty. "You know the community so well. Who do you think killed her? Who would have wanted to?"

But he just shook his head, looking up at the dark sky again. "I wish I knew, Ms. Cassidy, but I sure don't."

"And you don't know what secret she was talking about?"

"All she ever said to me was that she wouldn't lay

down like a dog and let people cheat and lie and hurt the people she loved."

"Was it about her family? Her sisters?" I said, thinking again about Sherri and wondering how close they actually were, and if an old rift had resurfaced.

But the pastor quashed that idea. "I don't know, Harlow. I think Coco and Sherri would have done anything for Delta. And hearing those stories about how she helped her friends, I think she would have done a lot for them, too. But really, do any of us know what goes on inside someone else's head?"

He considered me carefully. "Why are you so interested, Harlow?"

"Coco asked me to help," I said. "To try to figure out what happened to Delta."

"Isn't the sheriff doing that? Someone *killed* that woman. Murdered her. You should stay out of it."

"Are you friends with Gavin McClaine?" I asked, a little flippantly. They were singing the same tune.

Pastor Kyle's brows pulled together, puzzled. "The deputy sheriff? No, why?"

I waved it away. "It's nothing. He's my stepbrother and tells me to leave crime solving to the professionals." In fact, he'd told me more than a few times that I was not on the city of Bliss's payroll, so I should stick with solving sewing crises.

"Good advice," Pastor Kyle said. "We all have our expertise. From what I understand, you're quite the seamstress."

"Fashion designer," I clarified, keeping quiet about the luck I'd had solving crimes in Bliss since I'd moved back home. Maybe there was one secret still left in Bliss if he hadn't heard those stories.

"Of course, fashion designer." He smiled, but it felt placating rather than sincere, and a warning signal went off in my head again. I needed to be careful, and I suddenly realized that I wasn't one hundred percent convinced that the pastor wasn't involved.

"I should go," I said, taking a step backward.

He took a step forward, closing the gap I'd just created. "I think his point is that you're *not* in law enforcement. Best leave finding Delta's murder to the sheriff."

My heart raced, and I forced a smile. "I will. Thank you, Pastor."

He slid his hands into his pants pockets. "Will is quite fond of you, you know."

Was he trying to throw me off guard? "I'm fond of him, too." I threw up my hand in a quick wave and took a few steps in the opposite direction.

"We're going to Cynthia's house next," I said. "If you change your mind and want to come back."

"Thank you, but I won't." He got into his SUV, turning back to me before he shut his door. "Someone killed Delta, Miss Cassidy, and I reckon that whoever it is wants nothing more than to keep that under wraps. You might find yourself in danger if you're not careful."

As he drove away, another chill slithered through me. I didn't know whom to trust, was no closer to figuring out the truth, and the pastor had just put the fear of God squarely in my chest.

Chapter 21

When the evening started, Will's prediction that I could have the murder solved by the end of the night had seemed possible. But now, having a light tomato basil soup and a small spinach salad at Cynthia Homer's house, the next stop of the progressive dinner, it seemed entirely unrealistic. I needed some sudden new insight into Delta's character, or her relationships with the people around me, to lead me to the answer.

Instead I had too much information, and no real direction for my sleuthing. It was like the piles of fabric Randi had selected at the fabric store. Alone each bolt was fine, but together it was a hot mess.

"What d'ya learn?" Will asked me on the way to Cynthia's house.

I thought about how to answer him. "I feel like I learned something, only I'm not sure what," I finally said.

He gave me a sly grin. "Well, darlin', fear not. I got some good information."

My heart surged, and I grabbed his arm. "What did you find out?"

"Did you know that Delta went to college with Jeremy Lisle? Aggies, both of them," he said, a hint of competitive disdain in his voice. Will was a Longhorn through and through.

"Wait," I said, realizing what he'd just said. Radcliffe had said something about Delta questioning where Jeremy had gone to college. "Did they *know* they were both Aggies?"

Will lowered his chin, giving me a look that said, "You're kidding, right?"

Your college alma mater in Texas was a very big deal, especially the rivalry between the Longhorns from UT and the Aggies from Texas A&M.

I let this sink in. If Delta knew perfectly well that Jeremy Lisle had gone to A&M, then what had Mayor Radcliffe been talking about? Had he gotten it wrong? Was there someone else she suspected was lying about their college degree, and why did it even matter?

My head spun, my thoughts more jumbled and confused than ever. Delta was just as much a mystery to me today as she'd been before she died, and I couldn't make heads or tails of what had been on her mind before her death. I'd never even thought of her as having a soft side. But I was being proved wrong. She'd been looking out for someone. The question was still who.

Cynthia was the perfect hostess. The gathered front panel of the apron I'd made for her and the wide waistband complimented her figure beautifully. She had to admit that she loved it, even if she hadn't wanted it at first.

234 *Melissa Bourbon*

Cynthia and her husband whisked away the bowls as soon as the last spoonfuls of soup were gone, and the salad plates before the last lettuce leaves were speared. "This isn't turning out like it was supposed to," she said to the room, not speaking to anyone in particular. "I thought it might offer some comfort to talk about Delta. To still come together, but I think that was a mistake."

"We were right to hold the dinner," Randi said quietly.

But Cynthia shook her head. "Not like this. What Sherri said—"

"Sherri was wrong," Bennie said. "We're all thinking something horrible must have happened, but why does it have to be that way? Megan said it earlier. Delta was in the wrong place at the wrong time."

It was a good thought, but too simplistic. Sure, random crimes happened, but more often than not murderers killed for a specific reason. As the Red Hat ladies had already talked about, most people were killed by someone they knew. Hoss McClaine believed in that statistic, too.

"Come on, y'all. We haven't even had the main course yet. Let's go to Bennie's house and continue with the dinner."

The husbands looked at one another with expressions that said they'd each rather wrestle a passel of cottonmouths than hash out whatever had happened to Delta Mobley. But, almost like synchronized swimmers, the women made eye contact with their husbands and the men straightened up, pulled out keys, and led their wives to their respective trucks. Will and I met each other's gazes, our own smiles playing on our lips. Would we be that way one day? I tucked that thought away for another time and followed the group back outside, and just like before, we caravanned to the next house on the progressive dinner route.

As we drove, I considered the husbands. Could one of them be behind Delta's death? But just as quickly, I dismissed the idea. Not one of them seemed to have any connection with her beyond the friendships she'd had with their wives.

The trip was a quick five minutes, and, as it turned out, Bennie Cranford lived just three blocks away from me in a house nearly as old as mine. It was a restored Victorian, a painted lady done up in blue with red and pink trims. Gables and gingerbread trim gave it a dollhouse effect, and walking inside felt like stepping back in time. Every visible wall was papered in a classic Victorian pattern of some sort. The entryway was a blue geometric pattern with metallic ink running throughout. The parlor and dining room, on the other hand, were burgundy with three feet of horizontal borders running round the ceilings.

Heavy burgundy drapes hung from the windows under ornate valances, a deep gold trim along the edges making it feel just a bit like what I imagined a turn-of-the-century bordello might have been like. A heavy, ornate crystal chandelier hung above the dining table. The dining table itself was set with cream-colored china and crystal goblets and wineglasses. Gold-bordered cream cards sat at each place setting, telling us where to sit. Bennie had gone outside the down-home theme with her table décor. Her vintage ruffled apron added a little bit of whimsy, but still fit the period house, looking like it came from the same era as the wallpaper and drapery. The only difference was that the apron I'd made had a modern, contemporary touch to it that the house didn't.

"It looks beautiful," Georgia said, a slight hint of envy in her voice. "Like walking straight out of the present day and into the past."

There was a murmuring of agreement as we all found our places. Personally, I found the decorations stifling. Owning a Victorian house didn't mean every bit of it had to be historically rendered. It wasn't a setting I'd want to live in. I loved my own historical house, and I especially loved the vintage features that gave it so much character, but I liked having my own sensibility throughout, with modern touches and conveniences.

Bennie had intermixed the couples, separating the husbands and the wives, and me and Will. I ended up sandwiched between Jeremy Lisle and Jessie Pearl.

Bennie stood behind me, elaborating on the details of her house. "We had an architectural historian help us. She knows everything there is to know about the era. All the window coverings are custom, the wallpaper Bradbury and Bradbury. The floors are the original pine. I did the kitchen myself. It's redone with a custom island kit. Of course Delta never did like it," she said under her breath, "but that's not a surprise."

I turned to glance through the door, inwardly cringing at the blue Formica and traditional oak cabinets. The architectural historian couldn't have had a hand in those design elements. The style looked straight out of the

1980s, rather than 1900, and was completely at odds with the rest of the house. In a set of drawings asking which room didn't belong, there'd be no doubt that the kitchen was the sore thumb.

But everyone murmured politely. No one would burst Bennie's bubble by saying the kitchen was an eyesore. We were all too politely Southern for that. Only Delta would have been the unimpeded voice of opposition about the kitchen, but of course she wasn't here to say anything.

The question of whether Bennie could have killed Delta over some decorating slight crossed my mind, but I nixed it just as fast. Sure, murder happened for less rational reasons than that, but I couldn't see Bennie bashing a rock into Delta's head over a criticism of her kitchen.

Then again, at this point, I couldn't discount anyone. I needed a lead. Delta had rubbed too many people wrong and had made too many people angry along the way.

Bennie served the main course: pot roast with carrots and onions served on a bed of mashed Yukon gold potatoes. Next to me, Jessie Pearl moved the strands of beef around her plate, mixing it into the potatoes, but not eating. I also noticed Megan taking birdlike bites. The other women picked at their food as well, but the men . . . the men dug in and ate with gusto. Delta Mobley's demise hadn't interfered with their appetites.

Jessie Pearl's left hand curled into a loose fist next to her plate. It trembled, the thin skin and veins making her look more fragile with each passing glance. She'd been tough as nails just a week ago, but her drawn face, her

unsteady hands, and her sad eyes gave away her sorrow.
Her daughter was dead, and she was showing the signs
of the trauma. I rested my hand on hers. "Do you need
anything?" I said, my good Southern breeding front and
center. I may have grown up Texan, a breed in and of itself, but Southernness ran through my blood and always
would.

"Besides Delta back from the dead, I guess you
mean?" she said, not looking up from her plate.

My hand wavered from the bite in her tone, but I tried
not to let it show. "Yes, ma'am, besides that."

She turned, looking at me head-on. "I need to know
what happened." She lowered her voice, and it turned
hoarse. "What did she do that made someone kill her?"

Jeremy Lisle leaned my way, talking over me. "Ms.
Lea, Delta thought a great deal of you. The way I see it,
you need to focus on the good memories, ma'am. There
ain't no use in anything else. Nothing's gonna bring her
back."

Jessie Pearl raised her eyes to him. They were blazing
with fire. "There's plenty of use for the truth, Mr. Lisle."

He gawked at the force of her words but recovered
quickly. Jeremy was a politician, and I suspected the
truth was more of a vague idea to him rather than something set in stone. "There is, you're right, ma'am. That
was thoughtless of me."

"My daughter didn't support you for mayor. You'll see
the sign for Radcliffe in our yard. But did you ever wonder why, exactly? Don't you want to know why she
turned away from you and toward the mayor?"

Jeremy drew back, but again, his expression turned

sour only for a split second before it was placid again. The consummate politician, well versed at masking his true emotions. I already knew that Jeremy was bitter over Delta's decision not to support his campaign. She was well known and respected as an institution in town. Not having her endorsement could have had a negative effect on his campaign. I'd already pondered whether this was enough of a reason for Jeremy to eliminate Delta from the political equation. Suddenly Sherri was being pushed to the side and I was leaning toward yes as the answer to that question. "She didn't respect the Historic District," he said, "or believe in preserving the past. Or at least not to the degree that the Historic Council does."

"That's right. She cared more about tearing down the old and putting up new. Pretense and perception," Jessie Pearl said, taking her hand back. And then her eyes brightened, as if she'd just realized something. "I've come to know my daughter better in death than I did in life. She didn't do anything without a reason." She turned back to Jeremy. "She either wanted something from the mayor, or she wanted to thwart you for some reason."

Jeremy's face clouded, but before he could respond, we were distracted by a brouhaha from across the room. Pastor Kyle was back, and he had Sherri with him. "I shouldn't be here," she said, her voice low and desperate.

Coco was on her feet, ushering her sister to a vacant seat. "It'll all be okay, Sher. I'm glad you're here."

"It won't bring her back," Sherri said, not bothering to mask her despair.

But was it guilt rather than grief that spawned the tears? Family rivalry wasn't a strong motive in and of itself, but who knew what skeletons were in the Lea sisters' closet? But one look at her face told me that her anguish was real. Palpable. Family was family, no matter the depth of the complexities or the scars that remained from days gone by.

I shook my head. It sounded perfect for a Lifetime movie, but too melodramatic for real life, and I was muddying the waters by putting my own thoughts about family onto the Trapper/Mobley group.

Bennie stood, nodding her thanks to Pastor Kyle. I watched him closely, searching for the reason behind his reappearance. "I found her at the church," he said, answering my unasked question. "She said she wanted to find peace with all of you, so I convinced her to come back."

"Sit down and have some pot roast," Bennie said. She pulled out the chair next to her where the gold-rimmed card with Sherri's name marked her spot and ushered her into it, then brought the pastor to his seat.

Sherri hesitated, but finally plunked down, her body slack and dejected. Any suspicions that she could be the killer deflated. I knew that Sherri was distraught, but it didn't seem like it was from guilt.

Which left me nowhere.

Chapter 22

The dessert course was the final stop of the progressive dinner. One last chance to figure out what actually happened to Delta by the end of the night. I hoped it was still possible, but at this point, I wasn't convinced I could spin the mass of tangled threads into a tapestry that made any sense.

Todd and Megan left Bennie's house early to prepare the coffee and tea, and Will and I had offered to bring Jessie Pearl with us. "If it wasn't for these blasted crutches, I could walk," she said, as Will took her hand to lead her to the truck.

The air was crisp, and it was only three blocks, but in her current state, those three blocks might as well be all of Big Bend National Park. I tried to catch Will's eye, but he kept his focus squarely on Jessie Pearl. "It's a nice night," he said. "You'll be walking again soon enough."

She made a sound, but I couldn't tell whether it was to agree or disagree. More and more, I saw bits of Delta in her mother. "I'm not an invalid," she snapped, tucking her crutches more firmly under her arms, but they wobbled as she tried to make them move together. Her good foot tangled underneath her. She stumbled, her hold on the crutches giving way.

Will caught her, supporting her with one arm, holding on to the wayward crutches with the other. "I'm happy to walk with you, if you want to try," he said, and I saw what he was doing. Giving her the power to choose, so she could save face.

"Bah." She waved away the offer with one hand, all the while holding on to him with her other. "Why waste a good truck?"

I took the crutches from him and laid them in the bed of the truck, then climbed into the extended cab, careful not to catch my heel in the hem of my dress. Once I was settled, Will lifted Jessie Pearl into the passenger seat, and we started the quick trip to Mockingbird Lane. "It's a shame," Jessie Pearl said, one block into the drive.

"What is, Mrs. Trapper?" Will asked.

"That we'll probably never know what really happened in the cemetery with Delta, or what she was up in arms about before the end."

Will took the next right, an indirect route. I knew he was trying to stretch the trip, but I didn't think anything new would be revealed. "My daughter Gracie's sixteen now, and I've learned that she just is who she is. I've done all the influencing I can. I'm still her compass, but she's fully wired, and now it's up to her as to the kind of life she's going to live. I can't live it for her, just like you couldn't live Delta's."

"I suppose, but do you ever stop tryin'?" She turned to look at him, allowing me to see her profile. Her iron gray hair was done up in short, tight curls. There was a frailty to the way her skin was mapped with lines, the combination of them telling the story of her life. They seemed deeper and more ingrained than they had even a day ago. More evidence of how this ordeal was wearing on her.

"No," Will said, "I don't guess you ever do."

"I believe Delta was trying to help someone. She felt betrayed, somehow. You have no ideas, Miss Jessie Pearl?"

She turned her upper body, looking startled and like she'd forgotten for a moment that I was in the truck. Her voice rose, and for a moment she seemed even older than her eighty-three years. "She was poking around into someone's business. If she talked to that investigator and knew Anson wasn't cheatin' on her, then who was she talkin' about that day in the kitchen? She stood right there and said he couldn't be trusted, and that she would find out the truth if it killed her. What truth?"

Will pulled up in front of Jessie Pearl's house, but none of us moved to leave the truck. "Ma'am, you never mentioned that she said that the other day when I was over."

"I didn't think of it the other day. The problem with growing old, you see, is that the mind comes and goes."

Her mind seemed to come and go about as quick as her mood changed. She was steady and calm right now, but a short while ago, she'd been agitated and angry. I wondered how much of what she said could be trusted.

"But you didn't think she was talking about her husband?"

"Oh no, I *did* think she was talkin' about Anson. Absolutely. At least at the time. But you're tellin' us now that Anson *wasn't* the lout we were thinkin' he was, and if that's the case and she knew it, then she *had* to have been talkin' about someone else. And if she was tryin' to get the truth of somethin', then it means someone wasn't bein' honest with her. That's what's ironic. God says an eye for an eye, right? That's what happened with my girl. Whatever good she might have been tryin' to do there at the end . . . finding whatever truth she was after . . . well, that was her downfall."

I felt like she'd just talked in a giant circle, and yet it made sense in a way. Karma. An eye for an eye.

"Do you think it could have been Jeremy Lisle?" I asked.

"He's as good a suspect as any of them, I reckon."

"What about Mayor Radcliffe? Could she have found out something about him?"

"Well, now, I have no earthly idea. I'd say anythin's possible, wouldn't you say? *Someone* killed her."

That was the truest statement of the night. Jeremy Lisle and Mayor Radcliffe each had the strength to have overpowered Delta and wielded a rock against her. But which one had the bigger secrets? Did the mayor have any, in fact?

The passenger door of the truck wrenched open suddenly, a face appearing in the dark.

Jessie Pearl and I both jumped in our seats.

"Granny, it's just me!"

"Megan Mobley, you gave me a fright!" Jessie Pearl snapped. "What in heaven's name were you thinkin', scarin' me like that?"

Megan had taken a step back, the color draining from her face. "I'm so sorry, Granny. We were all just wondering where you were, and Pastor Kyle's kind of upset, so I said I'd come find you."

"Why's the pastor upset?" Will asked. He'd been listening to the conversation between Jessie Pearl and me, but when she whipped around at the sound of his voice now, I got the feeling she'd forgotten he was there.

"He's saying some of the things in the house belong to the church," Megan said. "He wants to know why they're there." She threw her hands up. "I don't know what to tell him!"

"What in tarnation are you talkin' about?" Jessie Pearl demanded. "What's he sayin' belongs to the church? Hogwash, pure and simple."

"Right? I bought everything, just like I bought the sideboard."

I remembered the sideboard Cynthia had seen, and her thinking Delta had stolen it. The pastor had defended that, but now it sounded like there were more items that needed to be accounted for.

Megan started to help her grandmother from the truck. Will hurried to her side, lifting her down and helping Megan prop her up while he grabbed the crutches from the back of the truck. I joined them, and together we walked slowly up the walkway to the Mobley/Trapper house.

Todd's strings of twinkle lights made the front yard

look fun and festive. If Delta had been a different kind of person, this whole evening might have been a celebration of her life. Instead, it felt like a disconnected moment. The entire night, in fact, had felt off-kilter, as if it had missed its mark with its intention. The Red Hat ladies had wanted to hold the progressive dinner, as planned, but the pall hanging over the group from her death was too much to overcome. It felt more like a funeral procession, and the twinkling lights didn't quite fit.

Todd met us at the door, holding it open and helping Jessie Pearl over the stoop. "The pastor's throwing a wall-eyed fit," Todd said under his breath, just loud enough for us to hear.

Jessie Pearl straightened her hunched spine as much as she could and hobbled forward on her crutches. "Where is he?"

Todd led the way through the maze of antiques to the dining room. It looked lovely. The twinkling lights continued inside, too, draped over the freestanding hutch and along the ceiling. With the interior lighting turned down low, they cast flickering shadows on the walls and pine floor.

The Red Hat ladies had gathered around the table, a few already holding dainty dessert plates. In their aprons, all lined up, they looked like a particularly fashionable group. Each apron seemed to say so much about the woman who wore it. Randi's spoke to her free spirit. Georgia's was romantic, while Cynthia's was tailored and classic. Bennie's was vintage flirty and Coco's Texas denim, with a twist, fit her to a tee. Megan and Jessie

Pearl wore theirs, too, but while I was sure I'd captured the personalities, the aprons hadn't helped either one accept what had happened to Delta. Megan had still lost her mother, and Jessie Pearl had still lost her daughter, and no magical Cassidy charm could take away the pain that went along with that.

Georgia picked at her slice of sopapilla cheesecake, a Texas classic. Randi nibbled on a sugar cookie. Coco stood over the banana pudding with Nilla Wafers, but hadn't taken any dessert. They were all down-home desserts, but it seemed none of the ladies were in the mood for sweets.

Their husbands, once again, were their opposites. They stood at the perimeter of the room, plates piled high with the different selections Todd and Megan had prepared, and watched as if the room were a theater and the people were actors in a play. Megan manned the sidebar, pouring coffee from a large carafe, and offering ice water and sweet tea.

From what I could see, Todd had exaggerated the pastor's state of mind. Either that, or he'd calmed down in the time it took us to get inside. There was no temper tantrum, but he was expressing a healthy dose of anger with a dollop of disbelief. He ran his hand through his sandy-colored hair, shaking his head. "How could this happen? I just don't understand."

He looked at each of the Red Hat ladies in turn, and in response, they each shook their heads. "You said all this was in the basement, Pastor," Coco said. "We come to church and sit in the sanctuary. We don't ever venture into the basement, do we, Sherri?"

"Why would we?" She looked at Coco, then at the pastor, but to me her eyes seemed vacant, and I wondered if she saw them at all.

"Exactly," Georgia said. "Cyn, you work there. Did you ever go in the basement?"

Cynthia had put her dessert plate down and was fiddling with the apron ties knotted at her waist. Her gaze darted about nervously. "Well, of course," she said. "Every once in a while, but—"

Pastor Kyle swept his arms wide. "Who took these things?"

Cynthia's eyes turned glassy from the accusatory stares. She took a hurried step backward. "I don't know."

Pastor Kyle looked around. "How could you not know?" He pointed first to an antique chair, then to an old trunk. "All of these are from the church basement."

"Delta didn't invite me over here."

The Red Hat ladies murmured their agreement. "Me, either," Randi said.

"Me, either," Georgia echoed.

I looked at Cynthia, recalling the conversation we'd had a few days ago. She'd told me the same thing about not being invited into Delta's house, and about discovering the stolen church items when she'd peeked through the window. Had that been the truth, or had she had enough foresight to plant that seed in my head so I could corroborate her story?

But even if it *was* a story she'd made up, that still didn't explain the murder. Unless Cynthia had turned to blackmail. But blackmail and murder over a few church antiques was a stretch. If Delta had even been behind it. Megan and

Rebecca were the ones who sold antiques, after all. Could one—or both—of them have stolen the goods?

I pulled out my cell phone and quickly texted Sheriff McClaine, asking him if Delta's bank account activity might indicate she was paying a blackmailer.

He responded right way. *Why?*

For the next minute, our texts flew back and forth.

Just a thought, I said.

Feel free to share that thought, he responded.

Hoss McClaine, dagnabbit, I typed with my thumbs, my frustration sky-high.

Hang on, he finally responded, and then thirty seconds later, he replied with, *There are regular deposits, but no regular outgoings. If anything, she was blackmailing someone, not the other way around.*

"Huh."

"What?" Will asked, raising one eyebrow.

I hadn't realized I'd spoken aloud. I quickly glanced around, but no one was paying attention to me. I handed my phone to Will, and a second later he was leading me out of the dining room and down the hallway toward the bedrooms. "Which one of them would she have been blackmailing?" he asked when we were sure no one could overhear us.

"Pastor Kyle? Maybe there's something shady in his past that we don't know about?"

But Will shook his head. "If Pastor Kyle's lying, he deserves an Oscar. Plus he drives a beat-up old car. He doesn't appear to have extra money lying around."

"I thought he drove an SUV," I said, puzzled. I'd seen him in it plenty of times, not to mention just this evening.

"That belongs to the church, but he basically *is* the church, so . . ."

That made perfect sense. "So he drives that around town when it's available."

"Right."

We moved on. "Jeremy Lisle?"

Will looked around to be sure we were still alone, then said, "If Delta had something on him, then I could see it. Ambition is a powerful motivator."

Once again, I thought back through everything I had discovered, trying to summon up something that would equate to dirt Delta might have had on Jeremy. He'd known she'd tried to block the Historic Council from giving a designation to Jessie Pearl's house. He'd also known she'd donated money to the Radcliffe campaign. From what Radcliffe had said, money had been donated by each one of Delta's family members. Surely there wasn't anything unethical there. They were all over the age of eighteen. I didn't know whether it looked better to have a whole family donate, each person individually, or to have a large donation come from one person. I also didn't know if it really mattered.

"Maybe he was trying to get her back on his side of the election. Delta was influential in town."

"Right, except *he* wasn't blackmailing *her*. Hoss said she's the one with the steady deposits in her account." Will leaned against wall. "Here's a hypothetical. What if Lisle turned the tables on her? He could have had *her* followed. She could have found out that he'd stooped to something underhanded and blackmailed him for her silence. Would anyone vote for a man who resorts to that kind of intimidation?"

"They wouldn't."

I jumped at the sound of a man's voice behind us. Jeremy Lisle came around the corner, his expression tight. "But that scenario you just painted didn't happen." He threw his arms wide. "If you want to ask me something, just do it. I got nothin' to hide."

"Mr. Lisle," I started weakly. "We were just throwing out ideas—"

He held up his hand, stopping me midsentence. "I heard you plain as day. Blackmail? I'm running for public office. Do you really think I'd succumb to blackmail?"

Will put his hand on my lower back, in encouragement and support. It was just what I needed to keep my voice steady and stand tall. "It happens, though. I've seen it. Good people making bad decisions."

He shrugged. "I'll give you that. There are certainly unethical people in the world. But Ms. Cassidy, Delta Mobley had nothing on me because there's nothing to be had. If anything, I knew things about *her*. Good thing *she* wasn't running for office," he said wryly.

Jeremy came back the way he'd come, anger still bubbling close to the surface. I didn't blame him. To overhear that you were a suspect in a murder investigation, even from the likes of me, had to be disconcerting, and if he was innocent, all the more upsetting.

Will returned to the group and was talking to the pastor, so I took the opportunity to sneak a peek at the rest of the house. I had no expectations of finding anything, but I was curious as to whether any other church antiques were hiding in plain sight, and how they might have gotten here.

Walking back down the hall, I glanced in each room. From the décor and clothes laid out on her bed, I guessed that Jessie Pearl's was at the end of the hallway. Across from it was a closed door. Tiptoeing closer, I turned the handle and opened the door a crack. Clothes were strewn about. Men's pants, shirts, sneakers, and dress shoes. A few ties dangled haphazardly from the back of a chair. This had to be Anson and Delta's room, the remnants of Anson's quick packing evident.

And there, in the middle of the room, was the mattress Jessie Pearl had tried to flip. I tried to picture the scene as she'd described it. She'd gotten up under the mattress, climbing onto the box spring to work it up higher and higher. But instead of being able to flip it over like she'd done before, it had fallen back down on her. Her leg had buckled under her, the bone snapping.

That's how Megan and Todd had found her.

I closed the door again, moving down the hall back toward the dinner guests, but stopped at another door. Acting on impulse, I slipped inside, closing the door behind me before I knew what room I was in. The queen-sized bed, the closet doors opened to reveal his and hers clothing, the boxes filled with antiques and knickknacks, all priced for a tag sale or flea market. This had to be Megan and Todd's room.

I stood back, taking it all in, feeling a sense of sadness close in around me. Megan had left three dresses discarded on the bed, one black, one multicolored, and one black, brown, and cream. She'd ended up in the faded floral number, the apron I'd made the perfect complement to it, but it had clearly taken her a while to figure out what to wear. Not surprising given how much her mother's sudden death seemed to have shaken her.

The poor girl would be in a bad place for a while, I was afraid. At least she had Todd, and her aunts and Jessie Pearl, and, hopefully, her father for support.

I started for the door, stopping when I remembered that Todd had been in possession of the private investigator's report. He'd said something about almost burning the entire file, or separating out the incriminating evidence to protect Megan and Jessie Pearl. Megan had gone on to say there wasn't much to the report, and I had to agree. From what I'd seen, and from what Kristina Boyd, the investigator, said, Anson hadn't been a cheating husband.

Hoss had the report now, but what if something *had* been removed from it? When Todd went to retrieve the file that day, it had taken him a good bit of time. Could there have been something more in the file that he had taken out? But why would he take that risk?

The only logical answer was to protect someone. Removing evidence was a crime, and a risk. The only person he'd take that chance for would be Megan.

The whole idea was a stretch, I realized, but since it was possible, I had to poke around to see if I could find any proof.

I got busy, working as quickly and quietly as I could. I searched the obvious places first. Rifling through the bedside tables, the closet shelves, behind the shoes in the closet revealed nothing. No stack of paper or pictures. No second goldenrod envelope. Nothing that screamed this was information that had been in the PI's report.

I stood in the center of the room, looking around. If information had been taken out of the report, where would it be hidden? I'd searched the box of antiques. The drawers of the bureau. There was no place else.

And then I heard voices. They came from down the hall, growing louder. The sound of footsteps followed. They slowed outside the room I was in and panic set in. I couldn't be found snooping. Quick as lightning, I sent up a prayer that whoever was in the hall would keep on walking, and then I did the only thing I could. I ducked into the closet to hide.

Chapter 23

From my hiding place, the voices were muffled, but I thought I recognized Will's voice.

The other person spoke with more force. "Georgia saw her back here." A man's voice. Yikes. Were they talking about me?

I'd spoken with Pastor Kyle and Jeremy Lisle enough to know it wasn't either of them. It could have been one of the Red Hat ladies' husbands . . . Georgia's husband?

I couldn't take any chances, so I flipped the little side button on my phone to SILENT just in case. I didn't anticipate a call, but I'd seen plenty of movies where stupid mistakes like leaving a phone on resulted in an awkward discovery. My phone ringing would be a dead giveaway, and I was not going to take any chances. My heartbeat pounded in my ears, heightening as the door handle turned and the voices outside in the hallway suddenly came into the room.

"Why do you need Harlow?" I heard Will ask.

That sweet man. He must have suspected that I was in one of these rooms and was trying to warn me.

"Megan said the ladies all want to take a picture in their aprons, and they want her in it with them." Ah, it was Todd's voice. Made sense.

"Maybe she went out front for some air," Will suggested. Bless his heart. He was giving me time to make a clean getaway.

Their footsteps retreated and the door clicked closed. I heaved a sigh of relief, but still waited a solid minute and then opened the door slowly, peeking through the crack to make sure the coast was clear. I started to slip out, my body rustling the clothes I moved against, but I stopped when my shoulder was pricked by the pointed edge of something. I pulled the hangers apart and there, hanging from the clips of a skirt hanger, was a blue file folder. My breath stalled. Could it be . . . ?

I held it from the bottom and gave a gentle pull, glancing inside. It held pages that seemed to match the type in the Boyd Investigations report, as well as a stack of photographs.

Very clever, Todd, I thought. Hanging the envelope between his clothes had been a smart way to hide the information he'd taken from the report. Quick as a lightning bug, I ran to the door, staying on my tiptoes to stop my heels from clicking against the hardwood floor. With my ear to the door, I listened. All was quiet and in seconds flat, I was across the hall, barricaded in the bathroom. Todd had said that the Red Hat ladies wanted a picture, so I didn't have time to look through the folder this second, and I couldn't very well carry it out with me.

Looking around, I noticed that even the bathroom was decked out in antiques and collectibles. A rattan storage table was across from the toilet. I opened the small doors to find a stash of toilet paper, two hand towels, and a spare container of liquid hand soap. Perfect. I slipped the file folder against the back wall of the chest, behind the supplies, closing the door and double-checking to be sure nothing looked disturbed.

Then I flushed the toilet, ran the water, and took a minute to calm my racing heart. I opened the door, fluffing my hair as I stepped into the hallway . . . and ran smack into Wayne Emmons, Georgia's husband and the one Red Hat husband who'd made an effort to chitchat.

"Found her!" he called over his shoulder. To me he said, "Everyone's been looking for you." He peered over my shoulder into the bathroom. The toilet was still running, and he looked back at me, so I guess he figured all was as it should be.

"Oh?" I smiled, playing innocent, since, of course, I couldn't let on that I'd overheard Will and Todd talking about the photo the Red Hat ladies wanted to take wearing their aprons.

"Picture time," he said, studying me. He seemed suspicious. Or maybe it was my guilty conscience that was making me feel like I'd done something wrong. Which, technically, I had. My head felt hot, my vision a little blurry. The after-effects of taking someone else's property. Or at least relocating it.

Could I leave the house with the file? It was going to be tricky to figure out how to sneak it out, forget about finding a way to look through it and then get it back into

Megan and Todd's closet. I blinked away the agitation bubbling inside me. I couldn't say why, but I felt sure that it held the key to understanding what had happened to Delta.

I refocused my thoughts and followed Wayne back toward the dining room. "I wouldn't have thought anyone was in the mood for pictures tonight," I said.

Actually, the way the evening had gone, I thought they'd all be running for the door to escape the first moment they could. But as we came back into the dining room, I saw the crowd had grown by two and the energy had changed. One Cassidy woman could have that effect. Two ensured it. My mother and grandmother sat at the table, each with a plate piled high with treats, smiles on their faces, and a lightness about them that they didn't normally possess, especially given the long-lasting feud between the Mobleys and Cassidys.

It's not that they weren't usually easygoing. They were. But at this moment, listening to them laugh and chat and generally lift the spirit of the room, it felt as if Meemaw were here, too, infusing the night with her otherworldly charm.

Mama met my eyes, and I drew my brows together in a silent question.

"We saw the twinkle lights in the yard, saw the cars, and when you weren't at home, darlin'," she said to me, "why we just decided to come on over." She turned to Jessie Pearl. "You don't mind, do you?"

Something knocked against the window. We all turned to look, but I recognized the *tat-tat-tat*. Thelma Louise.

Sure enough, the granddam of Nana's goat herd stood

on her hind legs, her forelegs resting on the outside windowsill, the horizontal pupils of her eyes staring at us.
Megan jumped, startled, then raced forward swinging a
dish towel. "Shoo! Go on, get outta here!"

"We're happy to have y'all join us, but I do mind the
goat," Jessie Pearl said, meeting Thelma Louise's gaze
with a challenge. Thelma Louise didn't budge and neither did Jessie Pearl. It was a standoff.

Nana pushed back in her chair, the legs scraping
against the old pine floors, and started toward the window. Thelma Louise blinked once and then vanished into
the night. The goat-whisperer in action. Nana's herd produced exquisite soap and delicious goat cheese, and it
was all due to the special rapport she had with the ani-
mals. It was an obscure charm, but a charm nonetheless.

The distraction gave me enough time to text Will and
tell him about the envelope I'd hidden in the bathroom.
Can you sneak it out so we can look at it before we leave?
I texted.

He shot me a look of clear disbelief from across the
room, but he texted back *Roger that*, and I heaved a sigh
of relief. I'd leave it to him, and we'd reconvene at some
point to find out whether that file held any other clues.

Coco clapped her hands, then swept her arms wide to
usher the Red Hat ladies together. "You, too, Harlow,"
she said, waving me over.

Wayne and Todd both appeared with cameras, Wayne's
a serious Nikon with a high-powered lens and a flash
sitting on top. Todd's the one on his phone.

The women gathered together in the front room of
the house, amid the antiques and collectibles. Aside from

Wayne and Todd, the men stayed behind in the dining room, refilling their plates with desserts. I saw Will head down the hall to the bathroom. So the plan was in action.

The Red Hat ladies wrapped their arms around one another, linking in Jessie Pearl and her crutches, Megan, and me. It might have been my imagination, but I felt Delta's presence in the room. It may have been just the idea of her, but I came back to Loretta Mae and her ghostly presence at 2112 Mockingbird Lane, wondering once again if that was an anomaly and something that happened only to the Cassidy women, or if there were ghosts all around us, including Delta Lea Mobley.

The cameras clicked, and we all smiled as best we could. "To Delta," Todd said, prompting us all to smile bigger.

"To Delta," we all echoed, and the cameras snapped again.

"Well," Coco said, "you may not cook, Cynthia, but now no one would ever know. Y'all'll have to send her that picture right away so she can pass it around and prove that she's worn an apron at least once in her life."

The women laughed ... all except Cynthia, who grimaced. "I may not like to cook, but I can look the part, and I'm okay with that. What people don't know won't hurt them."

I glanced down the hallway, looking for Will. No sign of him. I checked my phone, remembering that I'd left it turned to silent after my adventure in Megan and Todd's closet. Now I saw that he'd texted me. *Meet me on the back porch.*

The photo shoot was done. Wayne packed up his camera, Todd put his phone in his pocket, and they both wandered off. Cynthia had taken off her apron, tucking it away in her purse in the corner of the room. The Red Hat ladies milled about aimlessly, Jessie Pearl, with the help of Megan, hobbling back to the dining table to sit with Mama and Nana. The others went to their husbands or gathered around the sideboard with the coffee and tea.

The coast was clear. With a quick glance over my shoulder, I slipped through the kitchen and out the back door to the porch.

Chapter 24

There'd been enough light outside to see Thelma Louise a short while ago, so there was enough light to see Will and me if anyone was looking. I kept to the shadows. "Will?"

"Over here," he called softly.

He'd gone to the opposite side of the porch, away from the dining room, where we'd have privacy. He had the contents from the envelope spread on the small round table off to the side. "There you are." He straightened up and gave me a light kiss on the cheek. "Where'd you get this?" he asked, now that it was safe to press for information.

"Clipped to a hanger in Todd and Megan's closet," I whispered. "Clever. I never would have found it if I hadn't heard you and Todd coming and jumped in there to hide. Did you find anything?"

He shrugged. "I don't know what I'm looking for, so who knows?"

I stood next to him, and together we quickly looked at each piece of paper and each photo. I catalogued them in my mind as we flipped through the contents.

First was the intake form I'd seen the first time, but instead of Anson Mobley's name, the subject had been blacked out. Paper-clipped to the top sheet were snapshots of the five members of the household. The candid shots, each one of them in a different location, definitely hadn't been in the file the first time I'd seen it. In addition, there was a picture of Rebecca Masters, Megan's friend and partner in the antique business, who'd gone MIA.

Will pulled up his cell phone flashlight and shone it on the photos so I could get a better look. The one of Delta showed her bent over the RADCLIFFE FOR MAYOR sign in her front yard, a maroon Aggies flag right next to it. Anson was pictured on the golf course playing a round with Megan, Todd, and Rebecca. Another showed Todd in his car at the bank drive-through. In her candid shot, Megan held what looked like a heavy cardboard box in front of the church. In the background were Todd, Coco, and Sherri. Including a picture of Rebecca struck me as odd. She stood in the Mobley yard, arms folded, an envelope in her hand. The last photo was of Jessie Pearl on her porch, hands on her hips, unsmiling. Megan was in the corner of the yard, and Todd was hunched over a patch of flowers.

All the people Delta loved, plus Rebecca.

I skimmed the rest of the pages, none of which I'd seen the first time I'd looked at the file. Boyd Investigations hadn't just followed Anson Mobley. This was a list of each of the family member's comings and goings over a period of seven days. The notes were succinct.

Anson

10 a.m. Office. 3 hours
1 p.m. Met client at 3900 Magnolia Street
1:20 p.m. Fast food drive-through
2:20 p.m. Met Megan and Todd with boxes to deliver to church
3:33 p.m. Met Delta at listing

On and on it went, detailing everything he did, from playing five hours of golf at the municipal course to meeting Delta for dinner at a local cantina to a two-hour stop at the title company for a close of escrow.

Nothing seemed out of the ordinary, and there were no rendezvous at any hotels. In fact, other than one photo showing a hotel in the background, there was nothing even implying an affair. No wonder the investigator had seemed so adamant that Anson was not unfaithful. There was nothing to indicate anything suspicious. So why had Delta questioned her ability to trust him?

I flipped the page and saw a similar tracking of Megan's daily activities.

Megan

7 a.m. Yoga
8:15 a.m. Coffee shop with Rebecca
9:30 a.m. School

4 p.m. Church delivery with Todd
4:30 p.m. Met mother at nail salon

Megan's days were pretty much the same. She went to her classes at the local university, exercised, ran a few errands, and then it all repeated. Two days during the week included Rebecca coming to the Mobley house and staying for several hours, and a third day tracked Megan, Todd, and Rebecca at a flea market selling their antiques.

Todd's daily schedule was a little more varied. He worked in the yard, took boxes to the tag sale, worked in the church office, met Delta at a few of her listings to help, went to the bank, to the market, to the nursery. He was always on the go. A jack of all trades, just as he'd said, from the looks of it.

Jessie Pearl had barely half a page of notes. She rarely left the house. Walked around the garden. Moved the yard signs from one spot to another. Pulled weeds. It was an uneventful life.

The last page of notes was about Delta. "Do you think she knew the investigator was checking her out, too?" Will asked, reading over my shoulder.

"I don't know." I didn't understand any of this. She'd had her husband investigated, so why the details on everyone else, and why on herself?

Delta

8:15 a.m. Drive-through coffee shop
8:30 a.m. Office

10:05 a.m. House listing on Richland Lane
11 a.m. Church tag sale
11:30 a.m. Lunch with Randi
12:30 p.m. Post office
1:10 p.m. City offices
1:45 p.m. Bank with Todd
2:30 p.m. Megan haircut and color, Delta paid
4:00 p.m. Early dinner with Anson

On and on it went, each page giving a play-by-play. Before long, the details all blurred together, but something tickled at the back of my brain. I flipped back and forth between the pages, trying to figure out what it was that had put me on alert.

"Cassidy," Will prompted, "we've been out here for twenty minutes. We'd best get this file back."

"One sec," I said, holding up my index finger. I read through the detective's surveillance notes one more time, but whatever the red flag was eluded me.

I'd just gathered up all the papers and photos, sliding them back into the blue file, when we heard the kitchen door open, followed by voices. A group of people had come outside. In seconds flat, we'd be caught red-handed.

My heart lodged in my throat as I handed the folder back to Will, who quickly laid it against his chest. The second his jacket was zipped, Georgia, Wayne, and Randi came into view. "There you are," Randi said, looking from me to Will and back again. "A little alone time?"

I slipped one arm around Will's back, wrapping around his front as I snuggled up next to him. "A stolen moment," I said, inwardly cringing at the unintended double entendre. The stolen file hadn't given me answers, but it wasn't mine, and guilt flooded my pores.

"Everyone's getting ready to leave," Randi said. "Jeremy's going to take me home."

I drew in a sharp breath and threw a quick glance at Will. I couldn't say that Jeremy Lisle had killed Delta, but I felt there were enough questions to raise a red flag. "Will can give you a ride," I said.

Randi tilted her head and gave me a puzzled look. "Why in heaven's name would he want to do that?"

I stammered, no good answer coming to me.

"I'm fine, Harlow. Jeremy offered, and I'm kinda happy about that, truth be told."

"Oh, good. Good." I forced a smile and nodded.

Will gave me a squeeze, and I grounded myself. I had no solid reason to stop Randi from going with Jeremy. Even if he had killed Delta, he had no reason to do harm to anyone else. So maybe she'd be just fine.

Hopefully.

"I'll let y'all know how it goes," Randi said.

Wayne gave a low whistle, and Georgia batted his arm. "Wayne McCarthy Emmons," she scolded, and to us, she added, "Men."

Wayne met Will's gaze, lifting one brow. He directed a sheepish smile at his wife, put his arm behind her and gave her backside a pat. "Aw, come on now, you know you love it."

"I know your mama taught you manners."

"Guess I forgot to bring 'em tonight," he joked. "But I can still watch over you without 'em."

"Maybe so, but you should bring 'em everywhere," she chided, but one side of her mouth rose in a soft smile.

"Sweetums," Wayne said, "I have you. I don't need no manners."

"And no good grammar, neither," she said, mimicking his West Texas twang.

"Oh, Georgia," Randi said. "Leave him be. He's fine."

"That's right," he said, "I'm fine. Alls I'm sayin' is it's about time Randi found herself a man."

Randi brushed back her short shimmery hair, spiking it on top of her head. "Getting a little ahead of ourselves? It's just a ride home, is all."

"Romance has to start somewhere," Wayne said, "ain't that right, Georgia?"

She smiled at him, nodding. "That's true enough."

"I gave her a ride home after a pageant about a million years ago. The rest, as they say, is history." He looked at Will and me. "Where'd you two start?"

"Loretta Mae played matchmaker," Will volunteered, as Megan and Todd slipped out onto the porch. The party was migrating outside.

I almost added, *From beyond the grave*, but held it in. They didn't need the nitty-gritty details. Everyone knew that my great-grandmother got what she wanted, one way or another. No reason to draw more attention to that special Cassidy charm.

"We met in statistics class," Megan said. "He saw me and made a beeline right for me, like he knew just what he wanted."

"That's true," Todd said, but then he frowned. "Worst class ever, though. You were the only saving grace."

Megan smiled. "He thinks he's not very lovable."

"How did I get lucky enough to have you fall in love with me?" he asked, grinning.

She answered with a squeeze of his hand. "We have a story to tell our children. College is for learning, but also for falling in love."

Just then, the door to the kitchen opened again and Cynthia appeared, the light from the house like a glowing aura around her. "There y'all are. Jeremy's looking for you, Randi. And I'm heading out."

So the evening was drawing to a close, and the murderer, if he or she was among us, had hidden in plain sight. We followed the group back inside. Will immediately excused himself and headed down the hallway. The good-byes would give him enough time to replace the envelope on the clip hangers I'd described in Megan and Todd's closet, and no one would be the wiser.

Something about the file still bothered me. I kept coming back to what Coco had said about Cynthia and her apron. She could look like a kitchen diva, even if she barely knew how to scramble an egg.

The bottom line was that people were not always what they seemed, and we only let people see what we wanted them to see. This had proven true in the past, and whenever murder was involved, it was definitely the case. People hid out in the open, but they didn't always show others who they really were. It had happened time and time again. Meemaw always used to say that people reveal themselves if you let them. I had the feeling I'd seen the truth about whoever had killed Delta, I just hadn't realized it yet.

During the good-byes, I finally had a chance to pull Sherri aside. "How are you holding up?" I asked.

She shrugged. "My outburst aside? Okay, I guess."

"I wish I could have helped more," I said. Tears pooled in her eyes, and once again I felt as if I'd failed the Lea sisters. I hadn't been able to bring them any peace. I only hoped the sheriff would be able to.

"You tried," Sherri said. "You recovered Mother's Lladrós. You found those notes from Delta. You made us the aprons. You did everything you could."

She'd opened the door when she'd mentioned the notes, so I walked through, telling her about the note I'd found that she'd written so many months ago.

"When we were kids, we'd play spy," she said, her voice soft and nostalgic. "That teapot used to be one of the ways we'd pass secret messages. When she wouldn't listen to me, I guess I thought I'd write it down and put it there, and maybe one day she'd find it and realize that I'd tried to tell her."

"Tell her what?" I asked.

She looked over her shoulder, as if she were making sure we were alone. "There was something going on between Todd and that girl Rebecca," she said. "I didn't know how to tell Megan, so I told Delta."

My heart stalled in my chest. "You mean an affair?" My mind raced. The idea that Anson was having an affair, the private investigator, pages pulled from the report. What if Delta hadn't ever thought Anson was cheating on her? What if she'd been looking into the idea that Todd was cheating on Megan?

I remembered the up-and-down look Delta had given Rebecca the first day I'd met her in the Mobley kitchen. She'd questioned how Rebecca could work in the dress she'd been wearing. Rebecca's flirtatious reply had been that Todd was going to help.

"Did you see them together?" I asked.

She nodded. "At an antique fair in Plano about a month before Megan brought Todd home. Rebecca showed up a few weeks later, and at first I couldn't place her, but then it hit me. I'd seen them together."

"What did Delta say?"

"She told me I was imagining things. She said Megan was happy, Rebecca was a good friend, and Todd was the perfect son-in-law."

"So you dropped it?"

She nodded. "I dropped it."

"And you never mentioned it to Megan?"

"No, never," she said, her voice quiet. "If I was wrong, I didn't want to cause her pain."

"But if you were right?"

She shrugged. "Rebecca moved out of Randi's garage apartment, and from what Megan said, she's not returning her calls, so I guess it doesn't matter anymore."

I wasn't sure I believed that. Why had Rebecca vanished?

The Red Hatters converged at the front door, stopping us from talking any further. Jeremy led Randi outside. I watched them go, she still with her half apron on, he with his hand lightly touching her back, guiding her. A pool of anxiety settled in my chest, but I shook it away.

She'd be fine. Randi was soft-spoken, but she had the strength and wherewithal to defend herself, if she needed to.

Georgia and Wayne left next. Just like Jeremy had with Randi, Wayne guided Georgia, but his touch was more familiar. Suggestive, even, as his hand slipped over the curve of her backside. She batted his hand away, but the evening breeze carried her giggle back to us.

I wondered about my Cassidy charm and if I'd just seen it in action. Georgia had been flirtatious with Will earlier, but now she was playful with her husband. Maybe her deepest desire had been to strengthen their connection. And Randi had been happy as a clam leaving with Jeremy. I'd lay money down that her hopes and desires centered on finding a soul mate. Jeremy could be it. My suspicions about him could be completely off base.

Cynthia, Bennie, and their husbands left next, followed by Pastor Kyle and Sherri. "I'll see that she gets home," the pastor said. Like the other men, he led Sherri down the walkway, past the RADCLIFFE FOR MAYOR sign, past the Aggie flag and the twinkling lights, but he kept his hands to himself, instead walking slightly ahead of her so she'd follow.

Nana had slipped away out the back door. Her property backed up to my yard, and the Mobleys'. I peeked out the back window and saw her shadowy form trekking through the darkness, Thelma Louise trotting in front her.

Only Mama, Coco, and Delta's family—minus Anson,

of course—remained. "I'll stay and help clean up," I told Megan.

Mama slid her arm through mine, and we followed the others to the kitchen. "We both will. My husband'll be here in just a little bit to pick me up."

I turned to look at her. She'd been driving since she was thirteen, starting with a hardship license back when Nana and Granddaddy were barely making ends meet with their goats and she'd had to help by driving to the next town for farm supplies. Mama and her pickup truck were about as inseparable as my granddaddy and his cowboy hat. Which is to say they were rarely apart. Something was fishy, and I suspected it had to do with my mother wanting Sheriff Hoss McClaine to be in close proximity in case Delta's murderer decided to take out another victim. Not that that made a lick of sense, but Mama often didn't operate using logic. She felt her way through life using flowers and plants as her guide. Hoss kept her feet rooted even when she tried to flit away like an impatient butterfly.

Will had reappeared, nodding to me. I breathed a sigh of relief. The envelope was back where I'd found it. "Scotch?" Todd asked him. When Will agreed, they went back into the dining room.

"Aren't you going to help?" Megan called after him, but he didn't answer. Which was fine with me. I was happy for Will to keep him distracted while I dug a little deeper about Delta and the Red Hat ladies. Rebecca and Todd stayed in the back of my mind.

If Delta had actually believed Sherri and questioned

them, could one of them have killed her to keep their secret quiet?

But I shook my head, not believing that motive. Why would Todd marry Megan only to continue a relationship he'd already had going on with Rebecca? No, Sherri had to be mistaken. There had to be something I was missing. Some clue about someone that would crack everything wide open and let me see it in a new way.

"You don't have to help clean up at a party you didn't attend, Tessa," Jessie Pearl said.

Mama waved her hand like she was flitting the words right out of the air. "I'm not one to sit around when there's work to be done," she said.

Jessie Pearl held her crutches out in front of her where she sat at the kitchen table. "That's a good quality," she said, sending a pointed glance toward the dining room where Todd and Will had gone. "A mighty good quality."

"Come on, Granny," Megan said. "Todd worked hard all week doing up the yard, helping out around here, sorting through the antiques."

"I'm sure Granny doesn't disagree," Coco said, "but the point is, we're not done."

Megan's chin quivered. "That's not fair."

"He needs to find himself a lawyering job," Coco said.

Megan just shook her head. "He'd rather work with his hands."

"Waste of an education, if you ask me," Jessie Pearl said. "Three years in law school, how ever many in that culinary place, and he wants to do yard work."

As I listened, something Wayne Emmons had said to

Georgia out on the back porch came back to me. I'd been spinning in circles since Delta died, focusing on each of the people in her life, but not really understanding what she might have done to propel someone into killing her. But what if I looked at things from a different perspective? What if *she* had been trying to watch over someone, and she'd gotten in that person's way?

The only people she'd protect were her family members, and once again, I thought the most likely was Megan.

Mama had parked herself at the sink and had her arms submerged in soapy water as she washed the coffee cups and dessert plates. Megan brought in the rest of the treats from the dining room and Coco packaged up the leftovers. Jessie Pearl sat at the table watching the movement around her, a deep frown pulling the sides of her mouth down.

I felt a tingle at my hairline where the tuft of blond sprouted, and my skin pricked with apprehension. The threads were tangled and knotted, but the answer was there. For the first time since Delta died, I knew I was close to learning the truth, if only I could grab hold of an end thread and pull it free.

Mama flinched, bringing her arm up to her head and pressing her bicep against her hairline. Just like me, she had a streak of blond. It was a touchstone between us, all the Cassidy women.

She tossed a questioning look over her shoulder. In response, I straightened my glasses and darted a glance at Megan. I didn't know what Delta might have been protecting her from, or what trouble she might have encountered. And other than coming right out and asking her, which didn't seem like a good idea if she'd killed her mother over it, the only way to get answers was through her husband.

"I'll be right back," I said, and I scurried off in search of Will.

Chapter 25

Will and Todd were in the living room, each cradling a tumbler of scotch, the bottle on the table between them. I sat next to Will, and he took my hand, leaning close to give me a kiss on the cheek. "He's pretty buzzed," he whispered.

If Todd was on his second, or even his third, maybe his tongue would wag a little more loosely than normal and I could find out if Megan had some sort of problem she was trying to deal with. From the investigator's report, her days all followed the same pattern. Yoga or running, classes at the university, helping at the church tag sale or running errands, then home with her family. Could she have suspected something between Todd and Rebecca? An old fling? I thought back to the flirtatiousness. Rebecca called Todd "George" because he reminded her of a blond George Clooney.

A thought tickled at the back of my mind, but I couldn't pull it forward. Not yet anyway, but I'd keep trying. George . . .

Will and Todd finished their conversation about college sports teams. They were rivals, Will a Texas Longhorn and Todd an Aggie, but they kept the conversation civil. "I can fit in anywhere," Todd said, taking another drink. "Ask Delta." He sputtered, half laughing as he realized what he'd said. "Well, you can't actually ask her, but if you could, she'd have told you that I'm like a chameleon. I blend in."

"That's a good trait," I said, glad that Todd was a happy drunk and not an angry one. "It'll serve you well."

He raised his glass. "It already has," he said. "I can go from the garden to the church, to the city, to a law office and fit in at each of them."

"Are you still looking for a law firm to join?"

"Nah. Plenty to do with all Megan's antiques," he said, his words slurring just slightly. "Delta had a good collection of her own. And Jessie Pearl? There's a fortune in the curio cabinet alone."

"After all that schooling and taking the bar exam, don't you want to practice law?" Will asked.

Megan came in and perched on the arm of his chair as Todd shrugged. "I'll just stay here and be a kept man."

He nudged her leg and she smiled. "I don't mind that."

He tilted his head back to look up at her. "Your mother did."

"You can be a bookkeeper or a lawyer or a gardener or a garbage man. It doesn't matter to me. She's not here anymore to judge."

I held my breath, squeezing Will's hand. It was hardly a confession, but the conversation had just taken a turn in the right direction. "You didn't get along with Delta?" I asked Todd.

He lifted his shoulders again. "Eh. It doesn't matter."

"She didn't understand why you didn't practice law, that's all," Megan said. "Todd's got, what, three degrees?"

He nodded, and she continued. "But it's a tough economy. Hard to find a job right now."

He nudged her again, and she threw her hands up. "What? It's not like you haven't tried. It's not a secret, is it? I'm proud of you."

"Three degrees is impressive," I said. And it explained why he'd been taking a statistics class at the local university when he already had a law degree and who knew what else. "What are they in?"

He looked like he wanted to crawl into a hole, but he answered. "Political science. An MBA. History."

"And the culinary certificate," Megan added.

"And the law degree," I said, shaking my head. "It's a crazy world when someone like you can't get a job."

"He applied to Reynolds, Childs, and Briggs law office in town," Megan said. "Turned out they didn't have any openings, but —"

Todd threw back the rest of his scotch and interrupted her. "It's doesn't bother me. I like what I'm doing."

"My mother really tried to help him," Megan said. "She passed his resume around to everyone she knew." She squeezed his shoulder. "Something'll work out."

"I don't need charity," he snapped, but he quickly relaxed, correcting himself. "I like the antique business. There's a ton of money in it. People don't realize."

"Rebecca sure did," she said. To me, she added, "They knew each other a few years back when they both were in Plano. How long ago was that?"

But Todd waved the question away.

I pressed the subject, anyway. "How did you meet Rebecca?" I asked, going off what Sherri had just told me a short while ago.

"At the college here. What, about a month after I met you, right?" she asked Todd.

"Sounds right," he agreed, but even through his glassy eyes, his gaze had turned dark, and I could tell something was off. "But she bailed. We had a good business going, and she just up and left."

This time, Megan's eyes teared. "Why would she leave like that?"

Like a bulldozer in my mind, one of my conversations with Jeremy Lisle suddenly came back to me. He'd been the one to tell me about Anson having an affair, but something surfaced that I hadn't thought of before. Pastor Kyle had told him, but Delta had told Pastor Kyle. The way he'd relayed it stuck with me. *Some husbands can't be trusted.*

I suddenly felt as if I were an egg cracked open, spilling a million pieces of confetti, the bits forming a kaleidoscope of color. The feeling was deep in my bones. My stomach dropped and I stared at Todd. Could she have been talking about her son-in-law, and not Anson?

I remembered something else. Delta had been searching through the church files. I hadn't given it a second thought when Pastor Kyle mentioned it, but now I wondered. Was it about Todd? Megan had just said that

Delta had passed his resume around. Had she noticed something amiss?

Todd's gaze flashed to Megan, but then he focused on me and Will again so quickly that I wondered if I'd really seen the look of concern on his face that I imagined I had. The scotch had loosened his tongue, and he wasn't holding back. I forged ahead, asking the next obvious question. "I had no idea antiques were so profitable."

Todd nodded. Megan had her hand on his shoulder, rubbing it in circles for encouragement. "Oh yes, very. When I first met Rebecca and she told me what she did, I was floored. Aunt Sherri and my mom used to go to dealers and shows, but who knew?"

Aha, so that explained how Sherri may have seen Rebecca in Plano.

Coco appeared in the archway to the living room, beckoning me. She still wore the ruffled denim apron I'd made her, and like I had with the other women, I wondered what her deepest want was, and if the apron would help it come true.

Reluctantly, I left Will with Megan and Todd, following Coco back into the dining room. "I wanted to thank you for trying to help us," she started, but her voice faded away as the threads of clues began separating in my mind, pulling apart before braiding together in some semblance of order.

"Hang on," I told her, then I pulled out my cell phone and texted Madelyn, asking her the question in the forefront of my mind. *When we met with Mayor Radcliffe, he stopped to talk to his secretary about someone. Do you remember who?*

She texted me back not five seconds later. *No.*

It was a lawyer.

If you say so, love. I was busy getting my camera ready.

I waited. Madelyn was a self-proclaimed paranormal junkie and a crime aficionado. I knew she was racking her brain to come up with the answer to my question. My phone pinged and her text appeared. *Max? No, Lou? Something about a resume not checking out.*

That's exactly how I'd remembered it, but I had to be sure. All his degrees. All the universities he'd attended. Did they all check out?

My blood suddenly turned cold and I froze. "Oh my God."

Coco stared at me. "What?"

I grabbed her arm. "I've been looking at this all wrong."

She tapped the frame of her glasses, pushing them up into place. "Looking at what wrong?"

My mind flew back to the pictures in the investigator's file. I'd assumed that each one had been focusing on a different member of the family. Anson hadn't even been in the pictures, something I hadn't realized until this very second. But more than that was the fact that both Megan and Todd were in several of the pictures. The one with Delta had him in the background, and the flag of his alma mater front and center. The one I'd thought had been just about Megan had also shown Todd, Coco, and Sherri at the tag sale. Even the shot with Jessie Pearl had them both working in the yard.

Boyd Investigations hadn't followed each family member—there was one common denominator.

"Delta wasn't ever investigating Anson," I said.

Coco looked baffled. "She wasn't?"

I looked toward the living room, not liking the direction of my thoughts, but sure that I was finally on the right track. "It was Todd," I said softly, as if he'd be able to hear me accusing him from two rooms away. "He was the husband who couldn't be trusted. He was the one whose college background she didn't believe," I said.

The resume came back to mind, followed by something Mayor Radcliffe had said. He'd told me Delta had been investigating someone, sure they hadn't gone to the college they'd claimed. We'd assumed she'd been talking about Jeremy Lisle, but I knew that wasn't true. Jeremy and Delta had both attended Texas A&M. She knew his background.

Of course she knew her own daughter's history. She was still in college right here in town. But what about Todd? Three degrees, he said. Political Science, an MBA, and a history degree. Had she suspected, given his inability to find or keep a job, that he wasn't on the up and up? Had his interest in antiques given him away? Had Delta been digging for information about him and found some contradiction in his background? Or had she tried to help him and discovered the truth?

I thought about the photograph with Rebecca. The kaleidoscope of confetti pieces rearranged in my mind. Rebecca called Todd by the name George. Not because he looked like George Clooney, but because it was his real name. They'd known each other before. Had the investigator figured this out? No wonder she'd been so strange on the phone, telling me that Anson wasn't an adulterer and that she'd never heard of Jeremy Lisle. Because she'd only been investigating Todd Bettincourt.

Bigger fish to fry, Delta had said, and she'd tossed the investigator's report to Todd.

Had it been a warning or a threat?

Probably both, I thought, but most of all, it had been a motive for murder.

I texted Hoss McClaine with lightning speed. *Mayor Radcliffe got a call from someone named Lou saying that a resume didn't check out. I think it was Todd Bettincourt's. And I think it's a motive for murder.*

I hit SEND and tucked my phone away. It would take the sheriff a little while to track down the answer to my question. In the meantime, I kept processing through what I knew, telling Coco my suspicions. "What if he doesn't have those degrees and she figured it out? She'd want him away from Megan, right?"

"But he's married to her," Coco whispered, "and they adore each other."

I considered this. If he really did adore Megan, then he wouldn't want her finding out about his past with Rebecca and his falsehoods. Was *that* motive for murder? We both kept our voices low, afraid that someone else in the house would hear. "She would have gotten proof before breaking Megan's heart with the truth," I said.

Coco raised her gaze to the ceiling. "Maybe that's why they arranged to meet in the cemetery. She planned to confront him, away from the house and Megan, but things turned deadly."

My phone vibrated with a new text coming in. Hoss had been fast. I pulled it out of my pocket long enough to read the message. It was what I expected. *Lou Childs with Reynolds, Childs, and Briggs. Definitely Todd Bettincourt's. Lou checked the references and the degrees. Falsified.* He followed up with a second message. *Be there in 2 minutes.*

Coco inhaled sharply, just figuring out what I'd already concluded. "She gave that investigator's report right to him, didn't she?"

"Which was a threat. It told him that she knew everything." It had to have been his name blacked out on the sheet Will and I looked at on the back porch. Unease crept through me. He'd doctored the file to make it look as if Anson had been the target of the investigation.

We heard someone approach from behind us, and then a man's slurred voice said, "She wanted me to leave Megan. She didn't understand that I love her. I really love her."

Coco and I both jumped. Coco yelped, and my heart lodged in my throat.

Todd edged closer, but there was no murderous look in his eyes. Instead he just looked tired. More tired than he had just minutes ago. Dark circles ringed his eyes. His lips were cracked, and his shoulders hunched.

Will and Megan appeared behind him, but he didn't notice. He just stared past Coco and me, his whole body swaying. The scotch he'd had with Will had taken its full effect. His words were garbled, and I strained to make out what he said. "I didn't mean to kill her. I just wanted to talk. To get her to back off. I might not have always done things the right way, but I couldn't lose Megan." He leaned forward. "I can't lose her."

Briefly I met Will's eyes, then refocused on Todd. "You met her at the church that morning?"

His chin dropped toward his chest and he nodded. "I thought I could explain."

Suddenly Megan lunged at him from behind. He swung around as she careened into him. "Explain what?" she exclaimed. "That you've been lying to me this whole time?"

He reached for her. "No, Megs, it's not like that."

"I heard you," she said, her voice returning to calm but laced with a hard edge. "I heard everything you said." The questions flew from her mouth. "Did you even graduate from A&M? Did you actually go to law school? That's why you can't get a job, right?" She threw her hands up, spitting out a harsh laugh. "And Rebecca? You *knew* her? Were you actually playing me?"

"Megs . . ." His eyes fluttered and his body swayed.

She shoved him away. "Why did you marry me?"

He stumbled back, finally managing to right himself. "Because I love you. I never meant to hurt anyone, but then Rebecca showed up, and your mother kept pushing."

"Did you give Delta your resume to pass out?" I asked.

He shook his head. "She got a copy somehow. I never gave it to her."

I filled in the rest as best I could. She'd been caught red-handed by Pastor Kyle searching through the church files. Looking for Todd's resume, which she'd found. Maybe she'd given it to Lou Childs as a potential candidate for his law office so he could find out the truth. At this point we would likely never know exactly what she'd been thinking.

But before Childs could do his due diligence, thanks to the investigator Delta had hired, she already knew the resume was a fake. And that everything about Todd was, in fact, fake.

"So you arranged to meet her at the church," I prompted, circling back to the morning of Delta's death, hoping he'd tell us the rest.

His chin quivered, his eyes spilling tears. He raked his fingers through his hair then buried his face in his hands. "After she handed me the investigator's file, I didn't know what to do. She was going to work at the tag sale the next morning, so I asked if we could talk first. Alone. I didn't mean to do it," he wailed. "We argued, and she wouldn't listen."

He turned to Megan, reaching for her, but she backed away. "I didn't mean to hurt you."

She stared at him, her mouth agape. "You killed her?"

Todd staggered back until he was pressed against the wall. He sank down, crouching on his wobbly haunches. "I didn't mean to! When I told Rebecca, she freaked. She wanted me to go with her, but Megs, I couldn't leave you. You have to believe me, Megs . . . Megs . . ." His sobs grew frenzied. "Delta wouldn't listen to me. She kept saying that she'd figure out how to make me pay, and that she'd protect you from me. I . . . I . . . I snapped."

I looked at Coco. Her upper lip was raised in disgust, but her eyes had glazed with tears. "How could you do that?"

"I didn't mean to," he said again. "We were arguing,

and she was belligerent, and then she was just going to walk away. Before I knew what was happening, I'd picked up a rock and hit her with it."

He broke down again, his sobs matching Coco's and Megan's and now Jessie Pearl's, who had hobbled to the dining room on her crutches. Mama stood on the other side of the archway, and next to her, towering over her by a good five inches, was her husband. The sheriff.

Thank God.

"Not to Delta," Coco said, her voice cracking. "To Megan. How could you do that to the woman you say you love?"

A panicked, horrified expression came over him as he looked first at Coco then at Megan. "I'm sorry, Megs," he said through his tears. "I'm so sorry."

And then he collapsed on the floor, his body wracked with despair.

Chapter 26

Meemaw's old Mission-style rocking chair was in the corner of my bedroom. This was where I felt her presence more often than anywhere else in the house. The chair had a walnut finish and leather seat and sat next to the oval freestanding mirror, also Meemaw's. I'd spent thirty minutes rocking in the chair, thinking about everything that had happened next door. During my time in New York, I'd had plenty of time to observe models and designers and just people in general. What I'd found is that people acted one way when they thought others weren't watching, putting on a different face altogether when they knew people were. Delta, on the other hand, pretty much showed you what you were going to get. She had her core group of friends, the Red Hat ladies, and she had her family.

It was true that we all had more in us than we showed the world. It had been true for Delta, although she was more honest about who she was than most. It was true for Jeremy Lisle, Pastor Kyle, and even Mayor Radcliffe. And it was definitely true for Todd Bettincourt.

After I'd rehashed everything, I moved to the attic to dig through some of the Cassidy women's old clothes. I had an idea for a keepsake quilt. Something just for myself that honored the women who'd come before me, and would be a memory for those who came after. Meemaw had a stack of runners much like the pile Jessie Pearl had given to me. One or two of them could be included in the quilt.

I'd decided to offer a class on the keepsake quilt, letting local teens focus theirs on T-shirts. I needed a prototype first, and more than anything, I wanted to include some of Meemaw's creations. The relationship between Coco, Delta, and Sherri had made me appreciate being a Cassidy all the more. We were honest, we didn't hide who we were, and above all, we loved each other.

A part of me hoped Megan would want to come to the class. She needed a way to deal with the grief of losing her mother by her husband's hand, and then losing her husband to his lies and to the justice system. Coco and Sherri did, too. If I could, I'd help them make it a family affair, one that could heal and bond rather than tear apart.

I yanked on the drawer of an old sideboard, but it stuck. Something important was in the drawer, though. I was sure of it. What I wasn't sure of was whether Meemaw was playing games and keeping me out of it, or if it really was just stuck, the wood having swelled and contracted so many times over the years that the whole piece had given up trying to be functional.

"Cassidy, you in here?" Will's voice reached me about two seconds before I saw him round the corner. He'd maneuvered plenty of things in and out of the attic for me in the last year, so he knew his way around. "Thought I might find you here," he said.

"Why is that?" I asked. I had my grip on the drawer handle again, braced my feet, and pulled. The entire banquet lurched forward, but the drawer stayed shut.

"Just a hunch. If you're not in your workroom, or in the kitchen, it's a pretty good bet you're in the attic."

He reached over and grabbed hold of the handle. He looked around the attic and said, "Loretta Mae?"

And then he pulled. The drawer slid open easily, and from somewhere in the attic, the pipes creaked and it sounded like laughter. "Meemaw! You are incorrigible," I scolded. I crouched to look at the treasures the drawer held, and my breath caught.

"What is it?" Will asked, but a glass crashed to the ground behind him, pulling his attention. He hurried to the attic's entrance to see what had happened.

Alone for a moment, I pulled out the garment sitting on top of the folded clothes in the drawer. The soft flannel and the scent of the fabric mixed with the wood it had been sitting in for who knew how many years filled every bit of my being.

Will came back, a smile on his face. "What's that?" he asked.

I held up a pair of children's pajamas made from a vibrant, whimsical flannel printed with pink and gray elephants clutching umbrellas. The pajamas Meemaw had made me when I was six years old and we'd gone to the fabric store together for the very first time. My mind flooded with a wave of emotions. Meemaw, sewing, the comfort of wearing the garments she'd made for me. It hit me all at once, filling me with utter happiness, but also with a sense of loss. I wanted to go back to that moment when she'd shown me what she'd made for me, and when I'd known that I wanted to give people the very same joy she'd just given me.

We talked about Meemaw for a few minutes, and I shared my plan for the class and the quilt. "It'll be great," he said.

"Will Gracie come?" I asked.

"I don't think flying horses could keep her away."

"Darlin'," Will said to me a moment later.

"Mmm?" I folded the pajamas and placed them on the pile of clothes I'd already gathered for the keepsake quilt, then looked up at him.

Earl Grey scurried over to us, pausing at our feet and looking up at us, his little snout lifting as if he were smiling. Will crouched to pat his head, then stood again and looked squarely at me. Anxiety flitted through me. He had an expression I'd never seen before. It was equal parts determination, trepidation, and excitement.

"What's wrong?" I asked.

He moved closer, putting his hands on the banquet on either side of me. "We belong together, Harlow."

I gasped, perfect clarity coming over me. I understood what was happening. Meemaw seemed to get it, too, because the door to the attic slammed shut, and a few seconds later we heard scraping noises from downstairs. She was giving us privacy.

"We do," I said, my voice breathy with anticipation. We belonged together like Nana and my granddaddy Dalton did. Like Mama and Hoss did. Like leather and lace. I almost laughed as I thought of more ways to say that we were meant to be.

"I thought about planning a dinner or a little getaway to tell you how I feel, but I can't wait that long."

"No, let's not wait," I said, excitement bubbling up inside me. I'd known we'd end up together, but having it happen at this very moment was like nothing I'd ever experienced. Knowing that Will wanted it, too, and that he was too anxious to wait for our future made my stomach flutter.

"I want to marry you," he said. "I want to be your husband. I want you to be my wife. I want us to be a family. You. Me. Gracie."

"And Meemaw?" I asked, a smile forming on my lips that I couldn't tamp down. Will and I would be a force to be reckoned with as a married couple.

"Especially Meemaw." He put one hand in his jeans pocket. "She's been trying to tell me something for a while now."

"I've noticed."

"That broken jar a minute ago?"

I nodded. The shelves at the entrance of the attic were filled with Mason jars, and in those jars were buttons and trims and trinkets. I hadn't even begun to go through them, but it was on my list of things to do.

"She finally found what she's been looking for. What she wanted me to have."

I waited, not understanding.

"Really, it's what she wants *you* to have."

"What do you mean?"

"I've been looking at rings but haven't found anything quite right."

My heartbeat ratcheted up a notch, and suddenly I knew what he was going to say. What he was going to show me. He pulled his hand from his pocket and held out a ring, and I lost my breath. It was an Art Deco platinum ring with sapphires, a bejeweled, vaulted frame, and a bezel-set round diamond. The diamond floated on an etched frame and was surrounded by eight small diamonds, alternated with the channel-set French-cut sapphires. The whole thing reminded me of a flower, dainty and magical yet symmetrical and strong.

I knew without a doubt that this was the trinket so often referred to in our family lore. Butch Cassidy had given it to Texana, but it had disappeared, and no one was even sure that it had really existed. It had been more like folklore. We thought it existed, but no one knew for sure whether it did. Or even what it was. A trinket to show his love—that's all we'd ever known.

But Meemaw had known. She'd been searching for it so Will could give it to me. He held my left hand and slipped it on my finger. It fit perfectly, just like he and I fit, and in that instant I knew that it wasn't my charm or Meemaw's dreams that had brought Will into my life or that had brought us to this moment.

Like Butch's love for Texana, we were meant to be.

Harlow Cassidy's Sewing Tips

1. When making an apron, take care to choose a style that fits your personality! There are bib aprons, half aprons, cobble aprons (that cover both the front and the back of the body), and smocks (no strings).

2. When choosing fabric for your apron, consider how much wear and tear your apron is likely to receive. If it will be heavily used, choose machine washable and dryable, sturdy fabric that can withstand frequent cleaning. Natural fibers will probably require ironing!

3. If you're experimenting, roam through the fabric store and let the fabrics speak to you. Check out the home décor and remnant fabrics, too!

4. Embellishing an apron is a ton of fun! Use ruffles, rickrack, and ribbon, as well as lace, buttons, yo-yos, beads, and stenciling. The sky's the limit!

5. Adding black to a clothing design is like adding mascara to your lashes. It punctuates the other colors in the palette, so consider black as an accent.

Continue reading for more of Harlow's
crafty sleuthing in a special excerpt from

A KILLING NOTION

Available now from Obsidian

Go big or go home. That had to be the philosophy of the
people who spearheaded the Texas homecoming mum tradition. Big flowers made of ribbon, with trinkets and more ribbon, and even the occasional cowbell, to be worn by girls
across Texas during homecoming week, were a sign of status
in most Lone Star State schools. The grander, the better.
There was no other logical explanation, and at this particular
moment, I wanted those homecoming boosters strung up by
their toes.

"Everything's bigger in Texas," I said aloud to the three
people in my shop. Earl Grey, my little teacup pig, snorted
before going back to rooting his way into a mound of fabric
scraps I'd yet to bag up.

Mrs. Zinnia James stood framed beneath the French
doors that separated the front room of Buttons & Bows, my
custom dressmaking shop, from my workroom. Danica Ed-
wards stood on the fitting platform I'd pulled out next to the
cutting table, a length of black tulle draped over one shoulder. She was fairly new to Bliss, and she'd signed up to be

part of the Helping Hands community outreach program, so along with a mum, I was also making her homecoming dress.

And so far, the visions I normally saw of people in outfits that would help them realize their wishes and dreams weren't materializing. A black dress, even though it was a flirty, intricately silver-beaded embroidery number with a waist belt and a sheer illusion neckline and tulle underlay, felt far too serious for a seventeen-year-old. I'd have to go back to the drawing board for her.

My grandmother, Coleta Cassidy, stood next to the open window in the workroom, cooing at Thelma Louise, the grand-dam of her goat herd. Her Cassidy charm as a goat whisperer served her well. Every woman in my family had a magical gift, thanks to the wish my great-great-great-grandfather Butch Cassidy had made in an Argentinian fountain. Nana communicated with her goats. My mother had a powerful green thumb. And my gift had to do with dressmaking.

"All this . . ." Mrs. James waved one arm around at the mum paraphernalia, the right side of her top lip curling up. "It's just absurd."

She'd sprayed and teased her silver hair to within an inch of its life in a very Texas do. As she shook her head, not a strand of her hair even budged. I had to grin. She'd always had a heavy hand with her makeup and an affinity for Botox and fillers, but still, her papery skin revealed a map of blue veins.

She was the wife of Senator Jebediah James, which made her the quintessential Texas blue blood, and she'd fight her age until her dying breath. With both barrels blazing, I'd heard her say on more than one occasion.

Still, even with all her effort, the evidence of her years was there. Her skin pulled tautly over the hardscape of her cheeks and jawbones, but the indentation of fine lines curved around both sides of her mouth and her eyes.

She looked like a slightly odd, cloned version of herself, and I sometimes thought that if I squinted, I'd get a glimpse of the real Zinnia James. But then I'd blink and she'd have that frozen-in-time look she wore like a mask. It had been more than a year since I'd been back in Bliss, but I still hadn't grown completely used to the mannequin look of my biggest fan, Mrs. James.

"It wasn't always like this," she remarked.

"No?" I peered at the mounds of ribbon heaped on the cutting table in the center of the room. I'd amassed yard upon yard upon yard of red, black, and white grosgrain, satin, organza, wire-edged, double ruffled, and ultrathin curly ribbon, all in the name of the homecoming mum. Some of the ribbon was emblazoned with the words BLISS BRONCOS, CHEERLEADING, RODEO, FOOTBALL, and other extracurricular activities our high school offered to their student body.

"Good heavens, no, not in our day," Mrs. James said. "Isn't that right, Coleta?"

My grandmother tugged her cap down as she shook her head, the two dancing goats that formed the logo of her Sundance Kids dairy farm doing a jig as she forced it back into place over her wavy hair. "Got that right." She pointed at me as if it were my fault and she was setting me straight. "Your granddaddy gave me a *real* chrysanthemum."

I flung the back of my hand to my forehead, letting my mouth gape and my eyes widen. "What? No ribbons? No bows? No trinkets?" I said in my best Scarlett O'Hara drawl as I pointed to the pile of plastic adornments Bliss's teens wanted hanging from their mums.

Thelma Louise wrenched her lower jaw to one side, baring her teeth at me. Apparently she didn't like my sarcasm.

Nana lowered her chin. Neither did she. "That's right, ladybug." She waved her arm around. "None of this nonsense."

"A few ribbons," Mrs. James said.

"A few," Nana agreed. "You can't hardly count the three strands of ribbons we had back then to the million and one these girls wear today. Good Lord, I've heard people say they pay up to five hundred dollars for a mum. Five hundred dollars! That would buy a whole lot of grits and grain for my goats."

"And they were pinned to the bodice like a corsage,"

Mrs. James added, shaking her head. "Not like the mammoth mums today that need harnesses."

Danica stood on the fitting platform, riveted by the discussion. Nana leaned against the windowsill, crossing one white-socked foot over the other. "There aren't even any silk chrysanthemums on them anymore. Why they bother calling it a mum is a mystery."

Mrs. James and my grandmother had grown up together in Bliss, and had spent forty-some-odd years in a feud that had only recently ended. Now they were thick as thieves, their distaste over the state of the homecoming mum apparently fueling their camaraderie. "Why in heaven's name are you making them, anyway, Harlow?"

It was a good question, and one I'd wrestled with. The bottom line was, I wasn't going to *stop* the madness, so I'd decided that I might as well join it. "The girls want them. They're going to buy them. If I don't make them, they'll get them from the mega craft store or the local florist. So why not me? With all the bad press the *Bliss Tribune* has laid at my doorstep after the *D Magazine* fiasco, I figured this might help turn things around."

"Murder does have a way of putting a damper on business, I imagine," Mrs. James said.

I spread my arms wide. "Which is why I've been doing a million and one Buttons and Bows do-it-yourself mum parties. It's like Pampered Chef home parties, only with crafts."

They all three stared at me. "So let me get this straight," Nana said, her eyes sweeping the array of mum materials in the workroom. "You've been hauling all this stuff to people's homes and helping them make their own mums?"

I pushed my glasses back into place, nodding. "That's exactly right. I made some of the foundations ahead of time with the backings and the ribbon flowers over these polyurethane bases I have—they'll support twenty or thirty pounds—"

Danica gasped, clasping her chest with both hands. The tulle dropped from her shoulder to the floor. "Is that how much they weigh?"

"Some are even more, and if you want the crown jewel—a double mum that sandwiches the body, front and back—I bought these dog harnesses to support the weight."

She hopped down to retrieve her lost tulle, tossing it over her shoulder. "That's crazy," she said, gliding back into place. "My mom never—" She stopped short, swallowing the grief that instantly seemed to bubble up. She hadn't talked much about her mom, and whenever she mentioned her in passing, the hole inside her seemed to open wider.

"It is crazy," I said. I hadn't even attended the homecoming dance, let alone had a mum, so to hear the words "double mum" and "harness" coming from my mouth felt foreign and absurd. But business was business, Texas was Texas, and the craziness of the tradition notwithstanding, the crafting part of the project was fun.

Mrs. James patted me on the shoulder. "My dear, you never cease to amaze. You get tossed a bushel of lemons; you turn around and make lemon bars. Buttons and Bows will be just fine—you'll see."

Danica shifted around nervously. "But you ... you're making this for free," she finally said, gesturing toward the morose black tulle.

Mrs. James moved her attention from me to Danica. "My darling," she said, "Helping Hands is my special project. We have volunteers and the foundation pays for some services. Harlow's just fine.

"So while I don't adore the enormity of the mum, I do think every young woman should have a beautiful dress to wear to the homecoming dance. And if a girl wants a mum, she should have one."

"I don't have to have the mum—"

"Of course you're having a mum," I said. "We're going to make it together as a group. Don't you worry about a thing. Just think of yourself as Cinderella, and we're your fairy godmothers."

Mrs. James handed Danica an oversized notecard. "I need you to fill this out with your address, any dietary preferences, and such."

Danica arched a brow in question.

"It's for the Helping Hands brunch the day of the dance."

Danica obliged, carefully writing the information and handing the card back to Mrs. James, and then stepping back onto the fitting platform.

Mrs. James tucked the card into her purse. "Thank you, darlin'. And thank you for letting me put a little more light in your life."

Danica smiled shyly, gazing down at the platform and brushing back her black hair to reveal earbuds tucked in her ears. So, she was like every other teenager, listening to her music twenty-four seven. I wondered what her natural hair color was. A lighter brown, judging from how pale her skin was, but she died it raven black, emphasizing her fair complexion. "I don't know how to thank you."

Mrs. James gave her hand a squeeze. "You just have fun at the dance and look gorgeous. That's all the thanks I need."

"And don't turn into a pumpkin," Nana added with a chortle.

Mrs. James and Nana ambled into the kitchen, leaving Danica and me alone with our dress design. I looked long and hard at her, from her straight black hair to her wide shoulders and hips, to the trim indentation of her waist. Rather than stick thin, she was curvy in a way that reminded me of Jessica Rabbit, but so far, whenever I'd seen her, both here and at Villa Farina, the bakery where she worked part-time, her body was hidden under baggy tops and jackets.

"The black's not going to work," I said, tapping my finger against my lips. I was also making a dress for another Helping Hands girl, Leslie Downs. Hers, I already had clear in my mind. It had been easy: I'd looked at her and seen the exact dress, just like that.

It was a sapphire blue floor-sweeping semisheer tiered overlay with an explosion of confetti-colored sequin fabric as the main skirt and bodice. The strapless bandeau neckline, an A-line silhouette, a high-low hem, coming to the fingertips in front and sweeping the floor in back, would all set off her ebony skin beautifully. An updo for her hair, high-heeled black sandals, and she'd be a standout at the dance.

But Danica . . . She was a different story, and with her design, I was less confident. I'd had a vision of the short, flirty black dress I'd been planning, but it wasn't quite right. Everything around me faded away as I looked at her. Her blue eyes and pale skin reminded me of Emma Stone, but her black hair, heavy black boots, and patterned black stockings paired with a lacy black skirt gave her a hard look. Mostly, though, there was an underlying sadness to her. Completely understandable, given the fact that she'd been in foster care and now, at nearly eighteen, was finishing high school and would be living on her own soon. Not the way most teenagers envisioned their lives turning out.

I pulled the tulle away from her and wound it up in a haphazard ball. "Danica, I want to play a little game with you."

She took out her earbuds, turned off her music, and tucked it all away in her pocket, lifting her gaze and looking at me through her long, spidery eyelashes. "Okay?" she said, more like a question than acquiescence. "What kind of game?"

"Word association."

She pulled her lips in thoughtfully until they disappeared. "Okay," she said again. "Why?"

"I can't quite get a picture in my head of the right dress." Apparently my charm was failing me, but I couldn't tell her that. "This will help me get to know you better. I'll sketch tonight, and show you some ideas tomorrow. I want your input on this."

She batted her eyelashes, whisking away the thin layer of moisture glazing her eyes. I wished I knew her background. Had her relationship with her parents been okay, or strained? What about her foster family? Had they wanted her? Shown her love?

More than ever, I wanted to give Danica a Cinderella night at the dance.

"Let's give it a try," I said.

She nodded as I fired off my first word. "Homecoming."

"Parade," she said. No hesitation. So she liked the festivities.

"Monday."

"Day off."

"Saturday."

"Car shows."

"Sunday."

"Church."

So far, so good. Her answers didn't give me any insight to her psyche, but she was talking, so I was hopeful.

"Car."

"My dad," she said quietly. She wasn't with her dad anymore, but that's all I really knew. Now didn't feel like the right time to push for more information, so I moved on.

"High school."

"Torture."

I left that one alone. "Mums."

"Status."

Danica's perspective on school reflected her situation, namely that she was alone in the world. The next set of words that came to my mind were family, home, and vacation. Having her respond to them could give me more insight, but on the other hand, thinking about what she didn't have could drive her deeper into herself. I waffled back and forth, but finally made up my mind. If I had cancer or my husband—if I had a husband—had cheated, I wouldn't want my friends or the people I ran into to cower and pretend like my reality didn't exist. My grandmother, Loretta Mae—and all the Cassidy women, for that matter—had taught me to face adversity head-on. No pussyfooting around.

I decided Danica deserved the same honesty.

"Family," I said, but I held my breath.

Her lip twitched almost imperceptibly and she closed her eyes in a slow, sad blink. "The people you choose," she said softly, and once again, my heart went out to her.

She'd lost her family, so from here on out, the people she peppered her life with would be those she handpicked.

As I patted her arm and rattled off the next word—home—the front door opened, the strand of bells hanging from the inside of the front door jingling.

"Deceitful—" Danica said, stopping short when she saw Gracie Flores and her boyfriend, Shane Montgomery, tumble in, laughing. Gracie and Shane couldn't have heard what she'd said, nor would they know what she'd been talking about, but still, she looked as if she'd been caught sneaking cookies at midnight.

Gracie and Shane stopped just inside the door, Gracie's eyes growing wide and excited as she took in the trims and mum accessories. A shimmering trail of diffused light circled inside the house like the tail of a shooting star. It was the ghost of Meemaw, my grandmother Loretta Mae. Gracie's mouth drew into an O, her gaze following the glittery stream, but no one else seemed to pick up on Meemaw's presence.

She knocked the back of her hand against Shane's arm, grinning up at him. "It's like an enchanted land," she said.

He raised his eyebrows and I got the impression that Buttons & Bows was nothing like any enchanted land he'd want to spend time in, but then he nodded and pulled her forward. "This is, like, the total opposite of Bubba's."

Shane's family owned Bubba's Auto Repair, and Shane worked there part-time. I'd taken Buttercup, my old Ford pickup truck, there for service plenty of times. *Growing up with a dad who works on cars means I work on cars,* he'd told Gracie. She'd added that he made good money. "Enough so we can go out on real dates."

Two teenagers couldn't ask for more than that.

Danica stepped down from the fitting platform as Gracie and Shane came into the workroom. "Hey," Gracie said.

Danica dropped her gaze shyly, but threw up her hand in a quick wave. "Should I come back tomorrow?" she asked me.

"Perfect, yes. Thanks for playing along. I'll work up some sketches, and you can tell me what you like and what you don't."

"I've never had a dress like this, Ms. Cassidy. My dad died and my mother, she couldn't afford it—" She paused, her voice heavy with sorrow. This was the most she'd said about her parents. It wasn't much, but it was a start.

"I'm happy to do it, darlin'," I said, ushering her toward the front door.

The fact that I'd used a Southern endearment wasn't lost on me. The more time I spent back home in Bliss, the more my Southern roots took hold of me again. Sure, I was a Texan first and foremost, but like most of the folks I knew, unless they were from the border, I also felt Southern. Down-home accents and shared idioms could do that for people.

By the time I'd been twenty-four and living in New York, I'd all but ditched my accent, but it wasn't long before I'd had a big realization. You could take the girl out of the small town, but you couldn't ever take the small town out of the girl.

Now I was thirty-three, back home in Bliss, and before long, I'd sound just like my mama, dropping every G and saying *might could* and *right quick*.

"See you at the bakery," Mrs. James called, coming out from the kitchen.

Danica draped a Bliss High letterman's jacket over her arm, smiled, and waved to her. "Yes, ma'am. Skinny hazelnut latte—"

"And an Italian cream puff." Mrs. James touched her mouth as if she could taste the sweet cream on her lips.

"Good grief," Nana said, following her. "Pastries will clog your arteries. But a good smearing of persimmon chèvre on a thin slice of French bread? That's a treat worth havin'."

The bells on the door tinkled again as I shut it behind Danica. A minute later, her car revved and she was gone.

I went back to the workroom to get ready for Leslie's consultation, which I knew would go more smoothly than Danica's had. I pulled out the sapphire jacquard and the confetti-sequined fabric for the underskirt, setting it on the worktable. I already had my sketches for her dress, so I was good to go.

Gracie bopped up and down on her toes, looking like a child at her first rodeo who was trying desperately—and unsuccessfully—to stay cool and calm. She snuck a glance at Shane, who looked a bit stricken by the array of colorful ribbon assortments, small stuffed bears in cheerleading outfits, and cowbells.

But to his credit, he seemed to sense her excitement and put a grin on his face. "Go big or go home," he said. My exact sentiment just a little while ago.

It was all the encouragement Gracie needed. She went from toe-bopping to full-on bouncing, moving around the worktable and picking up different adornments. "I don't want a teddy bear," she said after a minute, referring to the center focal piece of the mum.

"Not even a bear holding a pair of sewing scissors?" he asked.

Wow, I was impressed. He knew Gracie and her passion for sewing—and respected it. That was pretty major for a fifteen-year-old girl and her sixteen-year-old new boyfriend.

But the moment was lost on Gracie. She just shook her head and said, "No. Something besides a teddy bear, for sure." Miniature bears were traditional, and while Gracie wanted a mum, I knew she was going to do it her own way. I could see her wanting squares of colorful fabric, an honest-to-goodness pair of Ginghers, or a rolled-up measuring tape.

He ran his hand through his hair, making it stand on end. The dark blond color set off his tanned skin. Gracie, on the other hand, had a beautiful olive complexion, courtesy of her father, Will. Shane and Gracie fit together, both sun-kissed and fresh-faced, clearly smitten, without a care in the world. "I guess we'll figure it out," he said.

"I'll make it," I volunteered. "You don't have to worry about a thing."

"Oh, but I want to help," Gracie said. "Can I?"

"Absolutely. Darlin', you and I are going to have a mum-making party," I said, just as Leslie, my second Helping Hands student, and another girl, came in the front door of the shop.

Leslie's brown doe eyes opened wide. "Where you, like, get together and everybody makes their mums?"

"Awesome," the second girl said.

"Everyone," Leslie said, gesturing to her friend, "this is Carrie. She's pretty new to Bliss. Carrie, this is everyone."

Carrie smiled, a faint dimple marking her cheek, and waved. She immediately headed across the room to look at the prêt-à-porter.

"Do you have one yet?" I asked Leslie.

She shook her head.

"Then you can come and help make yours." The more, the merrier. "You, too, if you like," I said to Carrie.

"I have mine," she said. "But thanks."

But Leslie's eyes grew even wider. "I get a mum?" Her gaze slid to Shane for the briefest second. "But I don't have a boyfriend," she said, her voice dropping.

"You don't need a boyfriend to wear a mum," Gracie said. "You just need a mum."

Leslie looked at Gracie, then at Shane, as if she was trying to decide if this were true. "It's the twenty-first century," I said. "You can give yourself a mum if you want to."

Leslie relaxed, but her shoulders lifted and her chest rose and fell with her excitement. "Then I want the biggest mum at Bliss High! I want to show those girls who ... who—"

She broke off, once again looking at Gracie and Shane, her attention focusing on Shane for an extra few seconds.

"Those girls who what?" I asked.

She rooted her feet to the ground and raised her chin slightly. "I want the shy girls and the geeky girls and the girls like me to believe in themselves," she said. "I want them to hear what you just said. That this is the twenty-first century and we can give ourselves mums."

I smiled at her, part of me wanting to applaud her confidence. She and Danica both came from foster homes, but they seemed to handle things so differently. Danica was quiet. Removed. Almost injured. But Leslie was bent on proving that she was as good as everyone else. If proving that was what she wanted, the dress I was going to make her would help her get there.

This was the second time I'd met Leslie, and when I closed my eyes, I still saw her in the sapphire confetti dress. The vibrant colors matched her vibrant personality. Carrie was in the love seat studying my lookbook, which was perfect. It gave us time to work.

"Come here, Leslie. I want to show you the sketches I came up with." I flipped open my sketchbook, turning to the pages where I'd drawn variations of the dress I envisioned for her.

She looked at the sketches, glanced in the freestanding oval mirror in the corner, and a slow smile lit her chocolate brown face, a rosy glow dusting her cheeks. "I love it!"

I hadn't realized I'd been holding air in my lungs, but now I breathed out, relieved. There was always a moment of apprehension when whomever I was designing for saw my ideas for the first time. What I visualized and what they thought they wanted didn't always mesh. But in this instance, Leslie saw my vision. And she liked it.

Shane's cell phone rang as I showed Leslie the fabric choices I'd come up with. He stepped back into the front room to answer it. Ten seconds later, the sound of his guttural cry sent a chill down my spine.

Gracie ran to the front, stopping short when she saw Shane's face. His cheeks had gone ruddy, his eyes glassy. His jaw pulsed, hollowing out his cheeks and giving him a drawn, angry look.

"What's wrong?" she asked, holding back as if she was afraid he might explode.

He shoved his phone back into his back pocket, looking shell-shocked. "This can't be happening," he said. He wheeled around, pacing the room, weaving among the paisley love seat, couch, and red settee. His hand tore through his hair, pulling angrily at it until it stood straight up.

Gracie took a step backward, her lips trembling.

I squeezed her hand as I scooted past her. Leslie came up next to her, looking more curious than anything else. Mrs. James and Nana had wandered out from the kitchen, and Carrie sat forward on the love seat.

"Shane?" I said sternly, trying to break through to him. "What happened?"

He abruptly stopped his pacing, digging all ten of his fingers through his hair. "There was a car accident," he said. His chin quivered and he struggled to get the rest of the words out. "My dad . . . my dad was in an accident. He's . . . he's dead."